L.T Meade

A Plucky Girl

L.T Meade

A Plucky Girl

1st Edition | ISBN: 978-3-75244-118-5

Place of Publication: Frankfurt am Main, Germany

Year of Publication: 2020

Outlook Verlag GmbH, Germany.

A PLUCKY GIRL

BY

MRS. L. T. MEADE

CHAPTER I

FORTUNE'S BALL

I was born a month after my father's death, and my mother called me after him. His name was John Westenra Wickham, but I was Westenra Wickham alone. It was a strange name for a girl, and as I grew up people used to comment on it. Mother loved it very much, and always pronounced it slowly. She was devoted to father, and never spoke of him as most people do of their dead, but as if he were still living, and close to her and to me. When a very little child, my greatest treat was to sit on her knee and listen to wonderful stories of my brave and gallant father. He was a handsome man and a good man, and he must have possessed, in a large degree, those qualities which endear people to their fellows, for surely it was no light cause which made my mother's beautiful brown eyes sparkle as they did when she spoke of him, and her whole face awake to the tenderest life and love and beauty when she mentioned his name.

I grew up, therefore, with a great passionate affection for my dead father, and a great pride in his memory. He had been a Major-General in a Lancer regiment, and had fought many battles for his country, and led his men through untold dangers, and performed himself more gallant feats than I could count. He received his fatal wound at last in rescuing a brother-officer under fire in Zululand, and one of the last things he was told was that he had received his Victoria Cross.

During my father's lifetime mother and he were well off, and for some years after his death there did not appear to be any lack of money. I was well educated, partly in Paris and partly in London, and we had a pretty house in Mayfair, and when I was eighteen I was presented to Her Gracious Majesty by mother's special friend, and my godmother, the Duchess of Wilmot, and afterwards I went a great deal into society, and enjoyed myself as much as most girls who are spirited and happy and have kind friends are likely to do. I was quite one and twenty before the collapse came which changed everything. I don't know how, and I don't know why, but our gold vanished like a dream, and we found ourselves almost penniless.

"Now what are we to do, Westenra?" said mother.

"But have we nothing?" I replied.

"Only my pension as your dear father's widow. Your pension as his child ceased when you came of age, and I believe, for so our lawyers tell me, that there is about fifty pounds besides. I think we can count on a hundred and fifty a year. Can we live on that sum, Westenra?"

"No," I answered proudly.

I was standing behind one of the silk curtains in the drawing-room as I spoke. I was looking down into the street. The room was full of luxury, and the people who passed backwards and forwards in their luxurious carriages in the street below were many of them our friends, and all more or less moved in what was called nice society. I was full of quite unholy pride at that moment, and poverty was extremely distasteful, and to live on a hundred and fifty pounds a year seemed more than impossible.

"What is it, West? What are you thinking of?" said mother, in a sad voice.

"Oh, too many things to utter," I replied. "We can't live on the sum you mention. Why, a curate's wife could scarcely manage on it."

"Don't you think we might just contrive in a very small cottage in the country?" pleaded mother. "I don't want much, just flowers round me and the country air, and your company, darling, and—and—oh, very small rooms would do, and the furniture of this house is ours. We could sell most of it, and send what we liked best down to the cottage."

"It can't be done," I answered. "Listen, mother, I have a proposal to make."

"What is it, my darling? Don't stand so far away—come and sit near me."

I walked gravely across the room, but I did not sit down. I stood before mother with my hands tightly locked together, and my eyes fastened on her dear, lovely, delicate old face.

"I am glad that the furniture is ours," I began.

"Of course it is."

"It is excellent furniture," I continued, looking round and appraising it quickly in my mind's eye: "it shall be part of our capital."

"My dear child, our capital? What do you mean?"

"We will take a house in Bloomsbury, put the furniture in, and have paying guests."

"West, are you mad? Do you remember who I am—Mrs. Wickham, the widow of—or no, I never will allow that word—the wife of your dear, dear, noble father."

"Father would approve of this," I answered. "He was a brave man and died fighting, just as I mean to die fighting. You are shocked at the idea to-night, mother, because it is fresh to you, but in a week's time you will grow accustomed to it, you will take an interest in it, you will even like it. I, bury myself in the country and starve!—no, no, no, I could not do it. Mother, darling, I am your slave, your devoted slave, your own most loving girl, but don't, don't ask me to vegetate in the country. It would kill me—it would kill me."

I had dropped on my knees now and taken both her hands in mine, and I spoke with great excitement, and even passion.

"Don't stir for a moment," said mother; "how like your father you look! Just the same eyes, and that straight sort of forehead, and the same expression round your lips. If your father were alive he would love you for being brave."

As mother looked at me I think she forgot for the moment the terrible plunge we were about to make into the work-a-day strata of society, but the next instant the horrid fact was brought back to her, for Paul, our pretty little page, brought in a sheaf of letters on a salver. Of course they were unpaid bills. Mother said sadly—

"Put them with the others, Westenra."

"All these bills must be met," I said stoutly, after Paul had closed the door behind him. "There will be just enough money for that purpose, so we need not start handicapped. For my part, I mean to enjoy our scheme vastly."

"But, my child, you do not realise—you will be stepping down from the position in which you were born. Our friends will have nothing to do with us."

"If they wish to give us up because we do something plucky they are not worthy to be called friends," was my reply. "I don't believe those friends we wish to keep will desert us, mother. On the contrary, I am certain they will respect us. What people cannot stand in these days is genteel poverty—its semi-starvation, its poor mean little contrivances; but they respect a hand-to-hand fight with circumstances, and when they see that we are determined to overcome in the battle, then those who are worth keeping will cling to us and help us; and if all our friends turn out to be the other sort, mother, why"—and here I rose and stretched out my arms wide—"let them go, they are not worth keeping. Those who won't be fond of us in our new home in Bloomsbury we can do without."

"You are enthusiastic and—and ignorant," said mother.

"I grant that I am enthusiastic," I answered. "It would be a great pity if I had none of that quality at one and twenty; but as to my ignorance, well, time will prove. I should like, however, to ask you a straight question, mother. Would father have sat beside his guns and done nothing when the fight was going against him? Was that the way he won his Victoria Cross?"

Mother burst out crying. She never could bear me to allude to that fatal and yet glorious occasion. She rose now, weak and trembling, and said that she must defer the discussion of ways and means until the next day.

I put on my hat and went for a walk alone. I was full of hope, and not at all depressed. Girls in these days are always glad to have something new to do, and in the first rush of it, the idea of leaving the humdrum path of ordinary society and of entering on a new and vigorous career filled me with ecstacy. I don't really think in the whole of London there was a prouder girl than the real Westenra Wickham; but I do not think I had ordinary pride. To know titled people gave me no special pleasure, and gay and pretty dresses were so common with me that I regarded them as the merest incidents in my life, and to be seen at big receptions, and at those "At Homes" where you met the most fastidious and the smartest folks, gave me no joy whatsoever. It is true I was very fond of my godmother, the Duchess of Wilmot, and of another dear little American friend, who had married a member of the Cabinet, Sir Henry Thesiger. But beyond these two I was singularly free from any special attachments. The fact is, I was in love with mother. Mother herself seemed to fill all my life. I felt somehow as if father had put some of his spirit into me, and had bound me over by a solemn vow to look after her, to comfort her, to guard her, until he himself came to fetch her, and now my thought of thoughts was how splendid and how necessary it would be to keep her usual comforts round my dainty, darling, lovely mother, to give her the food she required, and the comfortable rooms and the luxury to which she was born; and I felt that my pride, if I could really do that, would be so great and exultant, that I should hold my head higher than ever in the air. Yes, I would have a downright good try, and I vowed I would not fail. It seemed to me as I turned home again in the sweet golden summer evening that fortune's ball lay at my feet, that in the battle I would not be conquered, that like my father I in my own way would win the Victoria Cross.

CHAPTER II

FRIENDS OR QUONDAM FRIENDS

Mother used to say that there were times when her daughter Westenra swept her right off her feet.

"I can no more resist you," she used to remark on these occasions, "than if you were a great flood bearing me along."

Perhaps never did mother find my power so strong, so determined as on the present occasion. It was in vain for her, poor darling, to speak of our friends, of those dear, nice, good people who had loved father and for his sake were good to his widow. I had my answer ready.

"It is just this, mother," I said, "what we do will cause a gleaning—a sifting—amongst our friends. Those who are worth keeping will stay with us, those who are not worth keeping will leave us. And now do you know what I mean to do? I mean this morning, with your leave, to order the carriage, the carriage which we must put down at the end of the week, but which we can certainly keep for the next couple of days, and go round to our friends and tell them what we are about to do."

"You must go alone then, Westenra, for I cannot go with you."

"Just as you please, mother. I would rather you had the courage; but still, never mind, darling, I will do it by myself."

Mother looked at me in despair.

"How old are you?" she said suddenly.

"You know quite well," I replied, "I was twenty-one a month ago."

Mother shook her head sadly.

"If you really intend to carry out this awful idea, West, you must consider youth a thing of the past," she said.

I smiled and patted her cheek.

"Nothing of the sort," I answered; "I mean to be young and vigorous and buoyant and hopeful as long as I have you with me, so there! Now, may I ring the bell and tell Paul to desire Jenkins to bring the victoria round at eleven o'clock?"

Mother could not refuse, and having executed this order I sat down with considerable appetite to breakfast. I was really enjoying myself vastly.

Punctual to the hour, I stepped into our pretty carriage. First of all I would visit my dear old godmother, the Duchess of Wilmot.

Accordingly, early as it was, I told Jenkins to drive me to the Duchess's house in Park Lane. When we drew up at the house I jumped out, ran up the steps and sounded the bell. The man who opened the door informed me that her Grace was at home to no one at so early an hour.

I thought for a moment, then I scribbled something on a little piece of paper.

"Dear Duchess," I said, "I want to see you particularly, the matter is very urgent.—Your god-daughter,

WESTENRA WICKHAM."

This I twisted up and gave to the man.

"Give that to her Grace, I will wait to see if there is an answer," I said.

He came down in a moment or two.

"Her Grace will see you, Miss Wickham," he said.

I entered the house, and following the footman up some winding stairs and down some corridors, I was shown into the small boudoir where the Duchess generally sat in the morning. She was fully dressed, and busily writing notes.

"That will do, Hartop," she said to the man; "close the door, please. Now then, Westenra, what is the meaning of this? What eccentric whim has induced you to visit me at so early an hour?"

"I wanted to tell you something," I said; "mother is awfully distressed, but I thought you had better know."

"How queer you look, my child, and yet I seldom saw you brighter or handsomer. Take off your hat and sit near me. No, I am not specially busy. Is it about the Russells' reception? Oh, I can take you if your mother is not strong enough. You want to consult me over your dress? Oh, my dear Westenra, you must wear——"

"It has nothing to do with that," I interrupted. "Please let me speak. I want to say something so badly. I want to consult you."

"Of course," said her Grace.

She laid her jewelled hand on my arm. How I loved that white hand! How I adored my beautiful old friend! It would be painful to give her up. Was she going to give me up?

"I will tell you something quite frankly," I said. "I love you very much; you have always been kind to me."

"I am your godmother, don't forget."

"A great trouble has come to us."

"A great trouble, my dear, what do you mean?"

"Mother thinks it a fearful trouble, and I suppose it is, but anyhow there are two ways of taking it. There is the sinking-down way, which means getting small and poor and thin, anaemic, in short, and there is the bold way, the sort of way when you stand up to a thing, you know what I mean."

"You are talking school-boy language. My grandson Ralph would understand you; he is here; do you want to see him? I am a little too busy for riddles, Westenra."

"Oh! I do beg your pardon. I know I am taking a great liberty: no one else would come to you at so early an hour."

"Well, speak, my dear."

"We have lost our money."

"Lost your money!" cried the Duchess.

"Yes; everything, or nearly everything. It was through some bad investments, and mother was not at all to blame. But we have nothing left, or nearly nothing—I mean we have a hundred and fifty a-year, about the price of one of your dresses."

"Don't be personal, Westenra—proceed."

"Mother wants to live in a cottage in the country."

"I do not see how she could possibly do it," said the Duchess. "A cottage in the country! Why, on that pittance she could scarcely afford a workman's cottage, but I will speak to my friends; something must be arranged immediately. Your dear, lovely, fragile mother! We must get her a suite of apartments at Hampton Court. Oh! my poor child, this is terrible."

"But we do not choose to consider it terrible," I replied, "nor will we be beholden to the charity of our friends. Now, here is the gist of the matter. I have urged mother to take a house in Bloomsbury."

"Bloomsbury?" said the Duchess a little vaguely.

"Oh, please Duchess, you must know. Bloomsbury is a very nice, healthy part of the town. There are big Squares and big houses; the British Museum is there—now, you know."

8

"Oh, of course, that dreary pile, and you would live close to it. But why, why? Is it a very cheap neighbourhood?"

"By no means; but city men find it convenient, and women who work for their living like it also, and country folks who come to town for a short time find it a good centre. So we mean to go there, and—and make money. We will take our furniture and make the house attractive and—and take paying guests. We will keep a boarding-house. Now you know."

I stood up. There was a wild excited feeling all over me. The most daring flight of imagination could never associate the gracious Duchess of Wilmot with a lodging-house keeper, and mother had always hitherto been the Duchess's equal. I had never before felt *distrait* or nervous in the Duchess's presence, but now I knew that there was a gulf between us—that I stood on one side of the gulf and the Duchess on the other. I stretched out my hands imploringly.

"I know you will never speak to me again, you never can, it is not to be thought of. This is good-bye, for we must do it. I see you understand. Mother said that it would part us from our friends, and I thought she was wrong, but I see now that she was right. This is good-bye."

Before she could prevent me I dropped on my knees and raised the jewelled hand to my lips, and kissed it passionately.

"Oh, for heaven's sake, Westenra," said the Duchess then, "don't go into hysterics, nor talk in that wild way. Sit down again quietly, dear, and tell me what sort of person is a boarding-house keeper."

Her tone made me smile, and relieved the tension.

"Don't you really know?" I asked; "did you never hear of people who take paying guests? They swarm at the seaside, and charge exorbitant prices."

"Oh, and rob you right and left," said the Duchess; "yes, my friends have told me of such places. As a rule I go to hotels by preference, but do you mean, Westenra, that your mother is going to live in apartments for the future?"

"No, no," I answered wildly; "she will have a house, and she and I, both of us, will fill it with what they call paying guests. People will come and live with us, and pay us so much a week, and we will provide rooms for them, and food for them, and they will sit with us in the drawing-room and, and—*perhaps* we will have to amuse them a little."

The Duchess sank feebly back in her chair. She looked me all over.

"Was there ever?" she asked, "I scarcely like to ask, but was there ever any trace of insanity in your family?"

"I have never heard that there was," I replied. "It is certainly not developing in me. I have always been renowned for my common sense, and it is coming well to the fore now."

"My poor child," said the Duchess tenderly. She drew me close to her. "You are a very ignorant little girl, Westenra," she said, "but I have always taken a deep interest in you. You are young, but you have a good deal in your face— you are not exactly pretty, but you have both intelligence and, what is more important from my point of view, distinction in your bearing. Your father was my dear and personal friend. The man he rescued, at the cost of his own life, was my relation. I have known your mother too since we were both girls, and when she asked me, after your dear father's death, to stand sponsor to his child I could not refuse. But now, what confused rigmarole are you bringing to my ears? When did the first symptoms of this extraordinary craze begin?"

"A fortnight ago," I answered, "when the news came that our money, on which we had been living in great peace and comfort, had suddenly vanished. The investments were not sound, and one of the trustees was responsible. You ought to blame him, and be very angry with him, but please don't blame me. I am only doing the best I can under most adverse circumstances. If mother and I went to the country we should both die, not, perhaps, of physical starvation, but certainly of that starvation which contracts both the mind and soul. It would not matter at all doing without cream and meat, you know, and——"

"Oh dear," interrupted the Duchess, "I never felt more bewildered in my life. Whatever goes wrong, Westenra, people have to live, and now you speak of doing without the necessaries of life."

"Meat and cream are not necessary to keep one alive," I replied; "but of course you have never known the sort of people who do without them. I should certainly be hand and glove with them if I went into the country, but in all probability in the boarding-house in Bloomsbury we shall be able to have good meals. Now I must really say good-bye. Try and remember sometimes that I am your god-daughter … and that mother loves you very much. Don't *quite* give us both up—that is, as far as your memory is concerned."

The Duchess bustled to her feet. "I can't make you out a bit," she said. "Your head has gone wrong, that is the long and short of it, but your mother will explain things. Stay to lunch with me, Westenra, and afterwards we will go and have a talk with your mother. I can either send her a telegram or a note."

"Oh, I cannot possibly wait," I replied. "I drove here to-day, but we must give up the carriage at the end of the week, and I have other people to see. I must go immediately to Lady Thesiger. You know what a dear little Yankee she is, and so wise and sensible."

"She is a pretty woman," said the Duchess, frowning slightly, "but she does not dress well. Her clothes don't look as if they grew on her. Now you have a very lissom figure, dear; it always seems to be alive, but *have* I heard you aright? You are going to live in apartments. No; you are going into the country to a labourer's cottage—no, no, it isn't that; you are going to let apartments to people, and they are not to have either cream or meat. They won't stay long, that is one comfort. My poor child, we must get you over this craze. Dr. Paget shall see you. It is impossible that such a mad scheme should be allowed for a moment."

"One thing is certain, she does not take it in, poor darling," I said to myself. "You are very kind, Duchess," I said aloud, "and I love you better than I ever loved you before," and then I kissed her hand again and ran out of the room. The last thing I saw of her round, good-humoured face, was the pallor on her cheeks and the tears in her eyes.

Lady Thesiger lived in a large flat overlooking Kensington Gardens. She was not up when I called, but I boldly sent my name in; I was told that her ladyship would see me in her bathroom. I found her reclining on a low sofa, while a pretty girl was massaging her face.

"Is that you, Westenra?" she said; "I am charmed to see you. Take off your hat. That will do, Allison; you can come back in half-an-hour. I want to be dressed in time for lunch."

The young woman withdrew, and Lady Thesiger fixed her languid, heavily-fringed eyes on my face.

"You might shut that window, Westenra," she said, "that is, if you mean to be good-natured. Now what is it? you look quite excited."

"I am out of bondage, that is all," I said. I never treated Jasmine with respect, and she was a power in her way, but she was little older than I, and we had often romped together on rainy days, and had confided our secrets one to the other.

"Out of bondage? Does that mean that you are engaged?"

"Far from it; an engagement would probably be a state of bondage. Now listen, you are going to be awfully shocked, but if you are the good soul I think you are, you ought to help me."

"Oh, I am sure I will do anything; I admire you very much, child. Dear me, Westenra, is that a new way of doing your hair? Let me see. Show me your profile? I am not sure whether I quite like it. Yes, on the whole, I think I do. You have pretty hair, very pretty, but now, confess the truth, you do wave it; all those little curls and tendrils are not natural."

11

"As I love you, Jasmine, they are," I replied. "But oh, don't waste time now over my personal appearance. What do you think of my physical strength? Am I well made?"

"So-so," answered Lady Thesiger, opening her big dark eyes and gazing at me from top to toe. "I should say you were strong. Your shoulders are just a trifle too broad, and sometimes I think you are a little too tall, but of course I admire you immensely. You ought to make a good marriage; you ought to be a power in society."

"From this hour, Jasmine," I said, "society and I are at daggers drawn. I am going to do that sort of thing which society never forgives."

"Oh, my dear, what?" Lady Thesiger quite roused herself. She forgot her languid attitude, and sat up on her elbow. "Do pass me that box of Fuller's chocolates," she said. "Come near and help yourself; they are delicious, aren't they?"

I took one of the sweetmeats.

"Now then," said her ladyship, "speak."

"It is this. I must tell you as briefly as possible—mother and I have lost our money."

"Oh, dear," said the little lady, "what a pity that so many people do lose their money—nice people, charming people who want it so much; but if that is all, it is rather fashionable to be poor. I was told so the other day. Some one will adopt you, dear; your mother will go into one of the refined order of almshouses. It is quite the fashion, you know, quite."

"Don't talk nonsense," I said, and all the pride which I had inherited from my father came into my voice. "You may think that mother and I are low down, but we are not low enough to accept charity. We are going to put our shoulders to the wheel; we are going to solve the problem of how the poor live. We will work, for to beg we are ashamed. In short, Jasmine, this diatribe of mine leads up to the fact that we are going to start a boarding-house. Now you have the truth, Jasmine. We expect to have charming people to live with us, and to keep a large luxurious house, and to retrieve our lost fortune. Our quondam friends will of course have nothing to do with us, but our real friends will respect us. I have come here this morning to ask you a solemn question. Do you mean in the future to consider Westenra Wickham, the owner of a boarding-house, your friend? If not, say so at once. I want in this case to cut the Gordian knot quickly. Every single friend I have shall be told of mother's and my determination before long; the Duchess knows already."

"The Duchess of Wilmot?" said Lady Thesiger with a sort of gasp. She was sitting up on the sofa; there was a flush on each cheek, and her eyes were very bright. "And what did the Duchess say, Westenra?"

"She thinks I am mad."

"I agree with her. My poor child. Do let me feel your forehead. Are you feverish? Is it influenza, or a real attack of insanity?"

"It is an attack of downright common-sense," I replied. I rose as I spoke. "I have told you, Jasmine," I said, "and now I will leave you to ponder over my tidings. You can be my friend in the future and help me considerably, or you can cut me, just as you please. As to me, I feel intensely pleased and excited. I never felt so full of go and energy in my life. I am going to do that which will prevent mother feeling the pinch of poverty, and I can tell you that such a deed is worth hundreds of 'At Homes' and receptions and flirtations. Why, Jasmine, yesterday I was nobody—only a London girl trying to kill time by wasting money; but from this out I am somebody. I am a bread-winner, a labourer in the market. Now, good-bye. You will realise the truth of my words presently. But I won't kiss you, for if you decide to cut me you might be ashamed of it."

CHAPTER III

MY SCHEME

I arrived home early in the afternoon.

"Dear mother," I said, "I had an interview with the Duchess of Wilmot and with Lady Thesiger. After seeing them both, I had not the heart to go on to any more of our friends. I will describe my interview presently, but I must talk on another matter now. Our undertaking will be greatly prospered if our friends will stick to us and help us a little. If, on the other hand, we are not to depend on them, the sooner we know it the better."

"What do you mean?" asked my mother.

"Well, of course, mother dear, we will have our boarding-house. I have thought of the exact sort of house we want. It must be very large and very roomy, and the landlord must be willing to make certain improvements which I will suggest to him. Our boarding-house will be a sort of Utopia in its way, and people who come there will want to come again. We will charge good prices, but we will make our guests very comfortable."

Mother clasped my hand.

"Oh, my dear, dear child," she said. "How little you know about what you are talking. We shall have an empty house; no one will come to us. Neither you nor I have the faintest idea how to manage. We shall not only lose all the money we have, but we shall be up to our ears in debt. I do wish, Westenra, you would consider that simple little cottage in the country."

"If it must come to our living within our means," I said slowly, "I have not the least doubt that the Duchess of Wilmot would allow me to live with her as a sort of companion and amanuensis, and influence would be brought to bear to get you rooms in Hampton Court; but would you consent, mother darling, would you really consent that I should eat the bread of dependence, and that you should live partly on charity?"

Mother coloured. She had a very delicate colour, and it always made her look remarkably pretty. In her heart of hearts, I really do think she was taken with the idea of Hampton Court. The ladies who lived in those suites of apartments were more or less aristocratic, they were at least all well connected, and she and they might have much in common. It was, in her opinion, rather a distinction than otherwise to live there, but I would have none of it.

"How old are you, mother?" I asked.

"Forty-three," she answered.

"Forty-three," I repeated. "Why, you are quite young, just in the prime of middle-age. What do you mean by sitting with your hands before you for the rest of your life? You are forty-three, and I am twenty-one. Do you think for a single moment that able-bodied women, like ourselves, are to do nothing in the future; for if I did go to the Duchess my post would be merely a sinecure, and you at Hampton Court would vegetate, nothing more. Mother, you will come with me, and help me? We will disregard society; if society is ashamed of us, let it be ashamed, but we must find out, and I have a scheme to propose."

"You are so full of schemes, Westenra, you quite carry me away."

Dear mother looked bewildered, but at the same time proud of me. I think she saw gleaming in my eyes, which I know were bright and dark like my father's, some of that spirit which had carried him with a forlorn hope into the thickest of the fight, and which enabled him to win the Victoria Cross. There are a great many Victoria Crosses to be secured in this world, and girls can get and wear some of them.

"Now," I said, "we need not give up this house until the autumn. The landlord will then take it off our hands, and we shall move into our Bloomsbury mansion, but as I did not quite succeed to-day in knowing exactly how we stood with our friends, I propose that next week we should give an 'At Home,' a very simple one, mother, nothing but tea and sweet cakes, and a few sandwiches, no ices, nothing expensive."

"My dear Westenra, just now, in the height of the season, would any one come?"

"Yes, they will come, I will write to all the friends I know, and they will come out of curiosity. We will invite them for this day fortnight. I don't know any special one of our friends who has an 'At Home' on the third Friday in the month. But let me get our 'At Home' book and see."

I looked it out, and after carefully examining the long list of our acquaintances, proclaimed that I thought the third Friday in the month was a tolerably free day.

"We will ask them to come at three," I said, "a little early in the afternoon, so that those who do want to go on to friends afterwards, will have plenty of time."

"But why should they come, Westenra; why this great expense and trouble,

15

just when we are parting with them all, for if I go to Hampton Court, or the country, or to that awful boarding-house of yours, my poor child, my days in society are at an end."

"In one sense they are, mother, nevertheless, I mean to test our friends. People are very democratic in these days, and there is no saying, but that I may be more the fashion than ever; but I don't want to be the fashion, I want to get help in the task which is before me. Now, do hear me out."

Mother folded her hands in her lap. Her lips were quivering to speak, but I held her in control as it were. I stood before her making the most of my slender height, and spoke with emphasis.

"We will ask all our friends. Paul will wait on them, and Morris shall let them in, and everything will be done in the old style, for we have just the same materials we ever had to give a proper and fashionable 'At Home,' but when they are all assembled, instead of a recitation, or music, I will jump up and stand in the middle of the room, and briefly say what we mean to do. I will challenge our friends to leave us, or to stick to us."

"Westenra, are you mad? I can never, never consent to this."

"It is the very best plan, and far less troublesome than going round to everybody, and they will be slightly prepared, for the dear Duchess will have mentioned something of what I said this morning to her friends, and I know she will come. She won't mind visiting us here just once again, and Jasmine will come, and—and many other people, and we will put the thing to the test. Yes, mother, this day fortnight they shall come, and I will write the invitations to-night, and to-morrow you and I will go to Bloomsbury and look for a suitable house, for by the time they come, mother, the house will have been taken, and I hope the agreement made out, and the landlord will have been consulted, and he will make the improvements I suggest and will require. It is a big thing, mother, a great big venture for two lone women like ourselves, but we will succeed, darling, we *must* succeed."

"You are a rock of strength, West," she answered, half proudly, half sadly, "you are just like your father."

That night I sent out the invitations. They were ordinary notes of invitation, for on second thoughts I resolved not to prepare our many acquaintances beforehand. "Mrs. Wickham at home on such a day," nothing more.

I posted the letters and slept like a top that night, and in the morning awoke with the tingling sensation which generally comes over me when I have a great deal to do, and when there is an important and very interesting matter at stake. I used to feel like that at times when I was at school. On the day when I

16

won the big scholarship, and was made a sort of queen of by the other girls, I had the sensation very strongly, and I felt like it also when a terrible illness which mother had a few years ago came to a crisis, and her precious life lay in the balance. Here was another crisis in my career, almost the most important which had come to me yet, and I felt the old verve and the old strong determination to conquer fate. Fate at present was against me, but surely I was a match for it: I was young, strong, clever, and I had a certain *entrée* into society which might or might not help me. If society turned its back on me, I could assuredly do without it. If, on the other hand, it smiled on me, success was assured in advance.

I ran downstairs to breakfast in the best of spirits. I had put on my very prettiest white dress, and a white hat trimmed with soft silk and feathers.

"Why, Westenra, dressed already?" said mother.

"Yes, and you must dress too quickly, Mummy. Oh, there is Paul. Paul, we shall want the victoria at ten o'clock."

Paul seemed accustomed to this order now. He smiled and vanished. None of our servants knew that their tenure with us was ended, that within a very short time mother and I would know the soft things of life no more. We were dragging out our last delicious days in the Land of Luxury; we were soon to enter the Land of Hard Living, the Land of Endeavour, the Land of Struggle. Might it not be a better, a more bracing life than our present one? At least it would be a more interesting life, of that I made sure, even before I plunged into its depths.

Mother ate her breakfast quite with appetite, and soon afterwards we were driving in the direction of Bloomsbury.

Jenkins, who had lived with us for years, and who had as a matter of course imbibed some of the aristocratic notions of our neighbourhood, almost turned up his nose when we told him to stop at the house of a well-known agent in Bloomsbury. He could not, like the Duchess of Wilmot, confess that he did not know where Bloomsbury was, but he evidently considered that something strange and by no means *comme il faut* had occurred.

Presently we reached our destination, it was only half-past ten.

"Won't you get out, mother?" I asked as I sprang to the pavement.

"Is it necessary, dear child?" replied mother.

"I think it is," I answered; "you ought to appear in this matter, I am too young to receive the respect which I really merit, but with you to help me—oh, you will do *exactly* what I tell you, won't you?"

17

"My dear girl!"

"Yes, Mummy, you will, you will."

I took her hand, and gave it a firm grip, and we went into the house-agent's together.

CHAPTER IV

THE VERDICT

The first thing I noticed when I entered the large room where Messrs Macalister & Co. carried on their business, was a young man, tall and very well set up, who stood with his back to us. He was talking earnestly to one of Macalister's clerks, and there was something about his figure which caused me to look at him attentively. His hair was of a light shade of brown, and was closely cropped to his well-shaped head, and his shoulders were very broad and square. He was dressed well, and had altogether that man-of-the-world, well bred sort of look, which is impossible to acquire by any amount of outward veneer. The man who stood with his back to us, and did not even glance round as we came into the agent's office, was beyond doubt a gentleman. I felt curiously anxious to see his face, for I was certain it must be a pleasant one, but in this particular fate did not favour me. I heard him say to the clerk in a hurried tone—

"I will come back again presently," and then he disappeared by another door, and I heard him walking rapidly away. Mother had doubtless not noticed the man at all. She was seated near a table, and when the clerk in question came up to her, seemed indisposed to speak. I gave her a silent nudge.

"We want—ahem," said my mother—she cleared her throat, "we are anxious to look at some houses."

"Fourteen to fifteen bedrooms in each," I interrupted.

"Fourteen to fifteen bedrooms," repeated mother. "How many sitting rooms, Westenra?"

"Four, five, or six," was my answer.

"Oh, you require a mansion," said the agent. "Where do you propose to look for your house, madam?"

He addressed mother with great respect. Mother again glanced at me.

"We thought somewhere north," she said; "or north-west," she added.

"W.C.," I interrupted; "Bloomsbury, we wish to settle in Bloomsbury."

"Perhaps, Westenra," said my mother, "you had better describe the house. My daughter takes a great interest in houses," she added in an apologetic tone to the clerk. The face of the clerk presented a blank appearance, he showed

19

neither elation nor the reverse at having a young lady to deal with instead of an old lady. He began to trot out his different houses, to explain their advantages, their aristocratic positions.

"Aristocratic houses in Bloomsbury—aristocratic!" said mother, and there was a tone of almost scorn in her voice.

"I assure you it is the case, madam. Russell Square is becoming quite the fashion again, and so is"—he paused—"Would Tavistock Square suit you?" he said, glancing at me.

"I do not know," I answered. "I seem to be better acquainted with the names of Russell Square or Bloomsbury Square. After all, if we can get a large enough house it does not greatly matter, provided it is in Bloomsbury. We wish to see several houses, for we cannot decide without a large choice."

"You would not be induced, ladies, to think of a flat?" queried the agent.

Mother glanced at me; there was almost an appeal in her eyes. If I could only be induced to allow her to live in a tiny, tiny flat—she and I alone on our one hundred and fifty a year—but my eyes were bright with determination, and I said firmly—

"We wish to look at houses, we do not want a flat."

Accordingly, after a little more argument, we were supplied with orders to view, and returning to the carriage I gave brief directions to Jenkins.

During the rest of the morning we had a busy time. We went from one house to another. Most were large; some had handsome halls and wide staircases, and double doors, and other relics of past grandeur, but all were gloomy and dirty, and mother became more and more depressed, and more and more hopeless, as she entered each one in turn.

"Really, Westenra," she said, "we cannot do it. No, my darling, it is hopeless. Think of the staff of servants we should require. Do look at these stairs, it is quite worth counting them. My dear child, such a life would kill me."

But I was young and buoyant, and did not feel the stairs, and my dreams seemed to become more rosy as obstacles appeared in view. I was determined to conquer, I had made up my mind to succeed.

"Whatever happens you shall not have a tiring time," I said affectionately to my dear mother, and then I asked one of the caretakers to give her a chair, and she sat in the great wide desolate drawing-room while I ran up and down stairs, and peeped into cupboards, and looked all over the house, and calculated, as fast as my ignorant brain would allow me, the amount of furniture which would be necessary to start the mansion I had in view.

For one reason or another most of the houses on the agent's list were absolutely impossible for our purpose, but at last we came to one which seemed to be the exact thing we required. It was a corner house in a square called Graham Square, and was not so old by fifty years as the houses surrounding it. In height also it was a storey lower, but being a corner house it had a double frontage, and was in consequence very large and roomy. There were quite six or seven sitting rooms, and I think there were up to twenty bedrooms in the house, and it had a most cheerful aspect, with balconies round the drawing-room windows, and balconies to the windows of the bedrooms on the first floor. I made up my mind on the spot that the inmates of these special rooms should pay extra for the privilege of such delightful balconies. And the windows of the house were large, and when it was all re-papered and re-painted according to my modern ideas, I knew that we could secure a great deal of light in the rooms; and then besides, one whole side faced south-east, and would scarcely ever be cold in winter, whereas in summer it would be possible to render it cool by sun-blinds and other contrivances. Yes, the house would do exactly.

I ran downstairs to mother, who had by this time given up climbing those many, many stairs, and told her that I had found the exact house for our purpose.

"Seventeen Graham Square is magnificent," I said. "My dearest, darling mother, in ten years time we shall be rich women if we can only secure this splendid house for our purpose."

"We do not even know the rent," said mother.

"Oh, the rent," I cried. "I forgot about that. I will look on the order to view."

I held it in my hand and glanced at it. Just for a moment my heart stood still, for the corner house commanded a rental of two hundred and eighty pounds a year. Not at all dear for so big a mansion, but with rates and taxes and all the other etceteras it certainly was a serious item for us to meet, and would be considered even by the most sanguine people as a most risky speculation.

"Never mind, never mind," I cried eagerly, "we will secure this house; I do not think we need look at any of the others."

I crumpled up the remaining orders. Mother stepped into the carriage, and Jenkins took us back to the agent's.

"You must speak this time, Westenra," said mother. "Remember it is your scheme, darling; I am not at all accustomed to this sort of business; it will be necessary for you to take the initiative."

"Very well, mother, I will; and suppose you stay in the carriage." I uttered these last words in a coaxing tone, for the tired look on her face almost frightened me, and I did not want her to take any of the worry of what I already called to myself "Westenra's grand scheme."

I entered the office, and the man who had attended to us in the morning came forward. I told him briefly that of the many houses which we had looked over, the only one which would suit our purpose was No. 17 Graham Square.

"Ah," he answered, "quite the handsomest house on our list. Do you want it for your own occupation, Miss—Miss——"

"Wickham," I said. "Yes, of course we want the house for ourselves—that is, mother would like to rent it."

"It is a high rent," said the man, "not of course high for such a fine mansion, but higher than the rest of the houses in the Square. It contains a great many rooms." He glanced at me as though he meant to say something impertinent, but, reading an expression of determination on my face, he refrained.

"How soon can we take possession of the house?" I asked. "It would of course be papered and painted for us?"

"If you take a lease, not otherwise," answered Macalister's clerk.

"I think we would take a lease," I replied. "What is the usual length?"

"Seven, fourteen, twenty-one years," he answered glibly; "but I do not think the landlords round here would grant a longer lease than fourteen years."

"Oh, that would be quite long enough," I answered emphatically. "We should like to arrange the matter as soon as possible, we are greatly pleased with the house. Of course the drains must be carefully tested, and the entire place would have to be re-decorated from cellar to attic."

"For a fourteen years' lease I doubt not this would be done," said the man, "but of course there are several matters to be gone into. You want the house for a private residence, do you not?"

"Yes, and no," I said faintly. There was a room just beyond where I was seated, and at that moment I heard a book fall heavily to the ground. It startled me. Was any one in there listening to what we were saying?

The clerk stepped forward and quietly closed the door.

"To be frank with you," I said, "we wish to secure 17 Graham Square in order to start a boarding-house there."

The man immediately laid down the large book in which he had been taking my orders.

"That will never do," he said. "We cannot allow business of any sort to be carried on in the house, it would destroy all the rest of the property. It is far too aristocratic for anything of the kind."

"But our house would be practically private," I said; "I mean," I continued, stammering and blushing, and feeling ready to sink through the floor, "that our guests would be extremely nice and well-behaved people."

"Oh, I have no doubt whatever of that," replied the clerk, "but there is a condition in every lease in that special Square, that money is not to be earned on the premises. I presume your guests would not come to you for nothing?"

"Certainly not," I replied. I felt myself turning cold and stiff. All the angry blood of my noble ancestors stirred in my veins. I said a few more words and left the shop.

"Well?" asked mother. She was looking dreary and terribly huddled up in the carriage. It was a warm day, but I think going through those empty houses had chilled her. "Well, Westenra, have you taken No. 17?"

"Alas! no," I answered in some heat; "would you believe it, mother, the agent says the landlord will not let us the house if we make money in it."

"If we make money in it? I do not understand," answered mother. Her blue eyes were fixed on my face in an anxious way.

"Why, mother, darling, don't you know we meant to fill the house with paying guests."

"Oh, I forgot," said mother. "Home, Jenkins, as fast as possible."

Jenkins whipped up the horses, and we trotted home. Mother looked distinctly relieved.

"So you have not taken the house?" she said.

"I cannot get it," I answered. "It is more than provoking. What are we to do? I had taken such a fancy to the place."

"It did seem, for that benighted place, fairly cheerful," said my mother, "but, Westenra, there is a Providence guiding our paths. Doubtless Providence does not intend you to wreck your young life attending to lodgers."

"But, mother dear, don't you understand that we must do something for our living? It is disappointing, but we shall get over it somehow."

During the rest of that day mother refused even to discuss the boarding-house scheme. She seemed to think that because we could not get 17 Graham Square, there was no other house available for our purpose.

The next day I went out without mother. I did not visit the same agent. After finding myself in Bloomsbury I repaired to a post-office, and, taking down the big Directory, secured the names of several agents in the neighbourhood. These I visited in turn. I had dressed myself very plainly; I had travelled to my destination by 'bus. I thought that I looked exactly what I felt—a very business-like young woman. Already the gulf was widening between my old and my new life. Already I was enjoying my freedom.

Once more I was supplied with a list of houses, and once again I trotted round to see them. Alack and alas! how ugly empty houses did look; how dilapidated and dirty were the walls without the pictures and bookcases! How dreary were those countless flights of stairs, those long narrow windows, those hopelessly narrow halls; and then, the neighbourhood of these so-called mansions was so sordid. Could we by any possible means brighten such dwellings? Could we make them fit to live in? I visited them all, and finally selected three of these. Two had a clause forbidding the letting out of apartments, but the third and least desirable of the houses was to be the absolute property of the tenant to do what he liked with.

"That mansion," said the obliging agent, "you can sublet to your heart's content, madam. It is a very fine house, only one hundred and eighty pounds a year. There are ten bedrooms and five sitting-rooms. You had better close with it at once."

But this I could not do. The outlook from this house was so hideous; the only way to it was through an ugly, not to say hideous, thoroughfare. I thought of my delicate, aristocratic mother here. I thought of the friends whom I used to know visiting us in 14 Cleveland Street, and felt my castle in the clouds tumbling about my ears. What was to be done!

"I cannot decide to-day," I said; "I will let you know."

"You will lose it, madam," said the agent.

"Nevertheless, I cannot decide so soon; I must consult my mother."

"Very well, madam," said the man, in a tone of disappointment.

I left his office and returned home.

For the next few days I scarcely spoke at all about my project. I was struggling to make up my mind to the life which lay before us if we took 14 Cleveland Street. The street itself was somewhat narrow; the opposite houses seemed to bow at their neighbours; the rooms, although many, were comparatively small; and last, but by no means least, the landlord would do very little in the way of decoration.

24

"We can let houses of this kind over and over again," said the agent, "I don't say that Mr. Mason won't have the ceilings whitened for you, but as to papering, no; the house don't require it. It was done up for the last tenant four years ago."

"And why has the last tenant left?" I asked.

"Owing to insolvency, madam," was the quick reply, and the man darted a keen glance into my face.

Insolvency! I knew what that meant. It was another word for ruin, for bankruptcy. In all probability, if we took that detestable house, we also would have to leave on account of insolvency, for what nice, cheerful, paying guests would care to live with us there? I shook my head. Surely there must be somewhere other houses to let.

During the next few days I spent all my time searching for houses. I got quite independent, and, I think, a little roughened. I was more brusque than usual in my manners. I became quite an adept at jumping in and out of omnibuses. I could get off omnibuses quite neatly when they were going at a fairly good pace, and the conductors, I am sure, blessed me in their hearts for my agile movements. Then the agents all round Bloomsbury began to know me. Finally, one of them said, on the event of my fourth visit—

"Had you not better try further afield, Miss? There are larger, brighter, and newer houses in the neighbourhood of Highbury, for instance."

"No," I said, "we must live in Bloomsbury." Then I noticed that the man examined me all over in quite a disagreeable fashion, and then he said slowly —

"14 Cleveland Street is still to be had, Miss, but of course you understand that the landlord will want the usual references."

"References!" I cried. "He shall certainly have them if he requires them." And then I wondered vaguely, with a queer sinking at my heart, to whom of all our grand friends I might apply who would vouch for us that we would not run away without paying the rent. Altogether, I felt most uncomfortable.

The days passed. No more likely houses appeared on the horizon, and at last the afternoon came when our friends were to visit us, when I, Westenra, was to break to these fashionable society people my wild project. But I had passed through a good deal of the hardening process lately, and was not at all alarmed when the important day dawned. This was to be our very last entertainment. After that we would step down.

Mother, exquisitely dressed in dove-coloured satin, waited for her guests in the drawing-room. I was in white. I had given up wearing white when I was going about in omnibuses, but I had several charming costumes for afternoon and evening wear still quite fresh, and I donned my prettiest dress now, and looked at my face in the glass with a certain amount of solicitude. I saw before me a very tall, slender girl; my eyes were grey. I had a creamy, pale complexion, and indifferently good features. There were some people who thought me pretty, but I never did think anything of my looks myself. I gave my own image a careless nod now, and ran briskly downstairs.

"You'll be very careful what you say to our guests, Westenra?" queried mother. "This whole scheme of yours is by no means to my liking. I feel certain that the dear Duchess and Lady Thesiger will feel that they have been brought here unfairly. It would have been far franker and better to tell them that something singularly unpleasant was about to occur."

"But, dearest mother, why should it be unpleasant? and it is the fashion of the day to have sensation at any cost. Our guests will always look back on this afternoon as a sort of red letter day. Just think for yourself how startled and how interested they will be. Whether they approve, or whether they disapprove, it will be immensely interesting and out of the common, mother. O mother! think of it!" I gripped her hand tightly, and she said—

"Don't squeeze me so hard, Westenra, I shall need all my pluck."

Well, the hour came and also the guests. They arrived in goodly numbers. There was the usual fashionable array of carriages outside our door. There were footmen in livery and coachmen, and stately and magnificently groomed horses, and the guests poured up the stairs and entered our drawing rooms, and the chatter-chatter and hum-hum of ordinary society conversation began. Everything went as smoothly as it always did, and all the time my mother chatted with that courtly grace which made her look quite in the same state of life as the Duchess of Wilmot. In fact the only person in the room who looked at all nervous was the said Duchess. She had a way of glancing from me to mother, as if she was not quite sure of either of us, and once as I passed her, she stretched out her hand and touched me on my sleeve.

"Eh, Westenra?" she said.

"Yes, your Grace," I replied.

"All that silliness, darling, that you talked to me the other day, is quite knocked on the head, is it not? Oh, I am so relieved."

"You must wait and find out," was my reply. "I have something to say to every one soon, and oh please, try not to be too shocked with me."

"You are an incorrigible girl," she replied, but she shook her head quite gaily at me. She evidently had not the slightest idea of what I was going to do.

As to my special friend Jasmine Thesiger, she was as usual surrounded by an admiring group of men and women, and gave me no particular thought. I looked from one to the other of all our guests: I did not think any more were likely to come. All those who had been specially invited had arrived. My moment had come. Just then, however, just before I rose from my seat to advance into the middle of the room, I noticed coming up the stairs a tall, broad-shouldered man. He was accompanied by a friend of ours, a Mr. Walters, a well-known artist. I had never seen this man before, and yet I fancied, in a sort of intangible way, that his figure was familiar. I just glanced at him for a moment, and I do not believe he came into the room. He stood a little behind Mr. Walters, who remained in the doorway. My hour had come. I glanced at mother. Poor darling, she turned very white. I think she was almost terrified, but as to myself I felt quite cheerful, and not in the least alarmed.

"I want to say something to all my dear friends," I began. I had a clear voice, and it rose above the babel. There came sudden and profound silence.

I saw a lady nudge her neighbour.

"I did not know," I heard her say, "that Westenra recited," and then she settled herself in a comfortable attitude to listen.

I stood in the middle of the floor, and faced everybody.

"I have something to say," I began, "and it is not a recitation. I have asked you all to come here to-day to listen to me." I paused and looked round. How nice our guests looked, how kind, how beautifully dressed! What good form the men were in, and how aristocratic were the women. How different these men and women were from the people I had associated with during the week —the people who took care of the houses in Bloomsbury, the agents who let the houses, the people whom I had met in the busses going to and from the houses. These nice, pleasant, well-bred people belonged to me, they were part and parcel of my own set; I was at home with them.

I just caught the Duchess's eye for a moment, and I think there was alarm in those brown depths, but she was too essentially a woman of the world to show anything. She just folded her jewelled hands in her lap, leant back in her chair, and prepared to listen. One or two of the men, I think, raised their eye-glasses to give me a more critical glance, but soon even that mark of special attention subsided. Of course it was a recitation. People were beginning to be tired of recitations.

"I want to say something, and I will say it as briefly as possible," I commenced. "Mother does not approve of it, but she will do it, because she has yielded to me as a dear, good, *modern* mother ought."

Here there was a little laugh, and some of the tension was lessened.

"I want to tell you all," I continued, "for most of you have been our friends since I was a child, that mother and I are—poor. There is nothing disgraceful in being poor, is there? but at the same time it is unpleasant, unfortunate. We were fairly well off. Now, through no fault of our own, we have lost our money."

The visitors looked intensely puzzled, and also uncomfortable, but now I raised my eyes a little above them. It was necessary that if I went on putting them to the test, I should not look them full in the face.

"We are poor," I continued, "therefore we cannot live any longer in this house. From having a fair competence, not what many of you would consider riches, but from having a fair competence, we have come down to practically nothing. We could live, it is true, in the depths of the country, on the very little which has been saved out of the wreck, but I for one do not wish to do that. I dislike what is called decent poverty, I dislike the narrow life, the stultifying life, the mean life. I am my father's daughter. You have heard of my father, that is his picture"—I pointed as I spoke to an oil painting on the wall. "You know that he was a man of action, I also will act." I hurried my voice a trifle here—"So mother and I mean not to accept what many people would consider the inevitable; but we mean, to use a vulgar phrase, to better ourselves."

Now it is certain, our guests were a little surprised. They began to fidget, and one or two men came nearer, and I thought, though I am not sure, that I saw the tall man, with the head of closely cropped hair, push forward to look at me. But I never looked any one full in the eyes; I fixed mine on father's picture. I seemed to hear father's voice saying to me—

"Go on, Westenra, that was very good, you and I are people of action, remember."

So I went on and I explained my scheme. I told it very briefly. Mother and I would in future earn our own living.

I was educated fairly well, but I had no special gifts, so I would not enter the Arena where teachers struggled and fought and bled, and many of them fell by the wayside. Nor would I enter the Arena of Art, because in no sense of the word was I an artist, nor would I go on the Stage, for my talent did not lie in that direction, but I had certain talents, and they were of a practical sort. I could keep accounts admirably; I could, I believed, manage a house. Then I skilfully sketched in that wonderful boarding-house of my dreams, that house in dull Bloomsbury, which by my skill and endeavour would be bright and render an acceptable home for many. Finally, I said that my mother and I had made up our minds to leave the fashionable part of London and to retire to Bloomsbury.

"We will take our house from September," I said, "and advertise very soon for paying guests, and we hope the thing will do well, and that in ten or twelve years we shall have made enough money to keep ourselves for the future in comfort. Now," I continued, "I appeal to no one to help us. We do not intend to borrow money from anybody, and the only reason I am speaking to you to-day is because I wish, and I am sure mother agrees with me, to be quite frank with you. Mother and I know quite well that we are doing an absolutely unconventional thing, and that very likely you, as our friends of the past, will resent it. Those of you who do not feel that you can associate with two ladies who keep a boarding-house, need not say so in so many words, but you can give us to understand, by means known best to yourselves, whether you will know us in the future. If you want to cut us we shall consider it quite right, quite reasonable, quite fair. Then those who do intend to stick to us, even through this great change in our lives, may be the greatest possible help by recommending us and our boarding-house to their friends, that is, if any of you present have friends who would live in Bloomsbury.

"Mother and I thought it quite fair that you should know, and we thought it best that I should tell you quite simply. We are neither of us ashamed, and mother approves, or at least she will approve presently, of what I have done."

There was a dead silence when I ceased speaking, followed by a slight rustling amongst the ladies. The men looked one and all intensely uncomfortable, and the tall man who had come in with Mr Walters, the artist, disappeared altogether.

I had not been nervous while I was speaking, but I felt nervous now. I knew that I was being weighed in the balance, that I and my scheme were being held up before the mental eyes of these people with the keenest, most scathing criticism. Would one in all that crowd understand me? I doubted it. Perhaps in my first sensation of sinking and almost despair something of my feeling stole into my face, for suddenly Jasmine sprang to her feet and said in an excited, tremulous voice—

"I for one say that Westenra is a very plucky girl. I wish her God speed, and I hope her scheme will succeed."

This was very nice indeed of Jasmine, but I do not know that it relieved the situation much, for still the others were silent, and then one lady got up and went over to mother and took her hand and said—

"I am very sorry for you, dear Mrs. Wickham, very sorry indeed. I fear I must say good-bye now; I am very sorry. Good-bye, dear Mrs. Wickham."

And this lady's example was followed by most of the other ladies, until at last there was no one left in the room but the Duchess of Wilmot and Lady Thesiger and ourselves. Lady Thesiger's cheeks were brightly flushed.

"My dear Westenra," she said, "you are one of the most eccentric creatures in creation. Of course from first to last you are as wrong as you can be. You know nothing about keeping a boarding-house, and you are bound to fail. I could not say so before all those ridiculous people, who would not have understood, but I say so now to you. My dear girl, your speech was so much Greek to them. You spoke over their heads or under their feet, just as you please to put it, but comprehend you they did not. You will be the talk of the hour, and they will mention you as a girl whom they used to know, but who has gone a little mad, and then you will be forgotten. You would have done fifty times better by keeping this thing to yourself."

"That is precisely what I think," said the Duchess. "My dear Mary," she added, turning to my mother, "what is the matter with your child? Is she quite *right*?" The Duchess gave an expressive nod, and I saw mother's face turn pale.

"Oh, do listen to me for a moment," interrupted pretty Lady Thesiger, "what I say is this. Westenra is on the wrong tack. If she wishes to earn money, why must she earn it in this preposterous, impossible manner? It would be fifty times better for her to go as a teacher or a secretary, but to keep a boarding-house! You see for yourself, dear Mrs. Wickham, that it is impossible. As long as we live in society we must adhere to its rules, and for West calmly to believe that people of position in London will know her and respect her when she is a boarding-house keeper, is to expect a miracle. Now, I for one will not cut you, Westenra."

"Nor will I cut you, Westenra," said the Duchess, and she gave a profound sigh and folded her hands in her lap.

"Two of your friends will not cut you, but I really think all the others will," said Lady Thesiger. "Then I suppose you expect me to recommend nice Americans to come and stay with you, but it is my opinion that, with your no knowledge at all of this sort of thing, you will keep a very so-so, harum-scarum sort of house. How can I recommend my nice American friends to be made thoroughly uncomfortable by you? Oh, I am *very* sorry for you."

Lady Thesiger got up as she spoke; she kissed me, squeezed my hand, and said, "Oh child, what a goose you are!" and left the room.

The Duchess followed more slowly.

"I don't forget, my child," she said, "that I am your godmother, that I loved your dear father, that I love your mother, that I also love you. Do not be wilful, Westenra; give up this mad scheme. There are surely other ways open to you in this moment of misfortune. Above all things, try not to forget that you are your father's daughter."

CHAPTER V

JANE MULLINS

On the evening which followed our last "At Home," mother came to me, and earnestly begged of me to pause and reflect.

"Wherever you go I will go, Westenra," she said; "that may be taken as a matter of course, but I do think you are wrong to go against all the wishes of our friends."

"But our friends won't do anything for us, Mummy!" I answered, "and they will forget us just as soon in the cottage in the country, as they will in the boarding-house in town; sooner, in fact, if that is any consolation to you, and I do want to try it, Mummy, for I cannot be buried alive in the country at twenty-one."

"Then I will say no more," replied mother. "I only trust the way may be made plain for us, for at present I cannot see that it is; but if we can find a suitable house, and take it, I will go with you, West, although, darling, I hate the thing —I do truly."

After this speech of mother's it can easily be supposed that I slept badly that night. I began for the first time in my life to doubt myself, and my own judgment. I began even seriously to consider the cottage in the country with its genteel poverty, and I began to wonder if I was to spend the remainder of my youth getting thinner in mind and body, day by day, and hour by hour.

"Anæmic," I said to myself. "In the country with no money, and no interests, I shall become anæmic. My thoughts will be feeble and wanting in force, and I shall die long before my time a miserable old maid. Now, there are no real old maids in London. The unmarried women are just as full of force, and go, and common-sense, and ambition, and happiness as the married ones; but in the country, oh, it is different. There old age comes before its time. I knew that I was not the girl to endure having nothing to do, and yet that seemed to be my appointed portion. So during the night I shed very bitter tears, and I hated society for its coldness and want of comprehension. I longed more frantically than ever to find myself in the midst of the people, where "a man was a man for a' that," and mere veneer went for nothing. But if mother's heart was likely to be broken by my taking this step, and if there was no house for me but 14 Cleveland Street, I doubted very much whether I could go on with my scheme. Judge therefore of my surprise and delight, when on the following morning, mother handed me a letter which she had just received. It was from Messrs. Macalister & Co.

"Read it," she said, "I do not quite know what it means."

I read the letter quickly, it ran as follows:—

> "DEAR MADAM,—We write to acquaint you, that we have just had an interview with Mr. Hardcastle, the landlord of 17 Graham Square, and he desires us to say, that he is willing in your case to come to terms with regard to his house, and if you will take it for a lease of fourteen years, he will do it up for you, in the most approved style, and according to your own taste; he also withdraws his embargo to your letting apartments, or having paying guests in your house.

> "Under the circumstances, we shall be glad to hear if you still entertain the idea of taking this mansion.

> —Yours faithfully,

> MACALISTER & CO."

"Oh mother!" I cried, "this is just splendid!" My spirits rose with a bound. Anxious as I was to possess a boarding-house, I hated going to 14 Cleveland Street, but 17 Graham Square was a house where any one might be happy. It was charmingly built; it was large, commodious, cheerful, and then the landlord—he must be a delightful man when he withdrew his embargo, when he permitted us—*us* to have paying guests in our dwelling. Even Jasmine need not be ashamed to send her nice, rich American friends to 17 Graham Square.

"This is splendid, mother!" I repeated.

"Dear me, Westenra," said mother, looking pale and troubled, "what house is he alluding to? I saw so many that first day, darling, and the only impression they left upon me was, that they were all stairs and narrowness; they seemed to go up and up, for ever and ever, my legs ache even now when I think of them."

"But you cannot forget 17 Graham Square," I said, "the last house we saw … the corner-house. You recollect the hall, how wide it was, and you know there were darling balconies, and you shall have one, little mother, all to yourself, and such a sweet sun-blind over it, and you can keep your favourite plants there, and be, oh, so happy! Mother—mother, this is magnificent!"

"I do recall the house now," said mother, "it was not quite as bad as the other houses; but still, Westenra, what does this mean? Why should there be an exception made in our favour?"

"Oh, that I know nothing about," I answered, "I suppose the landlord was not going to be so silly as to lose good tenants."

"And what is the rent of the house … I forget."

"Two hundred and something," I said in a careless tone, "not at all high for such a house, and the landlord, Mr. Hardcastle, will do it up for us. Mother, we will have the carriage, and go and make our arrangements immediately."

"Then you are quite determined, West?"

"Mother, dear mother, I do think father would like us to do it."

Now, whenever I spoke of my dead father, mother looked intensely solemn and subdued. Once she told me that she thought there was a strong link between my father's spirit and mine, and that at times I spoke so exactly like him, and made use of the identically same expressions, and in short impressed her with the feeling that he was close to her. I did not often use my father's name, therefore, as a means of power over my mother, but I did use it now; and, with the usual result, she got up gently and said—

"We had better go and see the house once more."

We did go, we drove straight to the agents, and got the order to view, and went all over 17 Graham Square. Our second visit was far more delightful than the first, for the agent's clerk accompanied us. We found him in an excellent humour, most willing to offer suggestions and to accept any suggestions of ours. Not that mother made any, it was I who, with my usual daring, spoke of this improvement and the other.

But darling mother became a little cheerful when she stood in that noble drawing-room and saw the sun shining in bars across the floor, and the agent's clerk was quite astonishingly cheery; he knew just the colour the paper ought to be, for instance, and the tone of the paint, and he even suggested what curtains would go with such paper and such paint. I never saw a man so improved. He had lost his brusqueness, and was very anxious to please us.

"It is extraordinary," said mother afterwards; "really I never knew that house-agents could be such agreeable people. No. 17 Graham Square is a handsome house, Westenra, it is a great pity that it is not situated in Mayfair."

"But mother, dear mother, we could not have a boarding-house in the very midst of our friends," I said with a smile; "we shall do splendidly in Graham Square, and we should not do at all well in Mayfair."

When we returned to the agents, Mr. Macalister himself, one of the heads of the firm, came and interviewed us. After answering a great many questions, it was finally decided that he was to see Mr. Hardcastle, the landlord, and that the landlord was to have an interview the next day with mother; and the agent further agreed that the landlord should call on mother at our own house in Sumner Place, and then we drove home.

"I suppose it is completed now," said mother, "the thing is done. Well, child, you are having your own way; it will be a lesson to you, I only trust we shall not be quite ruined. I am already puzzled to know how we are to meet that enormous rent."

But at that moment of my career I thought nothing at all about the rent. That night I slept the sleep of the just, and was in high spirits the following day, when the landlord, a nice, jovial, rosy-faced man, arrived, accompanied by the agent. They both saw my mother, who told them frankly that she knew nothing about business, and so perforce they found themselves obliged to talk to me. Everything was going smoothly until Mr. Hardcastle said in the very quietest of tones—

"Of course you understand, Mrs. Wickham, that I shall require references. I am going to lay out a good deal of money on the house, and references are indispensable."

"Of course," answered mother, but she looked pale and nervous.

"What sort of references?" I asked.

"Tradesmen's references are what we like best," was his reply; "but your banker's will be all-sufficient—an interview with your banker with regard to your deposit will make all safe."

Then mother turned paler than ever, and looked first at me and then at Mr. Hardcastle. After a pause she said slowly—

"My daughter and I would not undertake our present scheme if we had capital —we have not any."

"Not any?" said Mr. Hardcastle, looking blank, "and yet you propose to take a house with a rental of two hundred and eighty pounds a year."

"We mean to pay the rent out of the profit we get from the boarders," I replied.

Mr. Hardcastle did not make use of an ugly word, but he raised his brows, looked fixedly at me for a moment, and then shook his head.

"I am sorry," he said, rising; "I would do a great deal to oblige you, for you are both most charming ladies, but I cannot let my house without references. If you, for instance, Mrs. Wickham, could get any one to guarantee the rent, I should be delighted to let you the house and put it in order, but not otherwise."

He added a few more words, and then he and the agent, both of them looking very gloomy, went away.

"I shall hear from you doubtless on the subject of references," said Mr. Hardcastle as he bowed himself out, "and I will keep the offer open until Saturday."

This was Wednesday, we had three days to spare.

"Now, Westenra," said my mother, "the thing has come to a stop of itself. Providence has interfered, and I must honestly say I am glad. From the first the scheme was mad, and as that nice, jovial looking Mr. Hardcastle will not let us the house without our having capital, and as we have no capital, there surely is an end to the matter. I have not the slightest doubt, West, that all the other landlords in Bloomsbury will be equally particular, therefore we must fall back upon our little cottage in——"

"No, mother," I interrupted, "no; I own that at the present moment I feel at my wits'end, but I have not yet come to the cottage in the country."

I think there were tears in my eyes, for mother opened her arms wide.

"Kiss me," she said.

I ran into her dear arms, and laid my head on her shoulder.

"Oh, you are the sweetest thing on earth," I said, "and it is because you are, and because I love you so passionately, I will not let you degenerate. I will find my way through somehow."

I left mother a moment later, and I will own it, went to my own lovely, lovely room, suitable for a girl who moved in the best society, and burst into tears. It was astonishing what a sudden passion I had taken, as my friends would say, to degrade myself; but this did not look like degradation in my eyes, it was just honest work. We wanted money, and we would earn it; we would go in debt to no man; we would earn money for ourselves. But then the thought came to me, "Was my scheme too expensive? had I any right to saddle mother with such an enormous rent?" I had always considered myself a very fair arithmetician, and I now sat down and went carefully into accounts. I smile to this day as I think of myself seated at my little table in the big bay window of my bedroom, trying to make out with pencil and paper how I could keep 17 Graham Square going—I, a girl without capital, without knowledge, without any of the sort of experience which alone could aid me in a crisis of this sort.

I spent the rest of the day in very low spirits, for my accounts would not, however hard I tried, show any margin of profit.

The more difficulties came in my way, however, the more determined was I to overcome them. Presently I took a sheet of paper and wrote a few lines to Mr. Hardcastle. I knew his address, and wrote to him direct.

"Dear sir," I said, "will you oblige me by letting me know what capital my mother will require in order to become your tenant for 17 Graham Square."

I signed this letter, adding a postscript, "An early answer will oblige."

I received the answer about noon the following day.

> "DEAR MISS WICKHAM,—Your letter puzzles me. I see you have a great deal of pluck and endeavour, and I should certainly do my utmost to please you, but I cannot let you have the house under a capital of five thousand pounds."

The letter fell from my hands, and I sat in blank despair. Five thousand pounds is a small sum to many people, to others it is as impossible and as unget-at-able as the moon. We, when our debts were paid, would have nothing at all to live on except the annuity which my mother received from the Government, and a small sum of fifty pounds a year.

I began dismally to consider what rent we must pay for the awful cottage in the country, and to what part of the country it would be best to retire, when Paul came into the room and presented me with a card.

"There's a lady—a person, I mean—downstairs, and she wants to see you, Miss."

I took the card and read the name—Miss Jane Mullins.

"Who is she?" I asked; "I don't know her."

"She's a sort of betwixt and between, Miss. I showed her into the li'bry. I said you was most likely engaged, but that I would inquire."

"Miss Jane Mullins." I read the name aloud. "Show her up, Paul," I said then.

"Oh, my dear West, what do you mean?" said mother; "that sort of person has probably called to beg."

"She may as well beg in the drawing-room as anywhere else," I said. "I have rather taken a fancy to her name—Jane Mullins."

"A hideous name," said mother; but she did not add any more, for the next moment there came a rustle of harsh silk on the landing, the drawing-room door was flung open by Paul in his grandest style, and Miss Jane Mullins walked in. She entered quickly, with a determined step. She was a little woman, stoutly built, and very neatly and at the same time quietly dressed. Her dress was black silk, and I saw at a glance that the quality of the silk was poor. It gave her a harsh appearance, which was further intensified by a kind of fixed colour in her cheeks. Her face was all over a sort of chocolate red. She had scanty eyebrows and scanty hair, her eyes were small and twinkling, she had a snub nose and a wide mouth. Her age might have been from thirty-five to forty. She had, however, a great deal of self-possession, and did not seem at all impressed by my stately-looking mother and by my tall, slender self.

As she had asked particularly to see me, mother now retired to the other end of the long drawing-room and took up a book. I invited Miss Mullins to a chair.

"I would a great deal rather you called me Jane at once and have done with it," was her remarkable response to this; "but I suppose Jane will come in time." Here she heaved a very deep sigh, raised her veil of spotted net, and taking out her handkerchief, mopped her red face.

"It's a warm day," she said, "and I walked most of the way. I suppose you would like me to proceed to business. I have come, Miss Wickham—Miss Westenra Wickham—to speak on the subject of 17 Graham Square."

"Have you?" I cried. Had the ground opened I could not have been more amazed. What had this little, rather ugly woman, to do with my dream-house, 17 Graham Square?

"It is a very beautiful, fine house," said the little woman. "I went all over it this morning. I heard from your agents, Messrs. Macalister & Co., that you are anxious to take it."

I felt that my agents were very rude in thus giving me away, and made no response beyond a stately bend of my head. I was glad that mother was occupying herself with some delicate embroidery in the distant window. She certainly could not hear our conversation.

Miss Mullins now pulled her chair forward and sat in such a position that her knees nearly touched mine.

"You'll forgive a plain question," she said; "I am here on business. Are you prepared to take the house?"

"We certainly wish to take it," I said.

"But are you going to take it, Miss Wickham?"

I rather resented this speech, and was silent.

"Now I'll be plain. My name is blunt, and so is my nature. I want the house."

I half rose.

"Sit down, Miss Wickham, and don't be silly."

38

This speech was almost intolerable, and I thought the time had come when I should call to mother to protect me, but Jane Mullins had such twinkling, good-humoured eyes, that presently my anger dissolved into a curious desire to laugh.

"I know, Miss Wickham, you think me mad, and I was always accounted a little queer, but I'll beat about the bush no longer. You want 17 Graham Square, and so do I. You have got beauty and good birth and taste and style, and your name and your appearance will draw customers; and I have got experience and"—here she made a long, emphatic pause—"*money*. Now my question is this: Shall we club together?"

I never in all my life felt more astonished, I was nearly stunned.

"Club together?" I said.

"Yes, shall we? Seven thousand pounds capital has been placed at my disposal. You, I understand, have got furniture, at least some furniture"—here she glanced in a rather contemptuous way round our lovely drawing-room. "You also, of course, have a certain amount of connection, and I have got a large and valuable connection. Shall we club together?"

"I do not think we have any connection at all," I said bluntly; "not one of our friends will notice us when we go to—to Bloomsbury, and we have not half enough furniture for a house like 17 Graham Square. But what do you mean by our clubbing together?"

"Let me speak, my dear. What I want is this. I want you to put your furniture, what there is of it, and your connection, what there is of it, and your good birth and your style, and your charming mother into the same bag with my experience and my capital—or rather, the capital that is to be given to me. Will you do it? There's a plain question. Is it to be yes, or is it to be no? I want 17 Graham Square, and so do you. Shall we take it together and make a success of it? I like you, you are honest, and you're nice to look at, and I don't mind at all your being stiff to me and thinking me queer, for by-and-by we'll be friends. Is it to be a bargain?"

Just then mother rose from her seat and came with slow and stately steps across the room.

"What is it, Westenra?" she said; "what does this—this lady want?"

"Oh, I'm not a lady, ma'am," said Jane Mullins, rising and dropping a sort of involuntary curtsey. "I'm just a plain body, but I know all about cooking, and all about servants, and all about house linen, and all about dusting, going right into corners and never slurring them, and all the rest, and I know what you ought to give a pound for beef and for mutton, and what you ought to give a

39

dozen for eggs, and for butter, and how to get the best and freshest provisions at the lowest possible price. I know a thousand things, my dear madam, that you do not know, and that your pretty daughter doesn't know, and what I say is; as we both want 17 Graham Square, shall we put our pride in our pockets and our finances into one bag, and do the job. My name is Jane Mullins. I never was a grand body. I'm plain, but I'm determined, and I am good-humoured, and I am true as steel. I can give you fifty-four references if you want them, from a number of very good honest tradesmen who know me, and know that I pay my debts to the uttermost farthing. Will you join me, or will you not?"

"Well," said mother, when this curious little person had finished speaking, "this is quite the most astounding thing I ever heard of in my life. Westenra dear, thank this person very kindly, tell her that you know she means well, but that of course we could not think of her scheme for a single moment."

Mother turned as she spoke, and walked up the drawing-room again, and I looked at Jane Mullins, and Jane Mullins looked at me, and her blue eyes twinkled. She got up at once and held out her hand.

"Then that's flat," she said; "you'll be sorry you have said it, for Jane Mullins could have done well by you. Good-bye, miss; good-bye, ma'am."

She gave a little nod in the direction of my stately mother, and tripped out of the room. I was too stunned even to ring the bell for Paul, and I think Jane Mullins let herself out.

Well, as soon as she was gone, mother turned on me and gave me the first downright absolute scolding I had received since I was a tiny child. She said she had been willing, quite willing, to please me in every possible way, but when I descended to talk to people like Jane Mullins, and to consider their proposals, there was an end of everything, and she could not, for my father's sake, hear of such an outrageous proposal for a moment. This she said with tears in her eyes, and I listened quite submissively until at last the precious darling had worn her anger out, and sat subdued and inclined to cry by the open window. I took her hand then and petted her. I told her that really my scolding was quite unmerited, as I had never heard of Jane Mullins before, and was as much amazed as she was at her visit.

"All the same," I added, "I have not the slightest doubt that, with Jane Mullins at the helm, we should do splendidly."

"My darling, darling West, this is just the straw too much," said mother, and then I saw that it was the straw too much, and at that moment who should come to visit us but pretty little Lady Thesiger. We turned the conversation instinctively. Lady Thesiger said—

"You have not yet gone under, either of you, you are only talking about it. You are quite fit to associate with me for the rest of the day. I want you to come for a long drive in my carriage, and afterwards we will go to the theatre together; there is a very good piece on at the Lyceum. Now, then, be quick, Westenra, get into your very smartest clothes, and Mrs. Wickham, will you also put on your bonnet and mantle?"

There was never any resisting Jasmine, and we spent the rest of the day with her, and she was absolutely winning, and so pleasant that she made mother forget Jane Mullins; but then during dinner, in the queerest, most marvellous way, she drew the whole story of Jane Mullins from us both, and mother described with great pride her action in the matter.

"Yes, that is all very fine," replied Jasmine; "but now I am going to say a plain truth. I am going to imitate that wonderful little Jane. My truth is this—I would fifty thousand times rather introduce my nice American friends to Jane Mullins's boarding-house than I would to yours, Westenra, for in Jane's they would have their wants attended to, and be thoroughly comfortable, whereas in yours goodness only knows if the poor darlings would get a meal fit to eat."

This was being snubbed with a vengeance, and even mother looked angry, and I think she thought that Lady Thesiger had gone too far.

During the play that followed, and the drive home and the subsequent night, I thought of nothing but Jane Mullins, and began more and more to repent of my rash refusal of her aid. Surely, if Providence had meant us to carry out our scheme, Providence had also supplied Jane Mullins to help us to do it, and if ever woman looked true she did, and if her references turned out satisfactory why should she not be a sort of partner-housekeeper in the concern?

So the next morning early I crept into mother's room, and whispered to her all about Jane and my thoughts during the night, and begged of her to reconsider the matter.

"It is very odd, West," said mother, "but what your friend Jasmine said has been coming to me in my dreams; and you know, darling, you know nothing about cooking, and I know still less, and I suppose this Miss Mullins would understand this sort of thing, so, Westenra, if your heart is quite, quite set on it, we may as well see her again."

"She left her address on her visiting-card. I will go to her the moment I have finished breakfast," was my joyful response.

CHAPTER VI

THE BERLIN WOOL ROOM

I ordered the carriage and set off, mother having declined to accompany me. Miss Mullins's address was at Highgate; she lived in a small, new-looking house, somewhere near the Archway. I daresay Jane saw me from the window, for I had scarcely run up the little path to her house, and had scarcely finished sounding the electric bell, before the door was opened by no less a person than herself.

"Ah," she said, "I felt somehow that you would call; come in, Miss Wickham."

Her manner was extremely cordial, there was not a trace of offence at the way in which we had both treated her the day before. She ushered me into a sort of little Berlin wool room, all looking as neat as a new pin. There was Berlin wool everywhere, on the centre-table, on the mantelpiece, on the little side-table. There were Berlin wool antimacassars and a Berlin wool screen, in which impossible birds disported themselves over impossible water, and there was a large waxwork arrangement of fruit and flowers in the centre of the mantelpiece, and there were six chairs, all with their backs decorously placed against the wall, and not a single easy chair. But the room was spick and span with cleanliness and brightness and the due effects of soap and water and furniture-polish. The little room even smelt clean.

Miss Mullins motioned me to one of the hard chairs.

"I must apologise for the absence of the rocking-chair," she said, "it is being mended, but I dare say being young you won't mind using that hard chair for a little."

"Certainly not," I replied.

"I observe that every one lounges dreadfully just now," she continued, "but I myself hate easy chairs, and as this is my own house I do not have them in it. The room is clean, but not according to your taste, eh?"

"It is a nice room of its kind," I said, "but——"

"You need not add any buts, I know quite well what you are thinking about," said Jane Mullins; then she stood right in front of me, facing me.

"Won't you sit down?" I said.

"No, thank you, I prefer standing. I only sit when I have a good deal on my mind. What is it you have come to say?"

I wished she would help me, but she had evidently no intention of doing so. She stood there with her red face and her twinkling eyes, and her broad, good-humoured mouth, the very personification of homely strength, but she was not going to get me out of my difficulty.

"Well," I said, stammering and colouring, "I have been thinking over your visit, and—and——"

"Yes, go on."

"Do you really mean it, Miss Mullins?" I said then. "Would you really like to join two such ignorant people as mother and me?"

"Hark to her," said the good woman. "Look here, Miss Wickham, you have reached quite the right frame of mind, and you're not a bit ignorant, my dear, not a bit, only your knowledge and my knowledge are wide apart. My dear Miss Wickham, knowledge is power, and when we join forces and put our united knowledge into the same bag, we will have huge results, huge results, my dear—yes, it is true."

"Let us talk it out," I said.

"Do you really mean, Miss Wickham, that you and your mother—your aristocratic mother—are seriously thinking of entering into partnership with me?"

"I don't know about mother, but I know that I am leaning very much towards the idea," I said; "and I think I ought to apologise, both for my mother and myself, for the rude way in which we treated you yesterday."

"I expected it, love; I was not a bit surprised," said Jane Mullins. "I thought it best to plump out the whole scheme and allow it to simmer in your minds. Of course, at first, you were not likely to be taken with it, but you were equally likely to come round. I stayed in this morning on purpose; I was almost sure you would visit me."

"You were right," I said. "I see that you are a very wise woman, and I am a silly girl."

"You are a very beautiful girl, Miss Wickham, and educated according to your station. Your station and mine are far apart, but having got capital and a certain amount of sense, it would be a very good partnership, if you really think we could venture upon it."

"I am willing," I said suddenly.

"Then, that is right; here's my hand upon it; but don't be more impulsive to-day, my dear, than you were yesterday. You must do things properly. Here are different references of mine." She walked across the room, took up a little packet, and opened it.

"This is a list of tradespeople," she said; "I should like you to write to them all; they will explain to a certain extent my financial position; they will assure you that I, Jane Mullins, have been dealing with them for the things that I require for the last seven years—a seven years' reference is long enough, is it not? But if it is not quite long enough, here is the address of the dear old Rector in Shropshire who confirmed me, and in whose Sunday-school I was trained, and who knew my father, one of the best farmers in the district.

"So much for my early life, but the most important reference of all is the reference of the friend, who does not choose his or her name to be mentioned, and who is helping me with capital; not helping you, Miss Wickham, mind—not you nor Mrs. Wickham—but me *myself*, with capital to the tune of seven thousand pounds. I could not do it but for that, and as the person who is lending me this money to make this great fortune happens to be a friend of Mr. Hardcastle's, I think he, Mr. Hardcastle, will let us have the house."

"Now this is all very startling and amazing," I said. "You ought to tell us your friend's name and all about it; that is, if we are to go properly into partnership."

"It can't be done, my dear. The friend is a very old friend and a very true one, and Mr. Hardcastle is the one to be satisfied. The friend knows that for years I have wanted to start a boarding-house, but the friend always thought there were difficulties in the way. I was too homely, and people are grand in these days, and want some society airs and manners, which you, my dear, possess. So if we put our fortunes into one bag everything will come right, and you must trust me, that's all."

I was quite silent, thinking very hard.

"When I saw 17 Graham Square yesterday," continued Miss Mullins, "I said to myself, if there is a suitable house for our purpose in the whole W.C. district it is that house. What a splendid drawing-room there is, or rather two drawing-rooms; just the very rooms to entertain people in in the evening. Now if we put all our fortunes into one bag, you, my dear Miss Wickham, shall have the social part of the establishment under your wing. I will arrange all about the servants, and will see that the cooking is right, and will carve the joints at dinner; and your beautiful, graceful, aristocratic lady mother must take the head of the table. She won't have a great deal to do, but her presence will work wonders."

"And do you think we shall make any money with this thing?" I said.

"It is my impression that we will; indeed I am almost sure of it, but the house must be furnished suitably."

"But what is your taste with regard to furniture, Miss Mullins?" I asked, and now I looked apprehensively round the little Berlin wool room.

"Well, I always did incline to the primitive colours. I will be frank with you, and say honestly that I never pass by that awful shop, Liberty's in Regent Street, without shuddering. Their greens and their greys and their pinks are not my taste, love—no, and never will be; but I shall leave the furnishing to you, Miss Wickham, for I see by the tone of that dress you are now wearing that you adhere to Liberty, and like his style of decoration."

"Oh, I certainly do," I replied.

"Very well then, you shall furnish in Liberty style, or in any style you fancy; it does not matter to me. You know the tastes of your own set, and I hope we'll have plenty of them at No. 17, my dear. As a matter of fact, all I care about in a room is that it should be absolutely clean, free from dust, tidily arranged, and not too much furniture in it. For the rest—well, I never notice pretty things when they are about, so you need not bother about that as far as I am concerned. The house is a very large one, and although you have some furniture to meet its requirements, and what I have in this little room will do for my own sitting-room, still I have not the slightest doubt we shall have to spend about a thousand pounds in putting the house into apple-pie order; not a penny less will do the job, of that I am convinced."

As I had no knowledge whatever on the subject I could neither gainsay Miss Mullins nor agree with her.

"The house must be the envy of all the neighbours," she said, and a twinkle came into her eyes and a look of satisfaction round her mouth.

"Oh, it shall be. How delightful you are!" I cried.

"What I propose is this," said Jane Mullins; "we—your mother, you and I—sign the lease, and we three are responsible. I take one third of the profits, you a third, and your mother a third."

"But surely that is not fair, for you are putting capital into it."

"Not at all, it is my friend's capital, and that is the arrangement my friend would like. Come, I cannot work on any other terms. I take a third, you a third, and your mother a third. I, having experience, do the housekeeping. Having experience, I order the servants. You arrange the decorations for the table, you have the charge of the flowers and the drawing-room in the

45

evenings. As funds permit and paying guests arrive you inaugurate amusements in the drawing-room, you make everything as sociable and as pleasant as possible. Your mother gives tone and distinction to the entire establishment."

"You seem to be leaving very little for mother and me to do," I said.

"Your mother cannot have much to do, for I do not think she is strong," said Miss Mullins. "She is older than I am too, and has seen a great deal of sorrow; but what she does, remember no one else can do, she gives *the tone*. It's a fact, Miss Wickham, that you may try all your life, but unless Providence has bestowed tone upon you, you cannot acquire it. Now I have no tone, and will only obtrude myself into the social circle to carve the joints at dinner; otherwise I shall be busy, extremely busy in my own domain."

"Well, as far as I am concerned, I am abundantly willing to enter into this partnership," I said. "I like you very much, and I am sure you are honest and true. I will tell mother what you have said to me, and we will let you know immediately."

"All I ask is that you prove me, my dear," said the little woman, and then she took my hand and gave it a firm grip.

CHAPTER VII

THE PAYING GUESTS

Everything went smoothly after my interview with Jane Mullins. In an incredibly short space of time the contract for the house was signed. It was signed by mother, by me, and by Jane Mullins. Then we had exciting and extraordinary days hunting for that furniture which Jane considered suitable, and consulting about the servants, and the thousand and one small minutiæ of the establishment. But finally Jane took the reins into her own hands, whisking my mother and me off to the country, and telling us that we could come and take possession on the 29th of September.

"There won't be any visitors in the house then," she said, "but all the same, the house will be full, from attic to cellar, before the week is out, and you had best be there beforehand. Until then enjoy yourselves."

Well, I did enjoy myself very much. It was quite terrible of me, for now and then I saw such a look of sorrow on mother's face; but I really did get a wonderful heartening and cheering up by Jane, and when the weeks flew by, and the long desired day came at last, I found myself in excellent spirits, but mother looked very pale and depressed.

"You will get accustomed to it," I said, "and I think in time you will learn to like it. It is a brave thing to do. I have been thinking of father so much lately, and I am quite certain that he would approve."

"Do you really believe that, West?" asked my mother; "if I thought so, nothing would really matter. West, dearest, you are so brave and masculine in some things, you ought to have been a man."

"I am very glad I am a woman," was my reply, "for I want to prove that women can do just as strong things as men, and just as brave things if occasion requires."

So we arrived at the boarding-house, and Jane Mullins met us on the steps, and took us all over it. It was a curious house, and at the same time a very beautiful one. There was a certain mixture of tastes which gave some of the rooms an odd effect. Jane's common-sense and barbarous ideas with regard to colour, rather clashed with our æsthetic instincts and our more luxurious ideas. But the drawing-room at least was almost perfect. It was a drawing-room after mother's own heart. In reality it was a very much larger and handsomer room than the one we had left in Sumner Place, but it had a home-like look, and the colouring was in one harmonious scheme, which took away from any undue effect of size, and at the same time gave a delicious sense of space. The old pictures, too, stood on the walls, and the old lovely curtains adorned the windows; and the little easy chairs that mother loved, stood about here and there, and all the nicknacks and articles of vertu were to be found in their accustomed places; and there were flowers and large palms, and we both looked around us with a queer sense of wonder.

"Why, mother," I said, "this is like coming home."

"So it is," said mother, "it is extraordinary."

"But Miss Mullins," I continued, "you told me you had no taste. How is it possible that you were able to decorate a room like this, and, you dear old thing, the carpet on the floor has quite a Liberty tone, and what a lovely carpet, too!"

Jane absolutely blushed. When she blushed it was always the tip of her nose that blushed—it blushed a fiery red now. She looked down, and then she looked up, and said after a pause—

"I guessed that, just what I would not like you would adore, so I did the furnishing of this room on that principle. I am glad you are pleased. I don't hold myself with cut flowers, nor nicknacks, nor rubbish of that sort, but you do; and when people hold with them, and believe in them, the more they have of them round, the better pleased they are. Oh, and there's a big box of Fuller's sweetmeats on that little table. I thought you would eat those if you had no appetite for anything else."

"But I have an excellent appetite," I answered; "all the same, I am delighted to see my favourite sweets. Come, mother, we will have a feast, both of us; you shall enjoy your favourite bon-bon this minute."

Mother got quite merry over the box, and Jane disappeared, and in five minutes or so, a stylishly dressed parlour-maid came in with a *recherché* tea, which we both enjoyed.

Mother's bedroom was on the first floor, a small room, but a very dainty one; and this had been papered with a lovely shade of very pale gold, and the hangings and curtains were of the same colour. There was a little balcony outside the window where she could sit, and where she could keep her favourite plants, and there in its cage was her old Bully, who could pipe "Robin Adair," "Home, sweet Home," and "Charlie is my Darling." The moment he saw mother he perked himself up, and bent his little head to one side, and began piping "Charlie is my Darling" in as lively a tone as ever bullfinch possessed.

I had insisted beforehand on having my room at the top of the house not far from Jane's, for of course the best bedrooms were reserved for the boarders, the boarders who had not yet come.

"But I have sheafs of letters, with inquiries about the house," said Jane, "and after dinner to-night, my dear Miss Wickham, you and I must go into these matters."

"And mother, too," I said.

"Just as she pleases," replied Jane, "but would not the dear lady like her little reading-lamp and her new novel? I have a subscription at Mudie's, and some new books have arrived. Would it not be best for her?"

"No," I said with firmness, "mother must have a voice in everything; she must not drop the reins, it would not be good for her at all."

Accordingly after dinner we all sat in the drawing-room, and Jane produced the letters. Mother and I were dressed as we were accustomed to dress for the evening. Mother wore black velvet, slightly, very slightly, open at the throat, and the lace ruffles round her throat and wrists were of Brussels, and she had a figment of Brussels lace arranged with velvet and a small feather on her head. She looked charming, and very much as she might have looked if she had been going to the Duchess's for an evening reception, or to Lady Thesiger's for dinner.

As to me, I wore one of the frocks I had worn last season, when I had not stepped down from society, but was in the thick of it, midst of all the gaiety and fun.

Jane Mullins, however, scorned to dress for the evening. Jane wore in the morning a kind of black bombazine. I had never seen that material worn by anybody but Jane, but she adhered to it. It shone and it rustled, and was aggravating to the last degree. This was Jane's morning dress, made very plainly, and fitting close to her sturdy little figure, and her evening dress was that harsh silk which I have already mentioned. This was also worn tight and plain, and round her neck she had a white linen collar, and round her wrists immaculate white cuffs, and no cap or ornament of any kind over her thin light hair. Jane was certainly not beautiful to look at, but by this time mother and I had discovered the homely steadfastness of her abilities, and the immense good nature which seemed to radiate out of her kind eyes, and we had forgotten whether she was, strictly speaking, good-looking or not.

Well, we three sat together on this first evening, and Jane produced her letters.

"Here is one from a lady in the country," she began; "she wishes to come to London for the winter, and she wishes to bring a daughter with her; the daughter requires lessons in something or other, some useless accomplishment, no doubt—anyhow that is their own affair. They wish to come to London, and they want to know what we will take them for as permanent boarders. The lady's name is Mrs. Armstrong. Her letter of inquiry arrived yesterday, and ought to be answered at once. She adds in a postscript —'I hope you will do me cheap.' I don't like that postscript; it has a low, mean sort of sound about it, and I doubt if we will put up with her long, but, as she is the very first to apply for apartments, we cannot tell her that the house is full up. Now I propose that we give Mrs. Armstrong and her daughter the large front attic next to my room. If the young lady happens to be musical, and wishes to rattle away on a piano, she can have one there, and play to her heart's content without anybody being disturbed. She cannot play anywhere else that I can see, for your lady mother, my dear Miss Wickham, cannot be worried and fretted with piano tunes jingling in her ears."

"West's mother must learn to put up with disagreeables," was my mother's very soft reply.

But I did not want her to have any disagreeables, so I said—

"Perhaps we had better not have Mrs. Armstrong at all."

"Oh, my dear," was Jane's reply, "why should my spite at that postscript turn the poor woman from a comfortable home? She shall come. We will charge three guineas a week for the two."

"But that is awfully little," I replied.

"It is quite as much as they will pay for the attic, and they will be awfully worrying, both of them. I feel it in my bones beforehand. They'll be much more particular than the people who pay five guineas a head for rooms on the first floor. Mark my words, Miss Wickham, it is the attic boarders who will give the trouble, but we cannot help that, for they are sure and certain, and are the backbone of the establishment. I'll write to Mrs. Armstrong, and say that if they can give us suitable references they can come for a week, in order that both parties may see if they are pleased with the other."

"Shall I write, or will you?" I asked.

"Well, my dear, after a bit I shall be very pleased if you will take the correspondence, which is sure to be a large item, but just at first I believe that I can put things on a more business-like footing."

"Thank you very much," I said in a relieved tone.

"That letter goes to-night," said Jane. She took a Swan fountain pen from its place by her waist, scribbled a word or two on the envelope of Mrs. Armstrong's letter, and laid it aside.

"Now I have inquiries from a most genteel party, a Captain and Mrs. Furlong: he is a retired army man, and they are willing to pay five guineas a week between them for a comfortable bedroom."

"But surely that is very little," I said again.

"It is a very fair sum out of their pockets, Miss Wickham, and I think we can afford to give them a nice room looking south on the third floor, not on the second floor, and, of course, not on the first; but on the third floor we can give them that large room which is decorated with the sickly green. It will turn them bilious, poor things, if they are of my way of thinking."

Accordingly Captain and Mrs. Furlong were also written to that evening, to the effect that they might enter the sacred precincts of 17 Graham Square as soon as they pleased.

Two or three other people had also made inquiries, and having talked their letters over and arranged what replies were to be sent, Miss Mullins, after a certain hesitation which caused me some small astonishment, took up her final letter.

"A gentleman has written who wishes to come," she said, "and I think he would be a desirable inmate."

"A gentleman!" cried mother, "a gentleman alone?"

"Yes, madam, an unmarried gentleman."

I looked at mother. Mother's face turned a little pale. We had neither of us said anything of the possibility of there being unmarried gentlemen in the house, and I think mother had a sort of dim understanding that the entire establishment was to be filled with women and married couples. Now she glanced at Jane, and said in a hesitating voice—

"I always felt that something unpleasant would come of this."

Jane stared back at her.

"What do you mean, Mrs. Wickham? The gentleman to whom I allude is a real gentleman, and it would be extremely difficult for me to refuse him, because he happens to be a friend of the friend who lent me the seven thousand pounds capital."

"There is a secret about that," I exclaimed, "and I think you ought to tell us."

Jane looked at me out of her honest twinkling eyes, and her resolute mouth

51

shut into a perfectly straight line; then nodding her head she said—

"We cannot refuse this gentleman; his name is Randolph. He signs himself James Randolph, and specially mentions the friend who lent the money, so I do not see, as the house is almost empty at present, how we can keep him out. I should say he must be a nice man from the way he writes. You have no objection to his coming, have you, Mrs. Wickham?"

Still mother made no answer, but I saw a hot spot coming into both her cheeks.

"Didn't I tell you, Westenra," she said after a pause, "that matters might be made very disagreeable and complicated? To be frank with you, Miss Mullins," she continued, "I would much rather have only married couples and ladies in the house."

"Then, my dear madam, we had better close within the week," said Jane Mullins in a voice of some indignation. "You ought to have arranged for this at the time, and if you had mentioned your views I would certainly not have joined partnership with you. What we want are ladies *and* gentlemen, and so many of them that the commonplace and the vulgar will not be able to come, because there will not be room to receive them. As to this gentleman, he has something to do in the city, and likes to live in Bloomsbury, as he considers it the most healthy part of London." Here Miss Mullins began to talk very vigorously, and the tip of her nose became suspiciously red once more.

"I propose," she continued, "as he is quite indifferent to what he pays, charging Mr. Randolph five guineas a week, and giving him the small bedroom on the drawing-room floor. It is a little room, but nicely furnished. He will be a great acquisition."

"May I see his letter?" asked mother.

"I am sorry, Madam, but I would rather no one saw it. It mentions my friend, and of course my friend would not like his name to get out, so I must keep the letter private, but if Mr. Randolph makes himself in any way disagreeable to you ladies I am sure he will go immediately, but my impression is that you will find him a great acquisition. I will write to him to-night, and say that he can have the accommodation he requires, and ask him to name the day when he will arrive."

After this we had a great deal of talk on other matters, and finally Jane retired to her premises, and mother and I sat together in the beautiful drawing-room.

"Well, Westenra," said mother, "it is done. What do you think of it?"

"It has only begun, mother dear. Up to the present I am charmed. What a treasure we have secured in Jane."

"It is all very queer," said mother. "Why would not she show us Mr., Mr.——what was his name, Westenra?"

"Randolph," I interrupted.

"Why would she not show us Mr. Randolph's letter? I must say frankly that I do not like it. The fact is, West, we are not in the position we were in at Sumner Place, and we must be exceedingly circumspect. You, for instance, must be distant and cold to all the men who come here. You must be careful not to allow any one to take liberties with you. Ah, my child, did we do wrong to come? Did we do wrong? It is terrible for me to feel that you are in such an equivocal position."

"Oh but, mother, I am not. I assure you I can look after myself; and then I have you with me, and Jane Mullins is such a sturdy little body. I am sure she will guide our ship, our new, delightful ship, with a flowing sail into a prosperous harbour; and I cannot see, mother, why we should not receive a man who is a real gentleman. It is the men who are not gentlemen who will be difficult to deal with. Mr. Randolph will probably be a great help to us, and for my part I am glad he is coming."

"Things are exactly as I feared," said mother, and I saw her anxious eyes look across the room as though she were gazing at a vision which gave her the greatest disquietude.

Early the next day I hung father's picture in such a position in the drawing-room that mother could have the eyes following her wherever she turned. She often said that she was never comfortable, nor quite at home, unless under the gaze of those eyes, and we made up our minds not to mind the fact of our new boarders asking questions about the picture, for we were intensely proud of my father, and felt that we could say in a few dignified words all that was necessary, and that my dear father would in a measure protect us in our new career.

Early the next week the first boarders arrived. Three or four families came the same day. Jane said that that was best. Jane was the one who received them. She went into the hall and welcomed them in her brusque tone and took them immediately to their rooms, in each of which printed rules of the establishment were pinned up, and mother and I did not appear until just before dinner, when the different boarders had assembled in the drawing-room.

"Dress for dinner and make yourself look as nice as you possibly can," was Jane's parting shot to me, and I took her advice in my own way.

CHAPTER VIII

THE FLOUR IN THE CAKE

"Put on the least becoming dress you have got, Westenra," said mother.

"And what is that?" I asked, pausing with my hand on the handle of mother's door.

"Well," said my mother, considering, "it is a little difficult, for all your dresses are perfectly sweet; but I think if there is one that suits you rather less than another it is that cloudy blue with the silver gauze over it."

"O mother! that is a great deal too dressy," I exclaimed.

"Well, there is the pale primrose."

"Too dressy again."

"One of your many white dresses—but then you look exquisite in white, darling."

"You had better leave it to me, mother," I said. "I promise to make myself look as plain and uninteresting and unpretentious as possible." And then I shut the door quickly and left her.

The stepping down had been exciting, but the first firm footfall on our new *terra firma* was more exciting still. The boarders and I were to meet at dinner. For the first time I was to be known to the world as Miss Wickham, who kept a boarding-house in company with her mother and a certain Miss Jane Mullins. It was not a high position according to that set in which I was born. But never mind. Just because my father had won the Victoria Cross would his daughter think nothing degrading which meant an honourable and honest livelihood. So I hastily donned a black net dress which was not too fashionable, and without any ornament whatsoever, not even a string of pearls round my neck, ran downstairs. But the dress was low and the sleeves were short, and I could not keep the crimson of excitement out of my cheeks, nor the fire of excitement out of my eyes. I ran into the drawing-room, exclaiming "Mother! mother!" and forgot for the moment that the drawing-room no longer belonged to mother and me, but was the property of our paying guests, and our house was no longer ours.

Mrs. and Miss Armstrong were standing near the hearth. Mrs. Armstrong was a thin, meagre little woman, of about forty years of age. Country was written all over her—provincial country. She had faded hair and a faded complexion, and at times, and when not greatly excited, a faded manner. When she was thinking of herself she was painfully affected; when she was not thinking of herself she was hopelessly vulgar. Her daughter was a downright buxom young person, who quite held her own. Neither Mrs. nor Miss Armstrong were in evening dress, and they stared with amazement and indignation at me. Miss Armstrong's cheeks became flushed with an ugly red, but I tripped up to them just as if there were no such thing as dress in the world, and held out my hand.

"How do you do?" I said. "I am glad to see you. Won't you both sit down? I hope you have found everything comfortable in your room."

Then, as Mrs. Armstrong still stared at me, her eyes growing big with amazement, I said in a low voice—

"My name is Wickham. I am one of the owners of this house."

"Oh, Miss Wickham," said Mrs. Armstrong, and there was a perceptible tone of relief in her voice. It did not matter how stylish Miss Wickham looked, she was still only Miss Wickham, a person of no importance whatsoever.

"Come here, Marion," said Mrs. Armstrong, relapsing at once into her commonest manner. "You must not sit too near the fire, for you will get your nose red, and that is not becoming."

Marion, however, drew nearer to the fire, and did not take the least notice of her mother's remark.

"So you keep this boarding-house," said Mrs. Armstrong, turning to me again. "Well, I am surprised. Do you mind my making a blunt remark?"

I did not answer, but I looked quietly back at her. I think something in my steady gaze disquieted her, for she uttered a nervous laugh, and then said abruptly—

"You don't look the thing, you know. You're one of the most stylish young ladies I have ever seen. Isn't she, Marion?"

"She is indeed," answered Miss Marion. "I thought she was a duchess at least when she came into the room."

"Come over here, Marion, and don't stare into the flames," was Mrs. Armstrong's next remark. "I didn't know," she added, "we were coming to a place of this kind. It is very gratifying to me. I suppose the bulk of the guests here will be quite up to your standard, Miss Wickham?"

"I hope so," I replied. I was spared any more of my new boarders' intolerable remarks, for at that moment Mrs. and Captain Furlong appeared. He was a gentleman, and she was a lady. She was an everyday sort of little body to look at, but had the kindest heart in the world. She was neither young nor old, neither handsome nor the reverse. She was just like thousands of other women, but there was a rest and peace about her very refreshing. She was dressed suitably, and her husband wore semi-evening dress.

I went up to them, talked a little, and showed them some of the most comfortable chairs in the room. We chatted on everyday matters, and then mother appeared. Dear, dear mother! Had I done right to put her in this position? She looked nervous, and yet she looked stately as I had never seen her look before. I introduced her not only to the Furlongs, who knew instinctively how to treat her, but also to Mrs. and Miss Armstrong, and then to a Mr. and Mrs. Cousins who appeared, and the three Miss Frosts, and some other people, who were all taking possession of us and our house. Oh, it was confusing on that first night. I could scarcely bear it myself. I had never guessed that the very boarders would look down on us, that just because we were ladies they would consider our position an equivocal one, and treat us accordingly. I hoped that by-and-by it might be all right, but now I knew that mother and I were passing through the most trying period of this undertaking. Some of our guests were people of refinement, who would know how to act and what to do under any circumstances, and some again were of the Armstrong type, who would be pushing and disagreeable wherever they went. Marion Armstrong, in particular, intended to make her presence felt. She had a short conversation with her mother, and then pushed her way across the room to where my own mother sat, and stood before her and began to talk in a loud, brusque, penetrating voice.

"I have not been introduced to you, Madam; my name is Marion Armstrong. I have come up to London to study Art. I was rather taken aback when I saw you. You and Miss Wickham are the people who are our landladies, so to speak, and you are so different from most landladies that mother and I feel a little confused about it. Oh, thank you; you wish to know if we are comfortable. We are fairly so, all things considered; we don't *mind* our attic room, but it's likely we'll have to say a few words to your housekeeper—Miss Mullins, I think you call her—in the morning. You doubtless, Madam, do not care to interfere with the more sordid part of your duties."

At that moment, and before my really angry mother could answer, the door was opened, and there entered Jane Mullins in her usual sensible, downright silken gown, and a tall man. I glanced at him for a puzzled moment, feeling sure that I had seen him before, and yet not being quite certain. He had good features, was above the medium height, had a quiet manner and a sort of distant bearing which would make it impossible for any one to take liberties with him.

Miss Mullins brought him straight across the room to mother and introduced him. I caught the name, Randolph. Mother bowed, and so did he, and then he stood close to her, talking very quietly, but so effectively, that Miss Armstrong, after staring for a moment, had to vanish nonplussed into a distant corner of the drawing-room. I saw by the way that young lady's eyes blazed that she was now intensely excited. Mother and I had startled and confused her a good deal, and Mr. Randolph finished the dazzling impression her new home was giving her. Certainly she had not expected to see a person of his type here. She admired him, I saw at a glance, immensely, and now stood near her own mother, shaking her head now and then in an ominous manner, and whispering audibly.

Suddenly Jane, who was here, there, and everywhere, whisked sharply round.

"Don't you know Mr. Randolph, Miss Wickham?" she said.

I shook my head. She took my hand and brought me up to mother's side.

"Mr. Randolph," she said, "this is our youngest hostess, Miss Westenra Wickham."

Mr. Randolph bowed, said something in a cold, courteous tone, scarcely glanced at me, and then resumed his conversation with mother.

CHAPTER IX

THE ARTIST'S EYE

During dinner I found myself seated next Miss Armstrong. Miss Armstrong was on one side of me, and her mother was at the other. I don't really know how I got placed between two such uncongenial people, but perhaps it was good for me, showing me the worst as well as the best of our position at once. I was having a cold douche with a vengeance.

As we were taking our soup (I may as well say that the ménu was excellent, quite as good as many a grand West End dinner which I had attended in my palmy days), Miss Armstrong bent towards me, spilling a little of her soup as she did so, and said, in a somewhat audible whisper—

"I wish you would give me a hint about him."

"About whom?" I asked in return.

"Mr. Randolph; he is one of the most stylish people I have ever met. What are his tastes? Don't you know anything at all about him? Is he married, for instance?"

"I never saw Mr. Randolph before, and I know nothing about him," I answered in a low, steady voice, which was in marked contrast to Miss Armstrong's buzzing, noisy whisper.

"Oh my!" said that young lady, returning again to the contemplation of her soup. Her plate was taken away, and in the interval she once more led the attack.

"He *is* distingué," she said, "quite one of the upper ten. I wish you *would* tell me where you met him before. You must have met him before, you know; he would not come to a house like this if he was not interested in you and your mother. He is a very good-looking man; I admire him myself immensely."

"I don't care to make personal remarks at dinner," I said, looking steadily at the young lady.

"Oh my!" she answered again to this; but as some delicious turbot was now facing her, she began to eat it, and tried to cover her mortification.

Presently my neighbour to my right began to speak, and Mrs. Armstrong's manners were only a shade more intolerable than her daughter's.

"Marion has come up to London to study h'Art," she said. She uttered the last word in a most emphatic tone. "Marion has a great taste for h'Art, and she wants to attend one of the schools and become an h'artist. Do you think you could give us any advice on the subject, Miss Wickham?"

I answered gently that I had never studied Art myself, having no leaning in that direction.

"Oh dear: now I should have said you had the h'artist's h'eye," said Mrs. Armstrong, glancing at my dress and at the way my hair was arranged as she spoke. "You are very stylish, you know; you are a good-looking girl, too, very good-looking. You don't mind me giving you a plain compliment, do you, my dear?"

I made no reply, but my cheeks had never felt more hot, nor I myself more uncomfortable.

Mrs. Armstrong looked me all over again, then she nodded across my back at Miss Armstrong, and said, still in her buzzing half-whisper, for the benefit of her daughter—

"Miss Wickham has got the h'artist's h'eye, and she'll help us fine, after she's got over her first amazement. She's new to this business any one can see; but, Marion, by-and-by you might ask her if she would lend you that bodice to take the pattern. I like the way it is cut so much. You have got a good plump neck, and would look well in one made like it."

Marion's answer to this was, "O mother, do hush;" and thus the miserable meal proceeded.

I was wondering how my own mother was getting on, and at last I ventured to glance in her direction. She was seated at the head of the table, really doing nothing in the way of carving, for the dishes, except the joints, were all handed round, and the joints Jane Mullins managed, standing up to them and carving away with a rapidity and *savoir faire* which could not but arouse my admiration. The upper part of the table seemed to be in a very peaceful condition, and I presently perceived that Mr. Randolph led the conversation. He was having an argument on a subject of public interest with Captain Furlong, and Captain Furlong was replying, and Mr. Randolph was distinctly but in very firm language showing the worthy captain that he was in the wrong, and Mrs. Furlong was laughing, and mother was listening with a pleased flush on her cheeks. After all the dear mother was happy, she was not in the thick of the storm, she was not assailed by two of the most terrible women it had ever been my lot to encounter.

The meal came to an end, and at last we left the room.

"Stay one minute behind, dear," said Jane Mullins to me.

I did so. She took me into her tiny little parlour on the ground floor.

"Now then, Miss Wickham, what's the matter? You just look as if you were ready to burst into tears. What's up? Don't you think our first dinner was very successful—a good long table all surrounded with people pleased with their dinner, and in high good humour, and you were the cause of the success, let me tell you, dear. They will talk of you right and left. This boarding-house will never be empty from this night out, mark my words; and I never was wrong yet in a matter of plain common-sense."

"But oh, dear!" I cried, and I sank into a chair, and I am sure the tears filled my eyes; "the company are so mixed, Miss Mullins, so terribly mixed."

"It takes a lot of mixing to make a good cake," was Jane's somewhat ambiguous answer.

"Now, what do you mean?"

"Well, any one can see with half an eye that you object to Mrs. and Miss Armstrong, and I will own they are not the sort of folks a young lady like yourself is accustomed to associate with; but all the same, if we stay here and turn this house into a good commercial success, we must put up with those sort of people, they are, so to speak, the support of an establishment of this sort. I call them the flour of the cake. Now, flour is not interesting stuff, at least uncombined with other things; but you cannot make a cake without it. People of that sort will go to the attics, and if we don't let the attics, my dear Miss Wickham, the thing won't pay. Every attic in the place must be let, and to people who will pay their weekly accounts regularly, and not run up bills. It's not folks like your grand Captain Furlong, nor even like Mr. Randolph, who make these sort of places 'hum,' so to speak. This establishment shall *hum*, my dear, and hum right merrily, and be one of the most popular boarding-houses in London. But you leave people like the Armstrongs to me. To-morrow you shall sit right away from them."

"No, I will not," I said stoutly, "why should you have all the burden, and mother and I all the pleasure? You are brave, Miss Mullins."

"If you love me, dear, call me Jane, I can't bear the name of Mullins. From the time I could speak I hated it, and three times in my youth I hoped to change it, and three times was I disappointed. The first man jilted me, dear, and the second died, and the third went into an asylum. I'm Mullins now, and Mullins I'll be to the end. I never had much looks to boast of, and what I had have gone, so don't fret me with the knowledge that I am an old maid, but call me Jane."

"Jane you shall be," I said. She really was a darling, and I loved her.

I found after my interview with Jane that the time in the drawing-room passed off extremely well, and this I quickly discovered was owing to Mr. Randolph, who, without making the smallest effort to conciliate the Armstrongs, or the Cousinses, or any of the other *attic strata*, as Jane called them, kept them all more or less in order. He told a few good stories for the benefit of the company, and then he sat down to the piano and sang one or two songs. He had a nice voice, not brilliant, but sweet and a real tenor, and he pronounced his words distinctly, and every one could listen, and every one did listen with pleasure. As to Mrs. and Miss Armstrong they held their lips apart in their amazement and delight. Altogether, I felt that Mr. Randolph had made the evening a success, and that without him, notwithstanding Jane's cheery words, the thing would have been an absolute failure.

Just towards the close of the evening he came up to my side.

"I must congratulate you," he said.

"On what?" I answered somewhat bitterly.

"On your delightful home, on your bravery." He gave me a quick glance, which I could not understand, which I did not understand until many months afterwards. I was not sure at that moment whether he was laughing at me or whether he was in earnest.

"I have something to thank you for," I said after a moment, "it was good of you to entertain our guests, but you must not feel that you are obliged to do so."

He looked at me then again with a grave and not easily comprehended glance.

"I assure you," he said slowly, "I never do anything I don't like. Pray don't thank me for exactly following my own inclinations. I was in the humour to sing, I sing most nights wherever I am. If you object to my singing pray say so, but do not condemn me to silence in the future, particularly as you have a very nice piano."

"You look dreadfully out of place in this house," was my next remark; and then I said boldly, "I cannot imagine why you came."

"I wonder if that is a compliment, or if it is not," said Mr. Randolph. "I do not believe I look more out of place here than you do, but it seems to me that neither of us are out of place, and that the house suits us very well. I like it; I expect I shall be extremely comfortable. Jane Mullins is an old friend of mine. I always told her, that whenever she set up a boarding-house I would live with her. For instance, did you ever eat a better dinner than you had to-night?"

"I don't know," I answered, "I don't care much about dinners, but it seemed good, at least it satisfied every one."

"Now I am a hopeless epicure," he said slowly. "I would not go anywhere if I was not sure that the food would be of the very best. No, Miss Wickham, I am afraid, whether you like it or not, you cannot get rid of me at present; but I must not stand talking any longer. I promised to lend your mother a book, it is one of Whittier's, I will fetch it."

He left the room, came back with the book in question, and sat down by mother's side. He was decidedly good-looking, and most people would have thought him charming, but his manner to me puzzled me a good deal, and I was by no means sure that I liked him. He had grey eyes, quite ordinary in shape and colour, but they had a wonderfully quizzical glance, and I felt a sort of fear, that when he seemed to sympathise he was laughing at me; I also felt certain that I had seen him before. Who was he? How was it possible that a man of his standing should have anything to do with Jane Mullins, and yet they were excellent friends. The little woman went up to him constantly in the course of the evening, and asked his advice on all sorts of matters. What did it mean? I could not understand it!

We took a few days settling down, and during that time the house became full. It was quite true that Mrs. Armstrong talked of us to her friends. The next day, indeed, she took a complete survey of the house accompanied by Jane; making frank comments on all she saw, complaining of the high prices, but never for a moment vouchsafing to give up her large front attic, which was indeed a bedroom quite comfortable enough for any lady. She must have written to her friends in the country, for other girls somewhat in appearance like Marion Armstrong joined our family circle, sat in the drawing-room in the evening, talked *at* Mr. Randolph, and looked at him with eager, covetous eyes.

Mr. Randolph was perfectly polite to these young ladies, without ever for a single moment stepping down from his own pedestal. Marion Armstrong, poke as she would, could not discover what his special tastes were. When she questioned him, he declared that he liked everything. Music?—certainly, he adored music. Art?—yes, he did sketch a little. The drama?—he went to every piece worth seeing, and generally on first nights. The opera?—he owned that a friend of his had a box for the season, and that he sometimes gave him a seat in it.

Miss Armstrong grew more and more excited. She perfectly worried me with questions about this man. Where did he come from? Who was he? What was his profession? Did I think he was married! Had he a secret care? Was he laughing at us?

Ah, when she asked me the last question, I found myself turning red.

"You know something about him, and you don't choose to tell it," said Marion Armstrong then, and she turned to Mrs. Cousins' daughter, who had come up to town with a view of studying music, and they put their heads together, and looked unutterable things.

Before we had been a fortnight in the place, all the other girls vied with me as to their dinner dress. They wore low dresses, with short sleeves, and gay colours, and their hair was fantastically curled, and they all glanced in the direction where Mr. Randolph sat.

What hopes they entertained with regard to him I could never divine, but he seemed to be having the effect which Jane desired, and the attics were filling delightfully.

Jane whispered to me at the end of the second week, that she feared she had made a great mistake.

"Had I known that Mr. Randolph would have the effect he seems to be having," she said, "I might have doubled our prices from the very beginning, but it is quite too late now."

"But why should it be necessary for us to make so much money?" I said.

Jane looked at me with a queer expression.

"So *much*!" she said. "Oh, we shall do, I am certain we shall do; but I am particularly anxious not to touch that seven thousand pounds capital; at least not much of it. I want the house to pay, and although it is a delightful house, and there are many guests coming and going, and it promises soon to be quite full, yet it must remain full all through the year, except just, of course, in the dull season, if it is to pay well. We might have charged more from the beginning; I see it now, but it is too late."

She paused, gazed straight before her, and then continued.

"We must get more people of the Captain Furlong type," she said. "I shall advertise in the *Morning Post*, and the *Standard*; I will also advertise in the *Guardian*. Advertisements in that paper are always regarded as eminently respectable. We ought to have some clergymen in the house, and some nice unmarried ladies, who will take rooms and settle down, and give a sort of religious respectable tone. We cannot have too many Miss Armstrongs about; there were six to dinner last night, and they rather overweighted the scale. Our cake will be heavy if we put so much flour into it."

I laughed, and counselled Jane to advertise as soon as possible, and then ran away to my own room. I felt if this sort of thing went on much longer, if the girls of the Armstrong type came in greater and greater numbers, and if they insisted on wearing all the colours of the rainbow at dinner, and very low dresses and very short sleeves, I must take to putting on a high dress without any ornaments whatsoever, and must request mother to do likewise.

Miss Armstrong was already attending an Art school, where, I cannot remember, I know it was not the Slade; and on bringing back some of her drawings, she first of all exhibited them to her friends, and then left them lying on the mantelpiece in the drawing-room, evidently in the hopes of catching Mr. Randolph's eye. She did this every evening for a week without any result, but at the end of that time he caught sight of a frightfully out-of-drawing charcoal study. It was the sort of thing which made you feel rubbed the wrong way the moment you glanced at it. It evidently rubbed him the wrong way, but he stopped before it as if fascinated, raised his eyebrows slightly, and looked full into Miss Armstrong's blushing face.

"You are the artist?" he said.

"I am," she replied; "it is a little study." Her voice shook with emotion.

"I thought so," he said again; "may I congratulate you?" He took up the drawing, looked at it with that half-quizzical, half-earnest glance, which puzzled not only Miss Armstrong and her friends but also myself, and then put it quietly back on the mantelpiece.

"If you leave it there, it will get dusty and be spoiled," he said. "Is it for sale?" he continued, as if it were an after-thought.

"Oh no, sir," cried Miss Armstrong, half abashed and delighted. "It is not worth any money—at least I fear it is not."

"But I am so glad you like it, Mr. Randolph," said Mrs. Armstrong, now pushing vigorously to the front; "I always did say that Marion had the h'artist's soul. It shines out of her eyes, at least I am proud to think so; and Marion, my dear, if the good gentleman would *like* the little sketch, I am sure you would be pleased to give it to him."

"But I could not think of depriving Miss Armstrong of her drawing," said Mr. Randolph, immediately putting on his coldest manner. He crossed the room and seated himself near mother.

"There now, ma, you have offended him," said Marion, nearly crying with vexation.

CHAPTER X

HER GRACE OF WILMOT

On a certain morning, between twelve and one o'clock, the inhabitants of Graham Square must have felt some slight astonishment as a carriage and pair of horses dashed up to No. 17. On the panels of the carriage were seen the coronet, with the eight strawberries, which denotes the ducal rank. The coachman and footman were also in the well-known livery of the Duke of Wilmot. One of the servants got down, rang the bell, and a moment later the Duchess swept gracefully into the drawing-room, where mother and I happened to be alone. She came up to us with both hands outstretched.

"My dears," she said, glancing round, "are they all out?"

"I am so glad to see you, Victoria," replied mother; "but whom do you mean? Sit down, won't you?"

The Duchess sank into the nearest chair. She really looked quite nervous.

"Are the boarders out?" she said again; "I could not encounter them. I considered the whole question, and thought that at this hour they would, in all probability, be shopping or diverting themselves in some way. Ah, Westenra, let me look at you."

"But do you really want to look at me, Duchess?" I asked somewhat audaciously.

"I see you have lost none of your spirit," said the Duchess, and she patted me playfully with a large fan which she wore at her side. "There, sit down in that little chair opposite, and tell me all about everything. How is this—this curious concern going?"

"You can see for yourself," I answered; "this room is not exactly an attic, is it?"

"No, it is a very nice reception-room," said the Duchess, glancing approvingly around her. "It has, my dear Mary—forgive me for the remark— a little of the Mayfair look; a large room, too, nearly as large as our rooms in Grosvenor Place."

"Not quite as large," I replied, "and it is not like your rooms, Duchess, but it does very well for us, and it is certainly better and more stimulating than a cottage in the country."

"Ah, Westenra, you are as terribly independent as ever," said the Duchess. "What the girls of the present day are coming to!" She sighed as she spoke.

"But you are a very pretty girl all the same," she continued, giving me an approving nod. "Yes, yes, and this phase will pass, of course it will pass."

"Why have you come to see us to-day, Victoria?" asked my mother.

"My dear friend," replied the Duchess, dropping her voice, "I have come to-day because I am devoured with curiosity. I mean to drop in occasionally. Just at present, and while the whole incident is fresh in the minds of our friends, you would scarcely like me to ask you to my receptions, but by-and-by I doubt not it can be managed. The fact is, I admire you both, and very often think of you. The Duke also is greatly tickled at the whole concern; I never saw him laugh so heartily about anything. He says that, as to Westenra, she is downright refreshing; he never heard of a girl of her stamp doing this sort of thing before. He thinks that she will make a sort of meeting-place, a sort of bond between the West and the—the—no, not the East, but this sort of neutral ground where the middle-class people live."

The Duchess looked round the big room, and then glanced out at the Square.

"Harrison had some difficulty in finding the place," she said, "but the British Museum guided him; it is a landmark. Even we people of Mayfair go to the British Museum sometimes. It is colossal and national, and you live close to it. Do you often study there, Westenra? Don't go too often, for stooping over those old books gives girls such a poke. But you really look quite comfortable here."

"We are delightfully comfortable," I said. "We enjoy our lives immensely."

"It is very nice to see you, Victoria," said mother.

Then I saw by the look on mother's face that while I had supposed her to be perfectly happy, all this time she had been more or less suffering. She had missed the people of her own kind. The Duchess looked her all over.

"You are out of your element here, Mary," she said, "and so is this child. It is a preposterous idea, a sort of freak of nature. I never thought Westenra would become odd; she bids fair to be very odd. I don't agree with the Duke. I don't care for odd people, they don't marry well as a rule. Of course there are exceptions. I said so to the Duke when——"

"When what?" I said, seeing that she paused.

"Nothing, my love, nothing. I have come here, Westenra, to let you and your mother know that whenever you like to step up again I will give you a helping hand."

"Oh, we are never going back to the old life," I said. "We could not afford it, and I don't know either that we should care to live as we did—should we, Mummy? We know our true friends now."

"That is unkind, my child. The fact is, it is the idea of the *boarding-house* that all your friends shrink from. If you and your mother had taken a nice house in the country, not a large and expensive house, but a fairly respectable one, with a little ground round, I and other people I know might have got ladies to live with you and to pay you well. Our special friends who wanted change and quiet might have been very glad to go to you for two or three weeks, but you must see for yourselves, both of you, that this sort of thing is impossible. Nevertheless, I came here to-day to say that whenever, Westenra, you step up, you will find your old friend——"

"And godmother," I said.

"And godmother," she repeated, "willing to give you a helping hand."

"When you became my godmother," I said slowly (oh, I know I was very rude, but I could not quite help myself), "you promised for me, did you not, that I should not love the world?"

The Duchess gazed at me out of her round, good-humoured brown eyes.

"We all know just what that means," she said.

"No, we do not," I answered. "I think very few people do know or realise it in the very least. Now stepping back again might mean the world; perhaps mother and I would rather stay where we are."

As I spoke I got up impatiently and walked to one of the windows, and just then I saw Mr. Randolph coming up the steps. As a rule he was seldom in to lunch; he was an erratic individual, always sleeping in the house, and generally some time during the day having a little chat with mother, but for the rest he was seldom present at any of our meals except late dinner. Why was he coming to lunch to-day? I heard his step on the stairs, he had a light, springy step, the drawing-room door opened and he came in.

"Ah, Jim," said the Duchess, "I scarcely expected to see you here."

She got up and held out her hand; he grasped it. I thought his face wore a peculiar expression. I am not quite certain about this, for I could not see him very well from where I was standing, but I did notice that the Duchess immediately became on her guard. She dropped his hand and turned to mother.

"I met Mr. Randolph last year in Italy," she said.

Mother now entered into conversation with them both, and I stood by the window looking out into the square, and wondering why the Duchess had coloured when she saw him. Why had she called him Jim? If she only met him last year abroad it was scarcely likely that she would be intimate enough to speak to him by his Christian name. A moment later she rose.

"You may take me down to my carriage, Jim," she said. "Good-bye, Westenra; you are a naughty girl, full of defiance, and you think your old godmother very unkind, but whenever you step up I shall be waiting to help you. Good-bye, good-bye. Oh hurry, please, Mr. Randolph, some of those creatures may be coming in. Good-bye, dear, good-bye."

She nodded to mother, laid her hand lightly on Mr. Randolph's arm, who took her down and put her into her carriage. They spoke together for a moment, I watched them from behind the drawing-room curtains, then the carriage rolled away, and the square was left to its usual solid respectability. Doctors' carriages did occasionally drive through it, and flourishing doctors drove a pair of horses as often as not, but the strawberry on the panels showed itself no more for many a long day in that region.

At lunch the boarders were in a perfect state of ferment. Even Captain and Mrs. Furlong were inclined to be subservient. Did we really know the Duchess of Wilmot? Captain Furlong was quite up in the annals of the nobility. This was one of his little weaknesses, for he was quite in every sense of the word a gentleman; but he did rather air his knowledge of this smart lady and of that whom he had happened to meet in the course of his wanderings.

"There are few women I admire more than the Duchess of Wilmot," he said to mother, "she is so charitable, so good. She was a Silchester, you know, she comes of a long and noble line. For my part, I believe strongly in heredity. Have you known the Duchess long, Mrs. Wickham?"

"All my life," answered mother simply.

"Really! All your life?"

"Yes," she replied, "we were brought up in the same village."

The servant came up with vegetables, and mother helped herself. Captain Furlong looked a little more satisfied.

Mrs. Armstrong gave me a violent nudge in the side.

"I suppose your mother was the clergyman's daughter?" she said. "The great people generally patronise the daughters of the clergy in the places where they live. I have often noticed it. I said so to Marion last night. I said, if only, Marion, you could get into that set, you would begin to know the upper ten, clergymen are so respectable; but Marion, if you'll believe it, will have nothing to do with them. She says she would not be a curate's wife for the world. What I say is this, she wouldn't always be a curate's wife, for he would be sure to get a living, and if he were a smart preacher, he might be a dean by-and-by, or even a bishop, just think of it. But Marion shuts her eyes to all these possibilities, and says that nothing would give her greater torture than teaching in Sunday-school and having mothers' meetings. With her h'artistic soul I suppose it is scarcely to be expected that she should take to that kind of employment. And your mother was the clergyman's daughter, was she not?"

"No," I answered. I did not add any more. I did not repeat either that the Duchess happened to be my godmother. I turned the conversation.

Mr. Randolph sat near mother and talked to her, and soon other things occupied the attention of the boarders, and the Duchess's visit ceased to be the topic of conversation.

On the next evening but one, Mr. Randolph came to my side.

"I heard your mother say, Miss Wickham, that you are both fond of the theatre. Now I happen to have secured, through a friend, three tickets for the first night of Macbeth. I should be so glad if you would allow me to take you and Mrs. Wickham to the Lyceum."

"And I should like it, Westenra," said mother—she came up while he was speaking. Miss Armstrong happened to be standing near, and I am sure she overheard. Her face turned a dull red, she walked a step or two away. I thought for a moment. I should have greatly preferred to refuse; I was beginning, I could not tell why, to have an uneasy feeling with regard to Mr. Randolph—there was a sort of mystery about his staying in the house, and why did the Duchess know him, and why did she call him Jim. But my mother's gentle face and the longing in her eyes made me reply—

"If mother likes it, of course I shall like it. Thank you very much for asking us."

"I hope you will enjoy it," was his reply, "I am glad you will come." He did not allude again to the matter, but talked on indifferent subjects. We were to go to the Lyceum on the following evening.

The next day early I went into mother's room. Mother was not at all as strong as I could have wished. She had a slight cough, and there was a faded, fagged sort of look about her, a look I had never seen when we lived in Mayfair. She was subject to palpitations of the heart too, and often turned quite faint when she went through any additional exertion. These symptoms had begun soon

69

after our arrival at 17 Graham Square. She had never had them in the bygone days, when her friends came to see her and she went to see them. Was mother too old for this transplanting? Was it a little rough on her?

Thoughts like these made me very gentle whenever I was in my dear mother's presence, and I was willing and longing to forget myself, if only she might be happy.

"What kind of day is it, Westenra?" she said the moment I put in an appearance. She was not up yet, she was lying in bed supported by pillows. Her dear, fragile beautiful face looked something like the most delicate old porcelain. She was sipping a cup of strong soup, which Jane Mullins had just sent up to her.

"O Mummy!" I said, kissing her frantically, "are you ill? What is the matter?"

"No, my darling, I am quite as well as usual," she answered, "a little weak, but that is nothing. I am tired sometimes, Westenra."

"Tired, but you don't do a great deal," I said.

"That's just it, my love, I do too little. If I had more to do I should be better."

"More visiting, I suppose, and that sort of thing?" I said.

"Yes," she answered very gently, "more visiting, more variety, more exchange of ideas—if it were not for Mr. Randolph."

"You like him?" I said.

"Don't you, my darling?"

"I don't know, mother, I am not sure about him. Who is he?"

"A nice gentlemanly fellow."

"Mother, I sometimes think he is other than what he seems, we know nothing whatever about him."

"He is a friend of Jane Mullins's," said mother.

"But, mother, how can that be? He is not really a friend of Jane Mullins's. Honest little Jane belongs essentially to the people. You have only to look from one face to the other to see what a wide gulf there is between them. He is accustomed to good society; he is a man of the world. Mother, I am certain he is keeping something to himself. I cannot understand why he lives here. Why should he live here?"

"He likes it," answered mother. "He enjoys his many conversations with me. He likes the neighbourhood. He says Bloomsbury is far more healthy than Mayfair."

"Mother, dear, is it likely that such a man would think much about his health."

"I am sorry you are prejudiced against him," said mother, and a fretful quaver came into her voice. "Well," she added, "I am glad the day is fine, we shall enjoy our little expedition this evening."

"But are you sure it won't be too much for you?"

"Too much! I am so wanting to go," said mother.

"Then that is right, and I am delighted."

"By the way," continued mother, "I had a note this morning from Mr. Randolph; he wants us to dine with him first at the Hotel Cecil."

"Mother!"

"Yes, darling; is there any objection?"

"Oh, I don't like it," I continued; "why should we put ourselves under an obligation to him?"

"I do not think, Westenra, you need be afraid; if I think it right to go you need have no scruples."

"Of course I understand that," I answered, "and if it were any one else I should not think twice about it. If the Duchess, for instance, asked us to dine with her, and if she took us afterwards to the theatre I should quite rejoice, but I am puzzled about Mr. Randolph."

"Prejudiced, you mean, dear; but never mind, you are young. As long as you have me with you, you need have no scruples. I have written a line to him to say that we will be pleased to dine with him. He is to meet us at the hotel, and is sending a carriage for us here. I own I shall be very glad once in a way to eat at a table where Mrs. Armstrong is not."

"I have always tried to keep Mrs. Armstrong out of your way, mother."

"Yes, darling; but she irritates me all the same. However, she is a good soul, and I must learn to put up with her. Now then, West, what will you wear to-night?"

"Something very quiet," I answered.

"One of your white dresses."

"I have only white silk, that is too much."

"You can make it simpler; you can take away ornaments and flowers. I want to see you in white again. I am perfectly tired of that black dress which you put on every evening."

I left mother soon afterwards, and the rest of the day proceeded in the usual routine. I would not confess even to myself that I was glad I was going to the Lyceum with Mr. Randolph and mother, but when I saw a new interest in her face and a brightness in her voice, I tried to be pleased on her account. After all, she was the one to be considered. If it gave her pleasure it was all as it should be.

When I went upstairs finally to dress for this occasion, which seemed in the eyes of Jane Mullins to be a very great occasion, she (Jane) followed me to my door. I heard her knock on the panels, and told her to come in with some impatience in my voice.

"Now that is right," she said; "I was hoping you would not put on that dismal black. Young things should be in white."

"Jane," I said, turning suddenly round and speaking with great abruptness, "what part of the cake do you suppose Mr. Randolph represents?"

Jane paused for a moment; there came a twinkle into her eyes.

"Well, now," she said, "I should like to ask you that question myself, say in a year's time."

"I have asked it of you now," I said; "answer, please."

"Let's call him the nutmeg," said Jane. "We put nutmeg into some kinds of rich cake. It strikes me that the cake of this establishment is becoming very rich and complicated now. It gives a rare flavour, does nutmeg, used judiciously."

"I know nothing about it," I answered with impatience. "What part of the cake is mother?"

"Oh, the ornamental icing," said Jane at once; "it gives tone to the whole."

"And I, Jane, I?"

"A dash of spirit, which we put in at the end to give the subtle flavour," was Jane's immediate response.

"Thank you, Jane, you are very complimentary."

"To return to your dress, dear, I am glad you are wearing white."

"I am putting on white to please mother," I replied, "otherwise I should not wear it. To tell the truth, I never felt less disposed for an evening's amusement in my life."

"Then that is extremely wrong of you, Westenra. They are all envying you downstairs. As to poor Miss Armstrong, she would give her eyes to go. They

72

are every one of them in the drawing-room, and dressed in their showiest, and it has leaked out that you won't be there, nor Mrs. Wickham, nor—nor Mr. Randolph, and that I'll be the only one to keep the place in order to-night. I do trust those attic boarders won't get the better of me, for I have a spice of temper in me when I am roused, and those attics do rouse me sometimes almost beyond endurance. As I said before, we get too much of the attic element in the house, and if we don't look sharp the cake will be too heavy."

"That would never do," I replied. I was hurriedly fastening on my white dress as I spoke. It was of a creamy shade, and hung in graceful folds, and I felt something like the Westenra of old times as I gathered up my fan and white gloves, and wrapped my opera cloak round me. I was ready. My dress was simplicity itself, but it suited me. I noticed how slim and tall I looked, and then ran downstairs, determined to forget myself and to devote the whole evening to making mother as happy as woman could be.

Mother was seated in the drawing-room, looking stately, a little nervous, and very beautiful. The ladies of the establishment were fussing round her. They had already made her into a sort of queen, and she certainly looked regal to-night.

The servant came up and announced that the carriage was waiting. We went downstairs. It was a little brougham, dull chocolate in colour. A coachman in quiet livery sat on the box; a footman opened the door for us. The brougham was drawn by a pair of chestnuts.

"Most unsuitable," I murmured to myself. "What sort of man is Mr. Randolph?"

Mother, however, looked quite at home and happy in the little brougham. She got in, and we drove off. It was now the middle of November, and I am sure several faces were pressed against the glass of the drawing-room windows as we were whirled rapidly out of the Square.

CHAPTER XI

WHY DID HE DO IT?

Mr. Randolph had engaged a private room at the hotel. We sat down three to dinner. During the first pause I bent towards him and said in a semi-whisper —

"Why did you send that grand carriage for us?"

"Did it annoy you?" he asked, slightly raising his brows, and that quizzical and yet fascinating light coming into his eyes.

"Yes," I replied. "It was unsuitable."

"I do not agree with you, Westenra," said mother.

"It was unsuitable," I continued. "When we stepped into our present position we meant to stay in it. Mr. Randolph humiliates us when he sends unsuitable carriages for us."

"It happened to be my friend's carriage," he answered simply. "He lent it to me—the friend who has also given me tickets for the Lyceum. I am sorry. I won't transgress again in the same way."

His tone did not show a trace of annoyance, and he continued to speak in his usual tranquil fashion.

As to mother, she was leaning back in her chair and eating a little, a very little, of the many good things provided, and looking simply radiant. She was quite at home. I saw by the expression on her face that she had absolutely forgotten the boarding-house; the attics were as if they had never existed; the third floor and the second floor boarders had vanished completely from her memory. Even Jane Mullins was not. She and I were as we used to be; our old house in Sumner Place was still our home. We had our own carriage, we had our own friends. We belonged to Mayfair. Mother had forgotten Bloomsbury, and what I feared she considered its many trials. Mr. Randolph talked as pleasantly and cheerfully as man could talk, keeping clear of shoals, and conducting us into the smoothest and pleasantest waters.

When dinner was over he led us to the same unsuitable carriage and we drove to the Lyceum. We had a very nice box on the first tier, and saw the magnificent play to perfection. Mr. Randolph made me take one of the front chairs, and I saw many of my old friends. Lady Thesiger kissed her hand to me two or three times, and at the first curtain paid us both a brief visit.

"Ah," she said, "this is nice; your trial scheme is over, Westenra, and you are back again."

"Nothing of the kind," I answered, colouring with vexation.

"Introduce me to your friend, won't you?" she continued, looking at Mr. Randolph with a queer half amused gaze.

I introduced him. Lady Thesiger entered into conversation. Presently she beckoned me out of the box.

"Come and sit with me in my box during the next act," she said, "I have a great deal to say to you."

"But I don't want to leave mother," I replied.

"Nonsense! that cavalier of hers, that delightful young man, how handsome and distinguished looking he is! will take care of her. What do you say his name is—Randolph, Randolph—let me think, it is a good name. Do you know anything about him?"

"Nothing whatever, he happens to be one of our boarders," I replied. "He has taken a fancy to mother, and gave us tickets and brought us to this box to-night."

Jasmine looked me all over.

"I must say you have not at all the appearance of a young woman who has stepped down in the social scale," she remarked. "What a pretty dress that is, and you have a nicer colour than ever in your cheeks. Do you know that you are a very handsome girl?"

"You have told me so before, but I detest compliments," was my brusque rejoinder.

"Oh! I can see that you are as queer and eccentric as ever. Now I tell you what it is, it is my opinion that you're not poor at all, and that you are doing all this for a freak."

"And suppose that were the case, what difference would it make?" I inquired.

"Oh! in that case," answered Lady Thesiger, "your friends would simply think you eccentric, and love you more than ever. It is the fashion to be eccentric now, it is poverty that crushes, you must know that."

"Yes," I answered with bitterness, "it is poverty that crushes. Well, then, from that point of view we are crushed, for we are desperately poor. But in our present nice comfortable house, even contaminated as we are by our paying guests, we do not feel our poverty, for we have all the good things of life around us, and the whole place seems very flourishing. Why don't you come to see us, Jasmine?"

"I am afraid you will want me to recommend my friends to go to you, and I really cannot, Westenra, I cannot."

"But why should you not recommend them?"

"They will get to know that you were, that you belonged, that you"—Jasmine stopped and coloured high. "I cannot do it," she said, "you must not expect it."

"I won't," I replied with some pride.

"But all the same, I will come some morning," she continued. "You look so nice, and Mr. Randolph is so—by the way, what Randolph is he? I must find out all about him. Do question him about the county he comes from."

I did not answer, and having said good-bye to Jasmine, returned to our own box.

The play came to an end, and we went home. Mother had gone up to her room. Mr. Randolph and I found ourselves for a moment alone.

"This evening has done her good," he said, glancing at me in an interrogative fashion.

"Are you talking of mother?" I replied.

"Yes, you must see how much brighter she appeared. Do you think it did really help her?"

"I do not understand you," I replied; "help her? She enjoyed it, of course."

"But can't you see for yourself," he continued, and his voice was emphatic and his eyes shone with suppressed indignation, "that your mother is starving. She will not complain; she is one of the best and sweetest women I have ever met, but all the same, I am anxious about her, this life does not suit her—not at all."

"I am sure you are mistaken; I do not think mother is as miserable as you make her out to be," I replied. "I know, of course, she enjoyed this evening."

"She must have more evenings like this," he continued; "many more, and you must not be angry if I try to make things pleasant for her."

"Mr. Randolph," I said impulsively, "you puzzle me dreadfully. I cannot imagine why you live with us; you do not belong to the class of men who live in boarding-houses."

"Nor do you belong to the class of girls who keep boarding-houses," he replied.

"No, but circumstances have forced mother and me to do what we do. Circumstances have not forced you. It was my whim that we should earn money in this way. You don't think that I was cruel to mother. She certainly did not want to come here, it was I who insisted."

"You are so young and so ignorant," he replied.

"Ignorant!" I cried.

"Yes, and very young." He spoke sadly. "You cannot see all that this means to an older person," he continued. "Now, do not be angry, but I have noticed for some time that your mother wants change. Will you try to accept any little amusements I may be able to procure for her in a friendly spirit? I can do much for her if it does not worry you, but if you will not enjoy her pleasures, she will not be happy either. Can you not understand?"

I looked at him again, and saw that his face was honest and his eyes kind.

"May I give your mother these little pleasures?" he continued; "she interests me profoundly. Some day I will tell you why I have a special reason for being interested in your mother. I cannot tell you at present, but I do not want you to misunderstand me. May I make up to her in a little measure for much that she has lost, may I?"

"You may," I answered; "you are kind, I am greatly obliged to you. I will own that I was cross for a moment—you hurt my pride; but you may do what you like in future, my pride shall not rise in a hurry again." I held out my hand, he took it and wrung it. I ran upstairs, mother was sitting before her fire. She looked sweet, and her eyes were bright, and there was a new strength in her voice.

"We have had a delightful evening," she said. "I hope you are not tired, my darling."

"I am quite fresh," I answered. "I am so pleased you enjoyed it."

"I did, dearest; did you?"

"Yes, and no," I answered; "but if you are happy I am."

"Sit down by me, Westenra. Let us talk a little of what has just happened."

I humoured her, of course. Mr. Randolph's words had rather alarmed me. Did he see more ill-health about mother than I had noticed? was he seriously anxious about her? But now as she sat there she seemed well, very well, not at all tired, quite cheerful, and like her own self. She took my hand.

Jane—dear, active, industrious Jane—had gone early to bed, but a little supper had been left ready for mother. She tasted some of the jelly, then laid the spoon down by her plate.

"You were rude to Mr. Randolph at dinner, West," she said.

"I am sorry if I vexed you," I answered.

"But what had he done to annoy you?"

"I could not bear him to send that carriage. It was so unsuitable, servants in livery and those splendid horses; and all the boarders did stare so. It seemed quite out of keeping with our present lot. But never mind, Mummy, he may bring any carriage—the Lord Mayor's, if you like—only don't look so unhappy." I felt the tears had come into my voice, but I took good care they should not reach my eyes. I bent and kissed mother on her cheek.

"You want your old life, your dear old life," I said, "and your old comforts. I am very happy, and I want you to be the same. If I have made a mistake, and you are injured by this, it will break my heart."

"I am not injured at all, I am happy," she said.

"You like Mr. Randolph?"

"I do. He belongs to the old life."

"Then he is no mystery to you?"

"I take him quite simply, as a good-natured fellow, who has plenty of money, and is attracted by our rather queer position," she answered, "that is all. I don't make mysteries where none may exist."

"Then I will do likewise," I said cheerfully.

The next morning when I awoke it seemed like a dream that we had dined at the Cecil and enjoyed the luxury of a box at the Lyceum, that we had for a brief time stepped back into our old existence.

The morning was a foggy one, one of the first bad fogs of the season. The boarders were cross—breakfast was not quite as luxurious as usual; even Jane was a little late and a little put out. The boarders were very fond of porridge, and it happened to be slightly burnt that morning. There were discontented looks, and even discontented words, from more than one uninteresting individual. Then Mr. Randolph came in, looking very fresh and neat and pleasant, and sat down boldly in the vacant seat near me, and began to talk about last night. Mother never got up until after breakfast. Mrs. Armstrong gazed at me, and Miss Armstrong tossed her food about, and the other boarders, even the Furlongs, cast curious glances in our direction; but I had determined to take him at his word, and to enjoy all the pleasures he could give us; and as to Mr. Randolph himself, I don't believe any one could upset his composure. He talked a good deal about our last night's entertainment, and said that he hoped to be able to take us to the theatre again soon.

Just at that moment a shrill voice sounded in his ears.

"Did I hear you say, Mr. Randolph," called out Mrs. Armstrong from her place at the opposite side of the board, "that you have a large connection with the theatrical managers?"

"No, you did not, Mrs. Armstrong," was his very quiet rejoinder.

"I beg your pardon, I'm sure." Mrs Armstrong flushed. Miss Armstrong touched her on her arm.

"Lor! mother, how queer of you," she said; "I am sure Mr. Randolph said nothing of the kind. Why, these play managers are quite a low sort of people; I'm ashamed of you, mother."

"I happen to know Irving very well," said Mr. Randolph, "and also Beerbohm Tree and Wilson Barrett, and I do not think any of these distinguished men of genius are a low sort of people."

"It is the exception that proves the rule," said Mrs. Armstrong, glancing at her daughter and bridling. "You should not take me up so sharp, Marion. What I was going to say was this, Mr. Randolph—can you or can you not get us tickets cheap for one of the plays. We have a great hankering to go, both me and Marion, and seeing that we are all in this house—one family, so to speak —it don't seem fair, do it, that *all* the favour should go to one?"—here she cast a withering glance at me.

Mr. Randolph turned and looked at me, and that quizzical laughing light was very bright in his eyes, then he turned towards Mrs. Armstrong, and, after a brief pause, said gently—

"What day would suit you best to go to the Lyceum?"

"Oh, Mr. Randolph!" said Marion Armstrong in a voice of rapture.

"Because if to-morrow night would be convenient to you two ladies," he continued, "I think I can promise you stalls. I will let you know at lunch-time." Here he rose, gave a slight bow in the direction of the Armstrongs, and left the room.

"Now I have done it, and I am glad," said Mrs. Armstrong.

"I do hope, ma," continued Marion, "that he means to come with us. I want to go just as Mrs. Wickham and Miss Wickham went, in the brougham with the coachman and the footman, and to have dinner at the Cecil. It must be delightful dining at the Cecil, Miss Wickham. They say that most dinners there cost five pounds, is that true?"

"I cannot tell you," I replied. "Mother and I were Mr. Randolph's guests."

Mrs. Armstrong looked me up and down. She thought it best at that moment to put on a very knowing look, and the expression of her face was most annoying.

"Don't you ask impertinent questions, Marion," she said; "you and me must be thankful for small mercies, and for those two stalls, even if we do go as lone females. But I hope to goodness Mr. Randolph won't forget about it. If he does, I'll take the liberty to remind him. Now be off with you, Marion, your h'Art awaits you. What you may become if you take pains, goodness only knows. You may be giving tickets yourself for the theatre some day— that is, if you develop your talents to the utmost."

Amongst other matters which Jane Mullins took upon her own broad shoulders was the interviewing of all strangers who came to inquire about the house. She said frankly that it would never do for me to undertake this office, and that mother was not to be worried. She was the person to do it, and she accordingly conducted this part of the business as well as—I began dimly to perceive—almost every other, for mother had next to nothing to do, and I had still less. I almost resented my position—it was not what I had dreamed about. I ought to help Jane, I ought to throw myself into the work, I ought to make things go smoothly. Dear Jane's fagged face began to appeal less to me than it had at first. Was I getting hardened? Was I getting injured? I put these questions to myself now and then, but I think without any great seriousness— I was sure that my plan was, on the whole, sensible, and I would not reproach myself for what I had done.

On the evening of the day which followed our visit to the Lyceum a new inmate appeared in the drawing-room. He was a tall man, considerably over six feet in height, very lanky and thin, with a somewhat German cast of face, pale-blue eyes, a bald forehead, hair slightly inclined to be sandy, an ugly mouth with broken teeth, and a long moustache which, with all his efforts, did not conceal this defect.

The new boarder was introduced to my mother and me by Jane Mullins as Mr. Albert Fanning. He bowed profoundly when the introduction was made, and gave me a bold glance. At dinner I found, rather to my annoyance, that he was placed next to me. Jane usually put strangers next to me at the table, as she said that it gave general satisfaction, and helped to keep the house full.

"What sort of man is Mr. Fanning?" I asked as we were going down to dinner.

"I don't know anything about him, dear," was her reply. "He pays well, generously, in fact—no less than five guineas a week. He has a room on the first floor, but not one of our largest. It is a very good thing to have him, for we don't often let the first floor rooms. It's the attics and third floors that go off so quickly. I don't know anything about him, but he seems to be somewhat of a character."

I made no reply to this, but the moment we seated ourselves at table Mr. Fanning bent towards me, and said in a low voice—

"I think myself extremely honoured to have made your acquaintance, Miss Wickham."

"Indeed," I answered in some surprise. "And why, may I ask?"

"I have often seen you in the Park. I saw you there last season and the season before. When I heard that you and Mrs. Wickham had taken this boarding-house, I made a point of securing rooms here as quickly as possible."

As he said this I felt myself shrinking away from him. I glanced in the direction of the upper part of the table, where Mr. Randolph was talking to mother. Mr. Fanning bent again towards me.

"I do not wish to say anything specially personal," he remarked, "but just for once I should like to say, if I never repeat it again, that I think you are a most enterprising, and, let me repeat, most charming young lady."

The servant was helping me just then to some bread. I turned my face away from Mr. Fanning, but when I looked round again he must have seen my flushed cheeks.

"I am a publisher," he said, lowering his voice, which was one of his most trying characteristics whenever he addressed me. "Most girls like to hear about publishers and about books. Has the writing mania seized you yet, Miss Wickham?"

"No," I replied, "I have not the slightest taste for writing. I am not the least bit imaginative."

"Now, what a pity that is; but there is a great deal of writing besides the imaginative type. What I was going to say was this, that if at any time a small manuscript of yours were put in my way, it would receive the most prompt and business-like attention. I am a very business-like person. I have an enormous connection. My place of business is in Paternoster Row. The Row is devoted to books, as you know. All my books are of a go-ahead stamp; they sell by thousands. Did you ever see a publisher's office, Miss Wickham?"

"No," I said.

"I should be most pleased to conduct you over mine, if you liked to call some day at the Row. I could take you there immediately after luncheon, and show you the premises any day you liked. Eh! Did you speak?"

"I am very much occupied with my mother, and seldom or never go anywhere without her," was my reply to this audacious proposal. I then turned my shoulder upon my aggressive neighbour, and began to talk frantically to a lady at my other side. She was a dull little woman, and I could scarcely get a word out of her. Her name was Mrs. Sampson; she was slightly deaf, and said "Eh, eh!" to each remark of mine. But she was a refuge from the intolerable Mr. Fanning, and I roused myself to be most polite to her during the remainder of the meal.

CHAPTER XII

TWO EXTREMES

Mr. Fanning followed us upstairs after dinner. I greatly hoped that he was the sort of man who would not often frequent the drawing-room, but I soon perceived my mistake. He not only entered that apartment, but attached himself as soon as possible to my side. He was beyond doubt the most disagreeable boarder we had yet secured. Indeed, Mrs. and Miss Armstrong were delightful compared to him. I now saw Miss Armstrong glance two or three times both at him and me, and rising deliberately, I crossed the room, and with a motion of my hand, asked him to accompany me. I then introduced him to that young lady. She blushed when I did so, and bridled a little. She did not evidently think him at all objectionable. I went back immediately to my seat near mother, and could scarcely suppress a feeling of pleasure at Mr. Fanning's too evident discomfiture.

I generally sang a couple of songs in the evening, and I was asked, as usual, to do so to-night. My voice was a rather sweet mezzo soprano, and I had been well taught. I sat down before the piano, as usual. When Mr. Randolph was in the room he always came and turned the pages of my music for me, but he was not present this evening, although he had dined with us; he had evidently gone out immediately afterwards. Now a voice sounded in my ears. I turned, and saw the objectionable and irrepressible Mr. Fanning.

"Why did you play me that trick?" he said.

"What trick?" I asked. "I do not play tricks; I do not understand you."

"You do understand me perfectly well. Oh, pray do sing this song; I am sure it is charming. It is an old English ditty, is it not?—'Begone, Dull Care, You and I will Never Agree.' Now, that is just my way of thinking. I hate dismal people, and as to care, I never bother with it. To hear such a sprightly song from your lips will be indeed what I may call a pick-me-up."

I almost rose from the piano, but knowing that such a proceeding would call public attention to Mr. Fanning's most unpleasant remarks, I said in a low, emphatic voice—

"I will not play for you, nor allow you to turn my music, if you talk to me as you are now doing. You must address me as you would any other lady, and I will not permit what you consider compliments."

"Oh, I am sure I have no wish to offend. Sorry I spoke," he said. He did not blush—I do not think he could—but he passed his hand across his rather ugly mouth, and gave me a peculiar glance out of his queer blue eyes. He then said in a low voice—

"Believe me, it will be my utmost endeavour to make myself agreeable. I quite see what you mean. You do not want folks to remark; that's it, and I absolutely understand. But you must not play me those sort of tricks again, you know. I really cannot be introduced to ladies of the sort you just gave me an introduction to."

"Miss Armstrong is an excellent girl," I said, "and I shall ask her to sing when I leave the piano. She is very talented, and has a love both for music and art."

I then sang my one song, enduring the odious proximity of this most unpleasant man. I fancied I saw a conscious expression on the faces of several of our guests, and resolved that whatever happened, Mr. Fanning must leave on the following day. Such a man could not be permitted to remain in the place.

Later on, as I was going to bed, there came a tap at my door. I opened it, half hoping, half fearing, that Jane herself might have come to see me. On the contrary, somewhat to my surprise, I saw Mrs. Furlong. She asked me if she might come in. I eagerly begged of her to do so, and drew a comfortable chair forward for her acceptance.

"What is the matter?" I said. "Do you want to say anything special?"

"I do, my dear Miss Wickham," replied the lady. "I have come for the purpose."

"Yes?" I said in a slight tone of query.

"How did that objectionable man, Mr. Fanning, get here?"

"I suppose he came because he wanted to," I replied. "The house is open to any one who will pay, and who bears a respectable character."

"The house ought only to be open to those who bear agreeable characters, and know how to act as gentlemen," replied Mrs. Furlong stoutly. "Now my husband and I dislike that person extremely, but after all the fact of whether we like him or not matters but little; it is because he tries to annoy you that we are really concerned. Would you not rather at dinner come and sit at our end of the table? It always seems very hard to us that you should sit with your housekeeper, Miss Mullins, and amongst the least nice members of the establishment."

"But you must please remember," I said, "that Jane is not a housekeeper, she is one of the partners in this concern. It is kind of you to think of me, but I cannot do what you propose. I must help Jane in every way in my power. You do not know how good and true she is, and how little I really do for her. If I sat with you we should have a regular clique in the place, and by degrees the boarders would go, at least those boarders who were not included in our set."

"I see," answered Mrs. Furlong. "It is all most unsuitable," she added, and she stared straight before her. After a moment's pause she looked at me again.

"It is the queerest arrangement I ever heard of in all my life. Don't you think you are peculiarly unsuited to your present life?"

"I don't know; I hope not."

"You are a lady."

"That is my birthright. The boarding-house cannot deprive me of it," I answered.

"Oh, I know all that, but the life is not suitable. You will find it less and less suitable as time goes on. At present you have got your mother to protect you, but——"

"What do you mean by at present I have got my mother?" I cried. "My mother is young, comparatively young; she is not more than three and forty. What do you mean, Mrs. Furlong?"

"Oh nothing, dear," she said, colouring, "nothing at all. One always has, you know, in this uncertain world to contemplate the possibility of loss, but don't think again of what I have said. The fact is the life is quite as unsuitable for her as for you. You are put in a position which you cannot possibly maintain, my dear Miss Wickham. That awful man felt to-night that he had a right to pay you disagreeable attentions. Now is this thing to go on? I assure you Captain Furlong and I were quite distressed when we saw how he behaved to you when you were at the piano."

The tears rushed to my eyes.

"It is kind of you to sympathise with me," I said. "I am going to speak to Jane Mullins to-morrow. If possible Mr. Fanning must go."

"But there is another thing," began Mrs. Furlong. She paused, and I saw that she was about to say something, even more disagreeable than anything she had yet uttered.

"You have your mother, of course," she continued slowly, "but you yourself are very young, and—now I don't want to compliment you—but you are much nicer looking than many girls; you have quite a different air and appearance from any other girl in this house. Oh, I hate interfering, but your mother, Miss Wickham, must be a particularly innocent woman."

"What do you mean?" I asked.

"I mean Mr. Randolph," she answered, and she raised her eyes and fixed them on my face.

"Mr. Randolph?" I said. "Surely you must admit that he at least is a gentleman?"

"He is not only a gentleman, but he is more highly born and has more money than any one else in the house; he does not belong to the set who fill this house at all. Why does he come? This is no place for him. In one way it is quite as unsuitable to have him here as it is to have a man like Mr. Fanning here. Those two men represent opposite extremes. People will talk."

"What about?" I asked.

"About you, dear."

"They cannot. I will not permit it." Then I said abruptly, standing up in my excitement, "After all, I don't care whether they talk or not; I was prepared for misunderstandings when I came here. Mother likes Mr. Randolph; he at least shall stay."

"But, my child, it is not nice to be talked about; it is never nice for a young girl. People like my husband and myself quite understand. We know well that you and your mother are at present out of your right position, but others will not be so considerate. Mr. Randolph is always here."

"You think," I said, stammering, "that he comes because——"

She smiled, got up and kissed me.

"What else could he come for, Westenra?" she said softly.

"He comes because—because of mother," I answered. "He likes her; he told me so. He is anxious about her, for he thinks she misses her old life very much; he wants to make things easier for her. He is a very good man, and I respect him. I don't mind what any one says, I know in my heart he comes here because——"

"No, you do not," said Mrs. Furlong, and she looked me full in the eyes, and I found myself colouring and stammering.

"Believe me I have not intruded upon you this evening without cause," said the little woman. "I talked the matter over with my husband. I would rather Mr. Fanning were here than Mr. Randolph. Mr. Fanning is impossible, Mr. Randolph is not. He does not come here on account of your mother, he comes here because he likes you. I am very sorry; I felt I must speak; my husband agrees with me."

"Do not say another word now," I said. "I am sure you mean all this kindly, but please do not say any more now. I will think over what you have said."

"I will leave you then, dear," she said.

She went as far as the door; she was a very kindly little woman, she was a real lady, and she meant well, but she had hurt me so indescribably that at that moment I almost hated her. When she reached the door she turned and said—

"If ever my husband and I can help you, Miss Wickham (but we are poor people), if ever we can help you, we will be glad to do so. I know you are angry with me now, but your anger won't remain, you will see who are your true friends by-and-by."

She closed the door softly, and I heard her gentle steps going downstairs. I will frankly say that I did not go to bed for some time, that I paced indignantly up and down my room. I hated Jane, I hated Mr. Fanning, I still more cordially hated Mr. Randolph at that moment. Mr. Fanning must go, Mr. Randolph must go. I could not allow myself to be spoken about. How intolerable of Mr. Randolph to have come as he had done, to have forced himself upon us, to have invited us to go out with him, to have——and then I stopped, and a great lump rose in my throat, and I burst into tears, for in my heart of hearts I knew well that I did not think what he did intolerable at all, that I respected him, and—but I did not dare to allow my thoughts to go any further.

I even hated myself for being good-looking, until I suddenly remembered that I had the same features as my father had. He had conquered in all the battles in which he had borne part through his life. My face must be a good one if it was like his. I would try to live up to the character which my face seemed to express, and I would immediately endeavour to get things on a different footing.

Accordingly, the next day at breakfast I studiously avoided Mr. Randolph, and I equally studiously avoided Mr. Fanning. The consequence was that, being as it were between two fires, I had a most uncomfortable time, for Mr. Randolph showed me by certain glances which he threw in my direction that he was most anxious to consult me about something, and Mr. Fanning seemed to intercept these glances, and to make his own most unpleasant comments about them; and if Mr. Fanning intercepted them, so did Mrs. and Miss Armstrong.

Miss Armstrong had now given up Mr. Randolph as almost hopeless with regard to a flirtation, and was turning her attention in the direction of Mr.

Fanning. She talked Art *at* Mr. Fanning assiduously all during breakfast, and having learned by some accident that he was a publisher, boldly demanded from him if he would not like her to illustrate some of his books. In reply to this he gave a profound bow, and told her, with a certain awkward jerk of his body, that he never gave orders in advance, that he never gave orders on the score of friendliness, that when it came to the relations between publisher and artist he was brutal.

"That's the word for it, Miss Armstrong," he said, "I am brutal when it comes to a bargain. I try to make the very best I can for myself. I never think of the artist at all. I want all the *£ s d* to go into my own pocket"—and here he slapped his waistcoat loudly, and uttered a harsh laugh, which showed all his broken teeth in a most disagreeable manner. Miss Armstrong and her mother seemed to think he was excellent fun, and Mrs. Armstrong said, with a quick glance first at Mr. Randolph and then at me, that it was refreshing to hear any man so frank, and that for her part she respected people who gave themselves no h'airs.

Breakfast came to an end, and I sought Jane in her sanctum.

"Now, Jane," I said, "you must put away your accounts, you must cease to think of housekeeping. You must listen to me."

"What is it, Westenra?" she said. "Has anything vexed you?" she continued; "sit down and tell me all about it."

"Several things vex me," I answered. "Jane, we must come to an understanding."

"What about?" she asked in some alarm; "an understanding! I thought that was all arranged when our legal agreement was drawn up."

"Oh, I know nothing about lawyers nor about legal agreements," I answered; "but, Jane, there are some things I cannot put up with, and one of them is ——"

"I know," she answered; "Mr. Fanning."

"He is horrible, hateful; he is going to make himself most hateful to me. Jane, dear Jane, he must go."

Jane looked puzzled and distressed. I expected her to say—

"He shall certainly go, my dear, I will tell him that his room is required, and that he must leave at the end of the week." But on the contrary she sighed. After a long pause she said—

"You want this house to be a success, I presume."

"I certainly do, but we cannot have it a success on the present arrangement. Mr. Fanning must go, and also Mr. Randolph."

"Mr. Randolph, Mr. James Randolph!" said Jane, now colouring high, and a sparkle of something, which seemed to be a curious mixture of fear and indignation, filling her eyes. "And why should he go? You do not know what you are talking about."

"I do. He must go. Ask—ask Mrs. Furlong. They talk about him here, these hateful people; they put false constructions on his kindness; I know he is kind and he is a gentleman, but he does me harm, Jane, even as much harm as that horrible Mr. Fanning."

"Now, look here, Westenra Wickham," said Jane Mullins. "Are you going to throw up the sponge, or are you not?"

"Throw up the sponge! I certainly don't mean to fail."

"You will do so if you send those two men out of the house. If you cannot hold your own, whatever men come here, you are not the girl I took you for. As to Mr. Randolph, be quite assured that he will never do anything to annoy you. If people talk let them talk. When they see nothing comes of their idle silly gossip, they will soon cease to utter it. And as to Mr. Fanning, they will equally cease to worry about him. If he pays he must stay, for as it is, it is difficult to let the first-floor rooms. People don't want to pay five guineas a week to live in Bloomsbury, and he has a small room; and it is a great relief to me that he should be here and pay so good a sum for his room. The thing must be met commercially, or I for one give it up."

"You, Jane, you! then indeed we shall be ruined."

"I don't really mean to, my dear child, I don't mean for a single moment to desert you; but I must say that if 17 Graham Square is to go on, it must go on commercial principles; and we cannot send our best boarders away. You ask me coolly, just because things are a little uncomfortable for you, you ask me to dismiss ten guineas a week, for Mr. Randolph pays five guineas for his room, and Mr. Fanning five guineas for his, and I don't know any other gentleman who would pay an equal sum, and we must have it to balance matters. What is to meet the rent, my dear? What is to meet the taxes? What is to meet the butcher's, the baker's, the grocer's, the fishmonger's bills if we dismissed our tenants. I often have a terrible fear that we were rash to take a great expensive house like this, and unless it is full from attic to drawing-room floor, we have not the slightest chance of meeting our expenses. Even then I fear!—but there I won't croak before the time; only, Westenra, you have to make up your mind. You can go away on a visit if you wish to, I do not counsel this for a moment, for I know you are a great attraction here. It is because you are pretty and wear nice dresses, and look different from the other boarders, that you attract them; and—yes, I will say it—Mr. Randolph also attracts them. They can get no small change out of Mr. James Randolph, so they need not try it on, but once for all we cannot decline the people who are willing to pay us good money, that is a foregone conclusion. Now you have got to accept the agreeables with the disagreeables, or this whole great scheme of yours will tumble about our heads like a pack of cards."

CHAPTER XIII

THE UGLY DRESS

On that very day I searched through mother's wardrobe and found a piece of brown barége. It was a harsh and by no means pretty material. I held it up to the light, and asked her what she was going to do with it.

"Nothing," she answered, "I bought it ten years ago at a sale of remnants, and why it has stuck to me all these years is more than I can tell."

"May I have it?" was my next query.

"Certainly," replied mother, "but you surely are not going to have a dress made of that ugly thing?"

"May I have it?" I asked again.

"Yes, dear, yes."

I did not say any more with regard to the barége. I turned the conversation to indifferent matters, but when I left the room I took it with me. I made it into a parcel and took it out. I went to a little dressmaker in a street near by. I asked her if she would make the ugly brown barége into an evening dress. She measured the material, and said it was somewhat scanty.

"That does not matter," I said, "I *want* an ugly dress—can you manage to make a really ugly dress for me out of it?"

"Well, Miss Wickham," she replied, fixing her pale brown eyes on my face, "I never do go in for making ugly dresses, it would be against my profession. You don't mean it, do you, Miss Wickham?"

"Put your best work into it," I said, suddenly changing my tone. "Make it according to your own ideas of the fashion. Picture a young girl going to a play, or a ball, in that dress, and make it according to your own ideas."

"May I trim it with golden yellow chiffon and turquoise blue silk bows?" she asked eagerly, her eyes shining.

"You may," I replied, suppressing an internal shudder. I gave her a few further directions; she named a day when I should come to be fitted, and I went home.

In less than a week's time the brown barége arrived back, ready for me to wear. It was made according to Annie Starr's ideas of a fashionable evening gown. It was the sort of garment which would have sent the Duchess or Lady Thesiger into fits on the spot. In the first place, the bodice was full of wrinkles, it was too wide in the waist, and too narrow across the chest, but this was a small matter to complain of. It was the irritating air of vulgarity all over the dress which was so hard to bear. But, notwithstanding all these defects, it pleased me. It would, I hoped, answer my purpose, and succeed in making me appear very unattractive in the eyes of Mr. Randolph.

That evening I put on the brown barége for dinner. The yellow chiffon and the turquoise blue bows were much in evidence, and I did really feel that I was a martyr when I went downstairs in that dress with its *outré* trimmings.

When I entered the drawing-room, mother glanced up at me as if she did not know me; she then started, the colour came into her face, and she motioned me imperatively to her side.

"Go upstairs at once and take that off," she said.

"Oh no, mother," I answered, "there is no time now, besides I—I chose it, I admire it."

"Take it off immediately, Westenra."

"But it is your dear barége that you have kept for ten years," I said, trying to be playful; "I must wear it, at least to-night."

I knew that I had never looked worse, and I quite gloried in the fact. I saw Mr. Randolph from his seat near mother glance at me several times in a puzzled way, and Mr. Fanning, after one or two astonished glances, during which he took in the *tout ensemble* of the ugly robe, began to enter into a playful bear-like flirtation with Miss Armstrong. Dear brown barége, what service it was doing me! I secretly determined that it should be my dinner dress every evening until it wore itself to rags. When the turquoise blue bows became too shabby, I might substitute them for magenta ones. I felt that I had suddenly found an opening out of my difficulty. If I ceased to appear attractive, Mr. Randolph and Mr. Fanning would cease to worry me, the rest of the boarders would accept me for what I was, and my Gordian knot would be cut. Little did I guess! It was by no means so easy to carry out my fixed determination as I had hoped. In the first place, poor darling mother nearly fretted herself into an illness on account of my evening dress. She absolutely cried when she saw me in it, and said that if I was determined to deteriorate in that way, she would give up the boarding-house and go to the cottage in the country without a moment's hesitation. After wearing the dress for three or four days I was forced, very much against my will, to put on one of my pretty black dresses, and the barége made by Annie Starr resumed its place in my wardrobe. I determined to wear it now and then, however—it had already done me good service. I began to hope that neither Mr. Randolph nor Mr. Fanning thought me worth looking at when I appeared in it.

On this evening, as I was dressing for dinner, I heard a wonderful bumping going on in the stairs. It was the noise made by very heavy trunks, trunks so large that they seemed scarcely able to be brought upstairs. They were arriving at the attics, too—they were entering the attic next to mine. Now that special attic had up to the present remained untenanted. It was the most disagreeable room in the house. Most of the attics were quite excellent, but this room had a decidedly sloping roof, and rather small windows, and the paper on the walls was ugly, and the accommodation scanty, and what those huge boxes were going to do there was more than I could tell. The boxes, however, entered that special attic, and then a bodily presence followed them briskly, a loud hearty voice was heard to speak. It said in cheerful tones—

"Thank you, that will do nicely. A large can of hot water, please, and a couple more candles. Thanks. What hour did you say the company dined?"

The reply was made in a low tone which I could not catch, and the attic door was shut.

I was down in the drawing-room in my black dress—(how comfortable I felt in it, how hateful that brown barége was, after all)—when the door was opened, and a large, stoutly-made woman, most richly dressed, came in. She had a quantity of grizzly grey hair, which was turned back from her expansive forehead; a cap of almost every colour in the rainbow bedizened her head, she wore diamond pendants in her ears, and had a flashing diamond brooch fastening the front of her dress. Her complexion was high, she had a broad mouth and a constant smile. She walked straight up to Jane Mullins.

"Well," she said, "here I am. I have not unpacked my big trunk, as your servant said there was very little time before dinner. Please can you tell me when Albert will be in?"

"Mr. Fanning generally comes home about now," I heard Jane say. "Mrs. Fanning, may I introduce you to my dear young friend, Miss Wickham—Mrs. Wickham has not yet appeared."

To my horror I saw Miss Mullins advancing across the drawing-room, accompanied by the stout woman; they approached to my side.

"May I introduce Mrs. Fanning," said Miss Mullins—"Mr. Fanning's mother."

"The mother of dear, godly Albert," said the stout lady. "I am proud to say I am the mother of one of the best of sons. I am right pleased to meet you, Miss Wickham. I may as well say at once that Albert Fanning, my dear and only son, has mentioned your name to me, and with an approval which would make your young cheeks blush. Yes, I am the last person to encourage vanity in the young, but I must repeat that if you knew all that Albert has said, you would feel that flutter of the heart which only joy brings forth. Now, shall we both sit in a cosy corner and enjoy ourselves, and talk about Albert until dinner is ready?"

This treat was certainly not likely to cause my young cheeks to blush. On the contrary, I felt myself turning pale, and I looked round with a desperate intention of flying to Jane for protection, when the stout lady took one of my hands.

"Ah," she said, "quite up to date, a slim young hand, and a slim young figure, and a slim young face, too, for that matter. All that Albert says is true, you are a *very* nice-looking girl. I should not say that you had much durance in you, that remains to be proved. But come, here's a cosy corner, I have a great deal to say."

That hand of Mrs. Fanning's had a wonderfully clinging effect; it seemed to encircle my fingers something like an octopus, and she pulled me gently towards the corner she had in view, and presently had pinned me there, seating herself well in front of me, so that there was no possible escape.

The rest of the boarders now entered the drawing-room. Mother amongst others made her appearance; she went to her accustomed corner, glanced at me, saw that I was in one of my black dresses, nodded approval, concluding in her dear mind that I had probably met some old friend in the extraordinary person who was shutting me into the corner, and took no further notice.

Captain and Mrs. Furlong were well pleased to see that I was only talking to a woman, it did not matter at all to them who that woman was. And as to me I sat perfectly silent while Mrs. Fanning discoursed on Albert. She never for a single moment, I will say for her, turned the conversation into another channel. Albert was her theme, and she stuck to him with the pertinacity which would have done any leader of a debate credit. The debate was Albert. She intended before dinner was announced to give me a true insight into that remarkable man's most remarkable character.

"Yes," she said, "what Albert thinks is always to the point. Since a child he never gave me what you would call a real heartache. Determined, self-willed he is; you look, the next time you see him, at his chin, you observe the cleft in the middle; there never was a chin like that yet without a mind according—a mind, so to speak, set on the duty ahead of it—a mind that is determined to conquer. That is Albert, that is my only, godly son. You observe, when you have an opportunity, Albert's eyes. Did you ever see anything more open than

94

the way they look at you? He don't mind whether it hurts your feelings or not; if he wants to look at you, look he will."

When she said this I nodded my head emphatically, for I had found this most disagreeable trait in Albert's eyes from the first moment I had been unfortunate enough to make his acquaintance. But Mrs. Fanning took my nod in high good humour.

"Ah, you have observed it," she said, "and no wonder, no wonder. Now, when you get an opportunity, do pull him to pieces, feature by feature; notice his brow, how lofty it is; there's talent there, and t'aint what you would call a fly-away talent, such as those art talents that make me quite sick. He has no talent, thank Heaven, for painting or for poetry, or for any fal-lal of that kind, his talent lies in a sound business direction. Oh, he has made me roar, the way he talks of young authors and young artists, how they come to him with their wares, and how he beats them down. It's in Albert's brow where his talent for business lies. You mark his nose too, it's somewhat long and a little pointed, but it's the nose of a man who will make his mark; yes, he'll make his mark some day, and I have told him so over and over."

Having gone through all Albert's features, she next proceeded to describe Albert's character, and then went on to Albert's future. From this it was an easy step to Albert's wife, and Albert's wife took up a great deal of the good woman's attention.

"It is because I am thinking he'll soon be falling into the snares of matrimony that I have come to stay at 17 Graham Square," continued Mrs. Fanning. "And it's because I want my dear and godly son to get a wife who will be on the pattern of Solomon's virtuous woman that I have given up my home and broken up my establishment and come here. Now, Miss Wickham, my dear young lady, did you or did you not hear the noise of my boxes being brought upstairs?"

"I certainly did," I replied.

"Then you happen to occupy the bedroom next to mine?"

"I do," I said.

"That is very nice indeed, for often of an evening we will keep each other company and discourse on Albert, to the joy of both our hearts. The boxes are receptacles for my household gods, dear, those dear mementoes of the past, that I could not quite part with. Don't suppose for a moment that they are full of dresses, for although my taste is light and festive, Albert likes gay colours, he says they remind him of the sales of remnants in the autumn. Dear fellow, it was the most poetical thing he ever uttered, but he has said it once or twice.

I can show you my household treasures when you feel disposed to have an evening's real recreation. The burden of this house, and with so delicate a mother as your good Ma, must be heavy upon a young lass like you, but Albert tells me—but there! I won't say any more just now, for you'll blush, and I don't want you to blush, and I don't want to encourage those hopes that may never be realised. I may as well whisper, though, that Albert is looking out for a wife who will be a pattern of Solomon's virtuous woman, and when he finds her, why she'll be lucky, that's all I can say."

Just then the pretty silver gong sounded, and people began to stand up preparatory to going down to dinner. It was difficult even then to move Mrs. Fanning, and for a wild moment I had a fear that I might be imprisoned behind her in the drawing-room all during dinner, while she still discoursed upon Albert and his attractions. Miss Mullins, however, came to the rescue.

"Come, Miss Wickham," she cried, "we must lead the way," and accordingly Jane, my mother, and I went down first, and the different boarders followed us.

To my infinite distress Mrs. Fanning, being a complete stranger, had her seat next mine. I had one comfort, however, she was better than Albert; and Albert, who arrived presently himself, found that he was seated next Miss Armstrong. He nodded across at his mother.

"How do, old lady," he said, "glad to find you cosily established; everything all right, eh?"

"Yes, Albert, my son," replied the good woman, "everything is all right, and I have been having a long conversation about you with my interesting young friend here, Miss Westenra Wickham. By-the-by, dear, would you kindly tell me how you got that outlandish name, I never heard it before, and I do not believe it belongs to the Christian religion."

"I did not know there was anything heathenish about it," I could not help answering; "it happens to be my name, and I was fully baptized by it."

"I will see presently whether I can take to it," responded the old lady. "Soup? Yes, please. I will trouble you, my good girl, for (turning to the maid) a table-spoon; I never take soup with a dessert spoon. Thanks; that's better."

Mrs. Fanning now gave me a few moments peace, and I found, to my great satisfaction, that she had an excellent appetite, and was also extremely critical with regard to her food. I introduced her to her next door neighbour, who happened to be a fat little woman, something like herself in build. They were both gourmands, and criticised adversely the meal to their mutual pleasure. Thus I had time to look around me, and to consider this new aspect of affairs.

Things were scarcely likely to be more comfortable if Albert had now got his mother to plead his cause with me. He glanced at me several times during the meal, and once even favoured me with a broad wink—he was really intolerable.

Meanwhile Miss Armstrong was all blushes and smirks. I heard her suggest to Mr. Fanning that she should go the next day to see him, and bring some of her drawings with her, and I heard him tell her in what he was pleased to call his brutal manner that he would not be at home, and if he were and she came would certainly not see her. This seemed to be considered a tremendous joke by Miss Armstrong, and her mother also joined in it, and gave Mr. Fanning a dig in the ribs, and told him that he was the soul of wit, and had the true spirit of heart.

Meanwhile, Mr. Randolph, my mother, Captain and Mrs. Furlong, and the more refined portion of the establishment enjoyed themselves at the other end of the table. I saw Mr. Randolph glance down in my direction once or twice, and I am sure, although he was not able to judge of the difference, the fact of seeing me once more in my properly made black evening dress relieved his mind, for he looked quite contented, and turned in a cheerful manner to my mother, and when dinner was over, and we returned to the drawing-room, I was lucky enough to be able to escape Mrs. Fanning and to go up to the other end of the room, where I seated myself close to mother, took hold of her hand, leant against her chair, and indulged in the luxury of talking to Mr. Randolph. He was in a very good humour, and suggested that we should make a party on the following evening to another play, which was then very much in vogue.

"But not in the chocolate-coloured brougham with the pair of horses," I said.

"We will have a cab from the nearest stand, if you prefer it," was his instant response.

"I should much," I answered.

"And we will not dine at the Cecil," he continued; "we can have a sort of high tea here before we start."

"That I should also like infinitely better," I answered.

"It shall be as you please," was his response. Then he began to tell us something of the play which we were about to see, and I forgot all about my discomforts, and enjoyed myself well.

I was putting things in order in the drawing-room that night, for this was always one of my special duties, when Mr. Fanning, who had left the room a long time ago, came back. He came up to me holding his lighted candle in his hand. I started when I saw him.

"Good night," I said coldly.

"Pray don't go for a moment," he said. "I have come back here on the express chance of seeing you."

"I cannot wait now, Mr. Fanning," I replied.

"But I really must have an interview with you, it is of the highest importance, —when can I see you alone? When can you give me an hour of your time quite undisturbed?"

"Never," I answered brusquely.

"Now you will forgive me for saying that that is pure nonsense. If you will not promise me an hour of your own free will I shall take the present opportunity of speaking to you."

"But I shall not stay," I answered with spirit, "and you cannot keep me here against my will. Mr. Fanning, I also will take the present opportunity of telling you that you and I have nothing in common, that I dislike your singling me out for special conversations of any kind, and that I hope in the future you will clearly understand that I do not wish you to do so."

"Oh, that is all very fine," he said, "but come now; what have I done to make myself obnoxious? There is the old lady upstairs, she has taken no end of a fancy to you, she says you are the most charming and the prettiest girl she has ever seen, and what have you to say against my mother? Let me tell you that she has come to this house on purpose to make your acquaintance."

"I have nothing whatever to say against your mother, Mr. Fanning, but I object to the subject of conversation which she chooses to occupy her time with while talking to me. I am not in the least interested in you, and I wish you and your mother clearly to understand this fact as quickly as possible."

I do not think it was in the nature of Mr. Fanning ever to look crestfallen, or my present speech might have made him do so. He did not even change colour, but he looked at me out of those eyes which his mother had so vividly described, and after a moment said softly—

"There will come a day when you will regret this. An honest heart is offered to you and you trample it in the dust, but there will come a day when you will be sorry. How do you think this establishment is working?"

I was so astonished and relieved at his change of conversation that I said—

"It seems to be going very well, don't you think so?"

"It is going well for my purpose," he replied, and then he added, "it is working itself out in a way that will only spell one word—RUIN. Now you ponder on that. Take it as your night-cap, and see what sort of sleep you'll have, and when next I ask for a few moments' conversation perhaps you'll not say no. I will not keep you any longer for the present."

He left the room, I heard his footsteps dying down the corridor, and the next instant he had slammed his bedroom door.

CHAPTER XIV

ANXIETY

After he had left me, and I was quite certain that I should not see him again that night, I went straight to Jane Mullins' room. Jane was generally up the last in the house, and I had not the slightest doubt I should still find her in her dinner dress, and ready for conversation. I had bidden mother good night long ago, and hoped she was sound asleep, but I did not mind disturbing Jane. I opened the door now and went in. As I expected, Jane was up; she was seated by the fire, she was looking into its depths, and did not turn round at once when I entered. The first thing she did when she became aware of the fact that there was some one else in the room besides herself, was to sigh somewhat deeply. Then she said in a low voice—

"What if it all turns out a mistake?" and then she jumped to her feet and confronted me. "Yes, dear, yes," she said. "Oh, my dear Westenra, why aren't you in bed? It is very bad indeed for young people to be up so late. You will get quite worn and wrinkled. Let me tell you, my love, that we can never get youth back again, and we ought to prize it while we have it. How old are you, Westenra, my love?"

"I shall be twenty-two my next birthday," was my answer.

"Ah, yes, yes, quite young, in the beautiful prime of youth. Nevertheless, the bloom can be rubbed off, and then—well, it never comes back, dear. But go to bed, Westenra, don't stay up bothering your head. I see by that frown between your brows that you are going to say something which I would rather not listen to. Don't tell me to-night, Westenra, love."

"I must tell you," I answered. "I have come to see you for the purpose. You are old enough, Jane, to bear the little disagreeable things I tell you now and then. You are our mainstay, our prop, in this establishment. I cannot go on without confiding in you, and you must listen to me."

"Well, child, sit down, here is a comfortable chair." Jane got up and offered me her own chair. I did not take it.

"What nonsense," I said, "sit down again. Here, this little hassock at your feet will suit me far better."

I seated myself as I spoke, and laid my hand across Jane's knee.

"Now, that is cosy," I said. She touched my arm as though she loved to touch it, and then she laid her firm, weather-beaten hand on my shoulder, and then, as if impelled by an unwonted impulse, she bent forward and kissed me on my cheek.

"You are a very nice girl. Since I knew you life has been far pleasanter to me," said Jane Mullins. "I thank you for giving me a bit of love. Whatever happens I want you to remember that."

"I do," I answered; "you have very little idea how much I care for you, Jane, and how immensely I respect you. There are, I think, very few women who would have acted as you have done. I am fully convinced there is a mystery in all your actions which has not yet been explained to me, but I have not come here to-night to talk about that. I have come here to ask you one or two questions, and to tell you one or two things, and my first question is this— Why were you sighing when I came in, and why did you murmur to yourself, 'What if it all turns out a mistake?' Will you explain those words, Jane."

"No," replied Jane stoutly, "for you were eavesdropping when you heard them, and there is no reason why I should explain what you had no right to listen to."

"Thank you; you have answered me very sensibly, and I won't say another word on the subject of your sigh and your remarkable speech. But now to turn to the matter which has brought me to your room so late in the evening."

"Well, dear, it is past midnight, and you know how early I am up. It is a little unreasonable of you; what has brought you, darling?"

"Mr. Fanning has brought me."

"Oh dear, oh dear, that tiresome man again," said Miss Mullins.

"You don't like him yourself, do you, Jane?"

"It is a great pity he is not different," said Jane, "for he is extremely well off."

"O Jane! pray don't talk nonsense. Do you suppose that a person with the name of Fanning could have any interest whatever for me? Now, please, get that silly idea out of your head once for all."

"Oh, as far as any use that there is in it, I have long ago got it out of my head," replied Jane; "but the thing to be considered is this, that he has not got it out of his head—nor has his mother—and that between them they can make things intensely disagreeable. Now, if Mr. Randolph was going to stay here, I should not have an anxious moment."

"What do you mean?" I cried; "is Mr. Randolph going away?" A deep depression seemed suddenly to come over me; I could not quite account for it.

"He is, dear; and it is because he must be absent for two or three months that I am really anxious. He will come back again; but sudden and important news obliges him to go to Australia. He is going in a fortnight, and it is that that frets him. You will be left to the tender mercies of Mr. Fanning and Mrs. Fanning, and you have got so much spirit you are sure to offend them both mortally, and then they will leave, and—oh dear, I do think that things are dark. My dear Westenra, I often wonder if we shall pull through after all."

"That is what I want to speak to you about," I answered. "Mr. Fanning came into the drawing-room just now, and was very rude and very unlike a gentleman. I was alone there, and he said he had something to say to me in private, and, of course, I refused to listen. He wanted to insist on my granting him an interview, and said that he could compel me to listen if he chose. Think of any gentleman speaking like that!"

"They don't mind what they say, nor what they do, when they're in love," muttered Jane.

"I won't allow you to say that," I answered, springing to my feet; "the man is intolerable. Jane, he must go; there is no help for it."

"He must stay, dear, and I cannot disclose all my reasons now."

I stood clasping and unclasping my hands, and staring at Jane.

"You knew beforehand, did you not, Westenra, that there would be disagreeables connected with this scheme?"

"Of course I knew it; but I never did think that the disagreeables would resolve themselves into Mr. Fanning."

"We never know beforehand where the shoe is going to pinch," remarked Jane in a sententious voice.

"Well, I have something else to say," I continued. "Mr. Fanning was not only very unpleasant to me, but he told me something which I can scarcely believe. He said that our boarding-house, which seemed to be going so well, was not going well at all. He said there was only one word to spell how it was going, and that word was RUIN. O Jane! it can't be true?"

"Let us hope not," said Jane, but she turned very white. "I will tell you one thing, Westenra," she continued. "If you don't want to have utter ruin you must go on behaving as nicely as ever you can, bearing with every one, being gentle and considerate, and trying to make every one happy. And in especial, you must bear with Mr. Fanning and with Mrs. Fanning; you must be particularly civil to them both, for if they go others will go; and whatever happens, Westenra, remember your mother is not to be worried. I know what I am saying, your mother is not to be worried. Your mother must never guess that things are not as right as they should be. When Mr. Randolph comes back everything will be right, but during his absence we will have to go through rather a tight place; and Albert Fanning is the sort of person who might take advantage of us, and what you must do, my dear girl, is to be guileful."

"Guileful!" I cried; "never."

"But you must, my love, you must be guileful and wary; you need not give him a single straw to go upon, but at the same time you must be civil. There now, that is all I can tell you for the present. Go to bed, child, for I have to do the daily accounts, and must be up at six in the morning. It's that new cook, she frets me more than I can say, she don't do things proper; and I noticed that Mrs. Fanning sniffed at her soup instead of eating it this evening, and the turbot was not as fresh as it ought to be. Go to bed, Westenra, go to bed."

I left the room. There was no use in staying any longer with Jane. She certainly had not reassured me. She seemed puzzled and anxious about the establishment; and why were not things going well? And what had Mr. Fanning to do with it; and why, why was Mr. Randolph going away?

The next morning after breakfast I went into the drawing-room for my usual task of dusting and arranging the furniture and refilling the vases with fresh flowers, when Mr. Randolph suddenly came in.

"It will be best for you and Mrs. Wickham to meet me at the Criterion to-night," he said. "As you won't give me the opportunity of offering you dinner at the Cecil, that seems the next best thing to do. I have got a box in a good part of the house, so we need not be there more than a few minutes before it commences. I shall meet you at the entrance and conduct you to your seats."

His manner showed some excitement, quite out of keeping with his ordinary demeanour, and I noticed that he scarcely glanced at me. His face was somewhat worn, too, in expression, and although he generally had himself in complete control, he now looked nearly as anxious and worried as Jane herself. He scarcely waited for my compliance with the arrangement he had proposed, but glancing at the door, spoke abruptly—

"Something unexpected and very grievous has occurred, and I am obliged to leave England by the *Smyrna*, which sails on Saturday week."

"Miss Mullins told me last night that you were going away," I replied. I also now avoided looking at him. I was playing with some large sprays of mimosa which had been sent in from the market. To my dying day I shall never forget how that mimosa seemed to slip about, and would not get into the best position in the vase in which I was placing it.

103

"Effective," he said, as he watched my movements, "but it withers quickly; it wants its native air."

"I suppose so," I answered.

"Have you ever seen it growing?"

"No; I have never been to the South."

"You have a good deal to see. I hope some day——" He broke off.

"Where are you going when you do go away?" I asked.

"To Sydney first, perhaps to Melbourne."

"It will be nice for you to leave England during our unpleasant winter weather."

"There is nothing nice about my visit," he said; "I dislike going more than I have any words to express. In particular, I am sorry to leave your mother; but before I go I want"—he dropped his voice and came a step nearer.

"What?" I asked.

"I am anxious that your mother should see a doctor—a specialist, I mean. I am not satisfied with her condition."

"But mother is really quite well," I said impulsively. "You have not known her long, Mr. Randolph; she never was really strong. She is quite as well as she ever was."

"A specialist could assure us on that point, could he not?" was his reply. "I want Dr. Reade to give me a diagnosis of her case."

"Dr. Reade," I cried.

"Yes; I should like her to see him between now and the day when I must leave England. I cannot possibly be back under from four to five months, and if my mind can be relieved of a very pressing anxiety, you would not deny me the satisfaction, would you?"

"But why should your mind be anxious?" I asked boldly. I looked full into his face as I spoke, and then I met a look which caused me to turn faint, and yet to feel happy, as I had never felt happy before. I lowered my eyes and looked out of the window. He gave a quick sigh, and then said suddenly—

"How like your father you are."

"My father? But you never knew him."

"I never knew him, but I have often looked at his picture. Can you tell me how he won his V.C.?"

104

"Saving a comrade, bringing one of his brother officers out of the thick of the fight; he received his own fatal wound in doing so. He did not survive the action two months."

"A fine fellow! A splendid action," said Mr. Randolph, enthusiasm in his voice. "You will think over what I have said, and I will not keep you now. We shall meet at the Criterion this evening. Good-bye for the present."

CHAPTER XV

DR. READE

I cannot recall anything about the play. I only know that we had excellent seats and a good view of the house, and that mother seemed to enjoy everything. As to Mr. Randolph, I doubt if he did enjoy that play. He was too much a man of the world to show any of his emotions, but I saw by a certain pallor round his mouth, and a rather dragged look about his eyes, that he was suffering, and I could not imagine why. I had always in my own mind made up a sort of story about Jim Randolph. He was one of the fortunate people of the earth; the good things of the world had fallen abundantly to his share. He was nice to look at and pleasant to talk to, and of course he had plenty of money. He could do what he pleased with his life. I had never associated him with sorrow or trial of any sort, and to see that look now in his eyes and round the corners of his somewhat sensitive and yet beautifully-cut mouth, gave me a new sensation with regard to him. The interest I felt in him immediately became accelerated tenfold. I found myself thinking of him instead of the play. I found myself anxious to watch his face. I even found, when once our eyes met (his grave and dark, mine, I daresay, bold enough and determined enough), that my heart beat fast, and the colour flew into my face; then, strange to say, the colour came into his face, dying his swarthy cheek just for a moment, but leaving it the next paler than ever. He came a little nearer to me, however, and bending forward so that mother should not hear, said in a semi-whisper—

"You have thought about what I said this morning?"

"I have thought it over a good deal," I replied.

"You think it can be managed?"

"Dr. Anderson, mother's family physician, would do what you require, Mr. Randolph."

"That is a good idea," he said. "Anderson can arrange a consultation. I will see him to-morrow, and suggest it."

I did not say any more, for just then mother turned and said something to Mr. Randolph, and Mr. Randolph bent forward and talked to mother in that worshipping son-like way with which he generally addressed her. If mother had ever been blessed with a son, he could not have been more attentive nor sweeter than Jim Randolph was, and I found myself liking him more than ever, just because he was so good to mother, and my heart ached at the prospect of his enforced and long absence. So much did this thought worry me, that I could not help saying to him as we were leaving the theatre—

"I am very sorry that you are going."

"Is that true?" he said. His face lit up, his eyes sparkled; all the tired expression left his eyes and mouth.

"Are you saying what you mean?" he asked.

"I am most truly sorry. You have become indispensable to mother; she will miss you sorely."

"And you—will you miss me?"

I tried to say "For mother's sake I will," but I did not utter the words. Mr. Randolph gave me a quick glance.

"I have not told your mother yet that I am going," he said.

"I wondered if you had," I replied. "I thought of telling her myself to-day."

"Do not say anything until nearer the time," was his somewhat guarded response. "Ah! here comes the carriage."

"So you did order the carriage after all," I said, seeing that the same neat brougham which he had used on the last occasion stopped the way.

"You never forbade me to see you both home in the carriage," he said with a laugh. "Now then, Mrs. Wickham."

Mother had been standing a little back out of the crowd. He went to her, gave her his arm, and she stepped into the carriage, just as if it belonged to her. Mother had always that way with Mr. Randolph's possessions, and sometimes her manner towards him almost annoyed me. What could it mean. Did she know something about him which I had never heard of nor guessed?

The next day about noon Mr. Randolph entered Jane's sitting-room, where I often spent the mornings.

"I have just come from Anderson's," he said. "He will make an appointment with Dr. Reade to see your mother to-morrow."

"But on what plea?" I asked. "Mother is somewhat nervous. I am sure it would not be at all good for her to think that her indisposition was so great that two doctors must see her."

"Anderson will arrange that," replied Mr. Randolph. "He has told your mother once or twice lately that he thinks her very weak, and would like her to try a new system of diet. Now Reade is a great specialist for diseases of the digestion. Both doctors will guard against any possible shock to your mother."

"Well," I said somewhat petulantly, "I cannot imagine why you are nervous about her. She is quite as well as she ever was."

He looked at me as if he meant to say something more, and I felt certain that he strangled a sigh which never came to the surface. The next moment he left the room, I looked round me in a state of bewilderment.

In Jane's room was a bookcase, and the bookcase contained a heterogeneous mass of books of all sorts. Amongst others was a medical directory. I took it up now, and scarcely knowing why I did so, turned to the name of Reade. Dr. Reade's name was entered in the following way:—

"Reade, Henry, M.D., F.R.C.P., consulting physician to the Brompton Hospital for Consumption, London, and to the Royal Hospital for Diseases of the Chest, Ventnor."

I read these qualifications over slowly, and put the book back in its place. There was nothing whatever said of Dr. Reade's qualifications for treating that vast field of indigestion to which so many sufferers were victims. I resolved to say something to Jane.

"What is it?" said Jane, as she came into the room. "What is fretting you now?"

"Oh, nothing," I answered. "Dr. Reade must be a very clever physician."

"First-class, of course. I am so pleased your mother is going to see him."

"But I thought mother was suffering very much from weakness and want of appetite."

"So she is, poor dear, and I am inventing quite a new sort of soup, which is partly digested beforehand, that I think she will fancy."

"But I have been looking up Dr. Reade's name. He seems to be a great doctor for consumption and other diseases of the chest. There is no allusion to his extraordinary powers of treating people for indigestion."

"Well, my dear, consumptives suffer more than most folks from indigestion. Now, don't you worry your head; never meet troubles half-way. I am extremely pleased that your mother is to see Dr. Reade."

On the following morning mother herself told me that Dr. Reade was coming.

"It is most unnecessary," she said, "and I told Dr. Anderson so. I was only telling him yesterday that I thought his own visits need not be quite so frequent. He is such a dear, kind man, that I do not like to hurt his feelings;

but really, Westenra, he charges me so little that it quite goes to my heart. And now we have not our old income, this very expensive consulting physician is not required. I told Dr. Anderson so, but he has made up his mind. He says there is no use in working in the dark, and that he believes I should be much stronger if I ate more."

Dr. Reade called in the course of the morning, and Dr. Anderson came with him. They stayed in mother's room for some little time, and then they both went out, and Jane Mullins had an interview with them first, and then she sent for me.

"Dr. Anderson wants to speak to you, Westenra," she said. She rushed past me as she spoke, and I could not catch sight of her face, so I went into her little sitting-room, where both the doctors were waiting for me, and closed the door behind me. I was not at all anxious. I quite believed that mother's ailment was simply want of appetite and weakness, and I had never heard of any one dying just from those causes.

"Let me introduce you to Dr. Reade," said Dr. Anderson.

I looked then towards the great consulting physician. He was standing with his back to the light—he was a little man, younger looking than Dr. Anderson. His hair was only beginning to turn grey, and was falling away a trifle from his temples, and he was very upright, and very thin, and had keen eyes, the keenest eyes I had ever looked at, small, grey and bright, and those eyes seemed to look through you, as though they were forcing a gimlet into the very secrets of your soul. His face was so peculiar, so intellectual, so sharp and keen, and his glance so vivid, that I became absorbed in looking at it, and forgot for the moment Dr. Anderson. Then I glanced round and found that he had vanished, and I was alone with Dr. Reade.

"Won't you sit down, Miss Wickham?" he said kindly.

I seated myself, and then seeing that his eyes were still on me, my heart began to beat a little more quickly, and I began to feel uncomfortable and anxious, and then I knew that I must brace myself up to listen to something which would be hard to bear.

"I was called in to-day," said Dr. Reade, "to see your mother. I have examined her carefully—Dr. Anderson thinks that it may be best for you Miss Wickham —you seem to be a very brave sort of girl—to know the truth."

"Yes, I should like to know the truth," I answered.

I found these words coming out of my lips slowly, and I found I had difficulty in saying them, and my eyes seemed not to see quite so clearly as usual; and Dr. Reade's keen face seemed to vanish as if behind a mist, but then the mist cleared off, and I remembered that I was father's daughter and that it behoved me to act gallantly if occasion should require, so I got up and went towards the little doctor, and said in a quiet voice—

"You need not mind breaking it to me; I see by your face that you have bad news, but I assure you I am not going to cry nor be hysterical. Please tell me the truth quickly."

"I knew you were a brave girl," he said with admiration, "and I have bad news, your mother's case is——"

"What?" I asked.

"A matter of time," he replied gravely; "she may live for a few months or a year—a year is the outside limit."

"A few months or a year," I said. I repeated the words vaguely; and then I turned my eyes towards the window and looked past it and out into the Square. I saw a carriage drawn by a spirited pair of bays, it passed within sight of the window, and I noticed a girl seated by herself in the carriage. She had on a fashionable hat, and her hair was arranged in a very pretty way, and she had laughing eyes. I was attracted by her appearance, and I even said to myself in an uncertain sort of fashion, "I believe I could copy that hat," but then I turned away from the window and faced the doctor.

"You are very brave," he repeated; "I did not think any girl would be quite so brave."

"My father was a brave man," I said then; "he won his Victoria Cross."

"Ah," replied Dr. Reade, "women often do just as brave actions. Their battles are silent, but none the less magnificent for that."

"I always meant to get the Victoria Cross if I could," was my reply.

"Well," he answered cheerfully, "I know now how to deal with things; I am very glad that you are that sort. You know that Jim Randolph is a friend of mine."

It was on the tip of my tongue to say, Who is Jim Randolph? why should he be a friend of everybody worth knowing? but I did not ask the question. I put it aside and said gravely—

"The person I want to talk about is mother. In the first place, what is the matter with her?"

"A very acute form of heart disease. The aortic valve is affected. She may not, and probably will not, suffer much; but at any moment, Miss Wickham, at any moment, any shock may"—he raised his hand emphatically.

"You mean that any shock may kill her?"

"That is what I mean."

"Then she ought to be kept without anxiety?"

"That is precisely what I intend."

"And if this is done how long will her most precious life be prolonged?"

"As I have just said, a year is about the limit."

"One year," I answered. "Does she know?"

"No, she has not the slightest idea, nor do I want her to be told. She is ready —would to God we were all as ready—why distress her unnecessarily? She would be anxious about you if she thought she was leaving you. It must be your province to give her no anxiety, to guard her. That is an excellent woman, Miss Mullins, she will assist you in every way. I am truly sorry that Jim Randolph has to leave England. However, there is not the slightest doubt that he will hurry home, and when he does come back, will be time sufficient to let your mother know the truth."

I did not answer. Dr. Reade looked at his watch.

"I must be off," he said. "I can only spare one more moment. I have made certain suggestions to my old friend Anderson, and he will propose certain arrangements which may add to your mother's comfort. I do not want her to go up and down stairs much, but at the same time she must be entertained and kept cheerful. Be assured of one thing, that in no case will she suffer. Now, I have told you all. If you should be perplexed or in any difficulty come to me at once. Come to me as your friend, and remember I am a very special friend of Jim Randolph's. Now, good-bye."

He left the room.

I sat after he had gone for a moment without stirring; I was not suffering exactly. We do not suffer most when the heavy blows fall, it is afterwards that the terrible agony of pain comes on. Of course I believed Dr. Reade—who could doubt him who looked into his face? I guessed him to be what he was, one of the strongest, most faithful, bravest men who ever lived—a man whose whole life was given up to the alleviation of the suffering of others. He was always warding off death, or doing all that man could do to ward it off, and in many many cases death was afraid of him, and retired from his prey, vanquished by that knowledge, that genius, that sympathy, that love for humanity, which overflowed the little doctor's personality.

Just then a hand touched me, and I turned and saw Jim Randolph.

"You know?" he said.

I nodded. Mr. Randolph looked at me very gravely.

"My suspicions have been confirmed," he said; "I always guessed that your mother's state of health was most precarious. I can scarcely explain to you the intense pain I feel in leaving her now. A girl like you ought to have some man at hand to help her, but I must go, there is no help for it. It is a terrible trial to me. I know, Miss Wickham, that you will guard your mother from all sorrows and anxieties, and so cheer her passage from this world to the next. Her death may come suddenly or gradually, there is just a possibility that she may know when she is dying, and at such a time, to know also that you are unprovided for, will give her great and terrible anxiety." Here he looked at me as if he were anxious to say more, but he restrained himself. "I cannot remove her anxiety, I must trust for the very best, and you must wait and—and *trust me*. I will come back as soon as ever I can."

"But why do you go away?" I asked, "you have been kind—more than kind—to her. O Mr. Randolph! do you think I have made a mistake, a great mistake, in coming here?"

"No," he said emphatically, "do not let that thought ever worry you, you have done a singularly brave thing, you can little guess what I—but there, I said I would not speak, not yet." He shut his lips, and I noticed that drawn look round his eyes and mouth.

"I must go and return as fast as I can," he said abruptly. "I set myself a task, and I must carry it through to the bitter end. Only unexpected calamity drives me from England just now."

"You are keeping a secret from me," I said.

"I am," he replied.

"Won't you tell me—is it fair to keep me in the dark?"

"It is perfectly fair."

"Does Jane know?"

"Certainly."

"And she won't tell?"

"No, she won't tell."

"Does mother know?"

"Yes, and no. She knows something but not all, by no means all."

"It puzzles me more than I can describe," I continued. "Why do you live in a place like this, why are you so interested in mother and in me? Then, too, you are a special friend of the Duchess of Wilmot's, who is also one of our oldest friends. You do not belong to the set of people who live in boarding-houses. I wish, I do wish, you would be open. It is unfair on me to keep me in the dark."

"I will tell you when I return," he said, and his face was very white. "Trust me until I return."

CHAPTER XVI

GIVE ME YOUR PROMISE

That afternoon I went out late to do some commissions for Jane. I was glad to be out and to be moving, for Dr. Reade's words kept ringing in my ears, and by degrees they were beginning to hurt. I did not want them to hurt badly until night, for nothing would induce me to break down. I had talked to mother more cheerfully than ever that afternoon, and made her laugh heartily, and put her into excellent spirits, and I bought some lovely flowers for her while I was out, and a little special dainty for her dinner. Oh, it would never do for mother to guess that I was unhappy, but I could not have kept up with that growing pain at my heart if it were not for the thought of night and solitude, the long blessed hours when I might give way, when I might let my grief, the first great grief of my life, overpower me.

I was returning home, when suddenly, just before I entered the Square, I came face to face with Mr. Randolph. He was hurrying as if to meet me. When he saw me he slackened his steps and walked by my side.

"This is very fortunate," he said. "I want to talk to you. Where can we go?"

"But it is nearly dinner-time," I answered.

"That does not matter," he replied. "I have but a very few more days in England. I have something I must say to you. Ah, here is the Square garden open; we will go in."

He seemed to take my assent for granted, and I did not at all mind accompanying him. We went into the little garden in the middle of the Square. In the midst of summer, or at most in early spring, it might possibly have been a pleasant place, but now few words could explain its dreariness. The damp leaves of late autumn were lying in sodden masses on the paths. There was very little light too; once I slipped and almost fell. My companion put out his hand and caught mine. He steadied me and then dropped my hand. After a moment of silence he spoke.

"You asked me to-day not to go."

"For mother's sake," I replied.

"I want to tell you now that if I could stay I would; that it is very great pain to me to go away. I think it is due to you that I should give you some slight explanation. I am leaving England thus suddenly because the friend who has helped Jane Mullins with a certain sum of money, in order to enable her to start this boarding-house, has suddenly heard that the capital, which he hoped was absolutely secure, is in great danger of being lost. My friend has commissioned me to see this matter through, for if his worst surmises are fulfilled Miss Mullins, and you also, Miss Wickham, and of course your mother, may find yourselves in an uncomfortable position. You remember doubtless that Mr. Hardcastle would not let you the house if there had not been some capital at the back of your proposal. Miss Mullins, who had long wished for such an opportunity, was delighted to find that she could join forces with you in the matter. Thus 17 Graham Square was started on its present lines. Now there is a possibility that the capital which Jane Mullins was to have as her share in this business may not be forthcoming. It is in jeopardy, and I am going to Australia in order to put things straight; I have every hope that I shall succeed. You may rest assured that I shall remain away for as short a time as possible. I know what grief you are in, but I hope to be back in England soon."

"Is that all you have to say to me?" I asked.

"Not quite all. I am most anxious that while I am away, although you are still kept in the dark, you should believe in me; I want you to trust me and also my friend. Believe that his intentions are honourable, are kind, are just, and that we are acting as we are doing both for your sake and for your mother's and for Miss Mullins'. I know that I ask quite a big thing, Miss Wickham; it is this —I ask you to trust me in the dark."

"It is a big thing and difficult," I replied.

"Your mother does."

"That is true, but mother would trust any one who had been as kind to her as you have been."

"Then will you trust me because your mother does? will you believe that when I come back I shall be in a position to set all her fears and yours also absolutely at rest? I am certain of this, I go away with a hope which I dare not express more fully; I shall come back trusting that that hope may be fulfilled in all its magnificence for myself. I cannot say more at present. I long to, but I dare not. Will you trust me? will you try to understand? Why, what is the matter?"

He turned and looked at me abruptly. Quick sobs were coming from my lips. I suddenly and unexpectedly lost my self-control.

"I shall be all right in a minute," I said. "I have gone through much to-day; it is—it is on account of mother. Don't—don't speak for a moment."

He did not, he stood near me. When I had recovered he said gently—

"Give me your promise. I wish I could say more, much, much more, but will you trust me in the dark?"

"I will," I replied. "I am sorry you are going. Thank you for being kind to mother; come back when you can."

"You may be certain on that point," he replied. "I leave England with extreme unwillingness. Thank you for what you have promised."

He held out his hand and I gave him mine. I felt my heart beat as my hand lay for a moment in his, his fingers closed firmly over it, then he slowly dropped it. We went back to the house.

A few days afterwards Mr. Randolph went away. He went quite quietly, without making the slightest commotion. He just entered the drawing-room quickly one morning after breakfast, and shook hands with mother and shook hands with me, and said that he would be back again before either of us had missed him, and then went downstairs, and I watched behind the curtain as his luggage was put on the roof of the cab. I watched him get in. Jane Mullins was standing near. He shook hands with her. He did not once glance up at our windows, the cab rolled out of the Square and was lost to view. Then I turned round. There were tears in mother's eyes.

"He is the nicest fellow I have ever met," she said, "I am so very sorry that he has gone."

"Well, Mummy darling," I answered, "you are more my care than ever now."

"Oh, I am not thinking of myself," said mother. She looked up at me rather uneasily. It seemed to me as if her eyes wanted to read me through, and I felt that I did not want her to read me through; I did not want any one to read what my feelings were that day.

Jane Mullins came bustling up.

"It is a lovely morning, and your mother must have a drive," she said. "I have ordered a carriage. It will be round in half-an-hour. You and she are to drive in the Park and be back in time for lunch, and see here, Mrs. Wickham, I want you to taste this. I have made it from a receipt in the new invalid cookery book. I think you will say that you never tasted such soup before."

"Oh, you quite spoil me, Jane," said mother, but she took the soup which Jane had prepared so delicately for her, and I ran off, glad to be by myself for a few moments.

At dinner that day Mrs. Fanning and Mrs. Armstrong sat side by side. Mrs. Fanning had taken a great fancy to Mrs. Armstrong, and they usually during the meal sat with their heads bent towards one another, talking eagerly, and often glancing in the direction of Albert Fanning and Miss Armstrong and me. Mrs. Fanning had an emphatic way of bobbing her head whenever she looked at me, and after giving me a steady glance, her eyes involuntarily rolled round in the direction of Mr. Fanning.

I was so well aware of these glances that I now never pretended to see them, but not one of them really escaped my notice. After dinner that evening the good lady came up to my side.

"Well, my dear, well," she said, "and how are you bearing up?"

"Bearing up?" I answered, "I don't quite understand."

Now of course no one in the boarding-house was supposed to know anything whatever with regard to mother's health. The consultation of the doctors had been so contrived that the principal boarders had been out when it took place, therefore I knew that Mrs. Fanning was not alluding to the doctors. She sat down near me.

"Ah," she said, "I thought, and I told my dear son Albert, that a man of that sort would not stay very long. You are bearing up, for you are a plucky sort of girl, but you must be feeling it a good bit. I am sorry for you, you have been a silly girl, casting your eyes at places too high for you, and never seeing those good things which are laid so to speak at your very feet. You are like all the rest of the world, but if you think that my Albert will put up with other people's leavings, you are finely mistaken."

"Really, Mrs. Fanning," I answered, "I am completely at a loss to know what you are talking about."

Here I heard Mrs. Armstrong's hearty and coarse laugh in my ear.

"Ha! ha!" said Mrs. Armstrong, "so she says she doesn't know. Well now then, we won't allude any further to the subject. Of course it ain't likely that she would give herself away. Few young ladies of the Miss Westenra Wickham type do. Whatever else they don't hold with, they hold on to their sinful pride, they quite forget that they are worms of the dust, that their fall will come, and when it comes it's bitter, that's what I say; that's what I have said to Marion, when Marion has been a little put out, poor dear, with the marked and silly attentions of one who never meant anything at all. It was only before dinner I said to Marion, 'You wouldn't like to be in Miss Wickham's shoes to-night, would you, Marion? You wouldn't like to be wearing the willow, would you, my girl?' And she said no, she wouldn't, but then she added, 'With my soul full of Art, mother, I always can have my resources,' and that is where Marion believes, that if she were so unlucky as to be crossed in love, she would have the advantage of you, Miss Wickham, for you have plainly said that you have no soul for h'Art."

"All that talk of Art makes me downright sick," here interrupted Mrs. Fanning. "That's where I admire you, Miss Wickham. You are very nice to look at, and you have no nonsense about you, and it's my belief that you never cared twopence about that high-falutin' young man, and that now he has gone, you'll just know where your bread is buttered. Sit along side of me, dear, and we will have a little discourse about Albert, it's some time since we had a good round talk about my dear and godly son."

CHAPTER XVII

A DASH OF ONIONS

It was about a fortnight later that one afternoon, soon after lunch, Mrs. Fanning came into the drawing-room. She was somewhat short-sighted, and she stood in the middle of the room, looking round her. After a time, to my great horror, she caught sight of me. If I had a moment to spare, I should have got behind the curtain, in order to avoid her, but I had not that moment; she discovered her prey, and made for me as fast as an arrow from a bow.

"Ah," she said, "here you are; I am going out driving in Albert's brougham this afternoon. You didn't know, perhaps, that Albert had a brougham of his own?"

"I did not," I answered.

"It is a recent acquisition of his; he is becoming a wealthy man is Albert, and he started the brougham a short time ago. He had the body painted red and the wheels dark brown—I was for having the wheels yellow, because I like something distinct, but Albert said, 'No, *she* would rather have dark brown.' Who do you think he meant by *she*, now? That's the puzzle I am putting to you. Who do you think *she* is?"

"You, of course," I answered boldly.

Mrs. Fanning favoured me with a broad wink.

"Ah now, that's very nice of you," she said, "but the old mother doesn't come in anywhere when the young girl appears on the horizon. It is about time for Albert to be meeting the young girl, and meet her he will. Indeed, it is my opinion that he has met her, and that the brougham which she likes is standing at the door. It is for the sake of that young girl he has had those wheels painted brown, it is not the wish of his old mother. But come for a drive with me, will you, dear?"

"I am sorry," I began.

"Oh no, I am not going to take any refusal. Ah, there is your precious dear mother coming into the room."

Before I could interrupt her, Mrs. Fanning had gone to meet my mother. She never walked in the ordinary sense of the word, she waddled. She waddled now in her stiff brown satin across the drawing-room, and stood before mother.

"And how are you feeling this morning, Mrs. Wickham?" she said; "ah! but poorly, I can tell by the look of your face, you are dreadfully blue round the lips, it's the effect of indigestion, isn't it, now?"

"I have suffered a good deal lately from indigestion," replied mother in her gentle tones.

"And a bad thing it is, a very bad thing," said Mrs. Fanning. "I cured myself with Williams' Pink Pills for Pale People. Did you ever try 'em, Mrs. Wickham?"

"No," replied mother gravely.

"Well, well, they pulled me round. Albert was terribly concerned about me a year ago. I couldn't fancy the greatest dainties you could give me, I turned against my food, and as to going upstairs, why, if you'll believe me, I could have no more taken possession of that attic next to your young daughter than I could have fled. Now there ain't a stair in Britain would daunt me; I'd be good for climbing the Monument any fine morning, and it's all owing to Williams' Pink Pills. They're a grand medicine. But what I wanted to say to you now was this: May Miss Wickham come for a drive with me in my son's own brougham? I am anxious to have an outing with her, and I see by her face she is desirous to come; may she? Say yes, madam; if you are wise, you will."

I saw that mother was becoming a little excited and a little agitated, and I knew that that would never do, so I said hastily—

"Don't worry mother, please, Mrs. Fanning; I will certainly come with you for an hour or so."

"We won't be back in an hour, dear," said Mrs. Fanning, "nor for two hours; we are going to enjoy ourselves with a tea out. You'll spare your daughter until she comes back, won't you, madam? I mean you won't fret about her."

I was just about absolutely to refuse, when Miss Mullins came into the room. To my astonishment and disgust she came straight over to where we were talking, and immediately took Mrs. Fanning's part.

"Oh yes," she said, "you must not disappoint dear Mrs. Fanning, Westenra; she was so looking forward to having a time out with you. Go with her. As to your mother, I will look after her. I have nothing at all to do this afternoon, and mean to go and sit with her in the drawing-room, or rather to bring her into my private room, where we will have a cosy tea to ourselves."

There was no help for it. After Jane's treachery in siding with Mrs. Fanning, I could only have refused by making a fuss, which would have been extremely bad for mother, so I went upstairs and spent a little time considering in which of my hats I looked worst, and which of my jackets presented the most dowdy appearance. Alack and alas! I had no dowdy jackets and no unbecoming hats. I put on, however, the quietest I could find, and ran downstairs. Mrs. Fanning was waiting for me in the hall. One of the servants of the establishment was standing near with a heavy fur rug over her arm. Mrs. Fanning was attired in a huge sealskin cape, which went down below her knees, and a bonnet with a large bird of paradise perched on one side of the brim. She had a veil, with huge spots on it, covering her broad face, and she was drawing on a pair of gloves a great deal too small for her fat hands.

"Here you are, Miss Wickham," she said; "now, then, we'll go. Open the door, please, Emma."

Emma did so, and we entered the carriage.

"Spread the rug, Emma," said Mrs. Fanning in a lordly tone. This was also accomplished, and the next moment we were whirling away. Mrs. Fanning laid her fat hand on my lap.

"Now, this is pleasant," she said; "I have been looking forward to this. Do you know where I am going to take you?"

"I am sure I cannot tell," I answered; "but as we are out, I hope you will let me look at the shops; I want to tell mother something about the latest fashions; it often entertains her."

"Well, I am glad to hear you speak in that strain, it sounds so human and womanly. Your tastes and mine coincide to a nicety. There's no one loves shop-gazing better than I do; I have flattened my nose against shop windows times and again, as long as I can remember. Before my dear Albert became so wealthy, I used to get into my bus, and do my hour of shop-gazing a-most every afternoon, but now it fidgets the coachman if I ask him to pull up the horses too often. You like the swing of the carriage, don't you, my dear? It's very comfortable, isn't it? nearly as nice as if it had the yellow wheels that Albert would not gratify his old mother by allowing. Ah, SHE has a deal to answer for—a deal to answer for—however nice she may be in herself." Here Mrs. Fanning favoured me with one of her broadest winks.

"The carriage is very nice," I replied.

"I fancied somehow that it would suit you, and I was most anxious to see how you looked in it. Some people don't look as if they were born to a carriage, others take to it like a duck takes to the water. Now, you look very nice in it; you and your mother in this carriage would look as genteel as two ladies could look. You don't know what a great admiration I have for your mother.

She is one of the most beautiful women on God's earth."

"And one of the best," I said impulsively, and as I thought of all that was going to happen to that most precious mother, and how soon that presence would be withdrawn from our mortal gaze, and how soon that spirit would go to the God who gave it, tears sprang to my eyes, and even Mrs. Fanning became more tolerable.

"Ah, you are feeling cut to bits about her great delicacy," said that good lady. "Any one can see that; but cheer up, cheer up, the young ought to rejoice, and you of all women under the sun have the most cause for rejoicement, Miss Wickham."

I did not ask her why, I did not dare, we drove on. It seemed to me that we were not going anywhere near the shops, we were steadily pursuing our way into the suburbs. After a drive of over an hour, we suddenly found ourselves in a part of Highgate quite unknown to me. We had been going uphill for some time, and we stopped now before some iron gates; a woman ran out of a lodge and opened the gates, and then we drove down a short avenue shaded by some fine trees. We drew up in front of a large, substantial red-brick house, the door of which was open, and on the steps stood Mr. Fanning. He ran down to meet us, with both his hands extended.

"Ah! and you have brought the little thing," he said to his mother.

"What little thing?" I said to myself. This was really the final straw. I had never, never even by my most intimate friends, been spoken of as the "little thing," for I was a tall girl and somewhat large in my ideas, and if anything rather masculine in my mind, and to be spoken of as a little thing, and by Albert Fanning, was about the final straw which broke the camel's back. My first intention was to refuse to budge from the carriage, to fiercely demand that the coachman should turn round and drive me straight back again to mother, but on second thoughts, I reflected that I should lose a good deal of dignity by this proceeding, and the best possible plan was to appear as if nothing at all extraordinary had occurred, and to follow Mrs. Fanning into the house.

"Yes, I have brought her," said that good woman; "here she is. She looks slim beside your old mother, eh! Albert? but she's young; as time goes on she'll spread like all the rest of us. Well, and here we are, and she likes the brougham extremely; don't you, my dear? I could see that if you had yielded to me with regard to the yellow wheels she would not have approved. We must all humour her while she is young; it is always the way, always the way, ain't it, Albert? And I never saw a girl look nicer in a brougham than she does. She did enjoy her drive; it was lovely to see her. Well, now, she'll enjoy still more what's before her—the house and the grounds. It's a bit of a surprise we have for you, my dear," continued the old lady, turning to me. "It is not every girl would have the luck to be brought here by *his* mother; but everything that can be made easy and pleasant for you, Miss Wickham, shall be made easy and pleasant. It was Albert's wish that you should come here with me, and he said you would much rather it was not bragged about at the boarding-house beforehand. This is my son Albert's new house, furnished according to his own taste, which is excellent, nothing showy nor gimcrack, all firm and good, bought at Maple's, dear, in Tottenham Court Road, and the very best the establishment could furnish. Everything new, shining, and *paid* for, dear, paid for. You can see the bills, not a debt to hang over your head by-and-by, love. But come in, come in."

I really felt that I could not stand much longer on the steps of the mansion, listening to this most extraordinary address made to me by Mrs. Fanning. What did it matter to me whether Albert Fanning paid for his household goods or not? and how could it concern me what shop he chose to buy them at? But I felt myself more or less in a trap, and knew the best way to prevent any crisis taking place was to put on an assumed air of absolute indifference, and to take the first possible opportunity of returning home.

"Jane must get the Fannings to leave to-morrow, whatever happens," I said to myself, "and I must cling now to Mrs. Fanning for dear life. I don't suppose Albert Fanning will propose for me while she is by." But alas! I little knew the couple with whom I had to deal. Albert Fanning had willed that I was not to cling close to his mother. Turning to the old lady, he said—

"You're fagged and flustered. You have done things uncommonly well, and now you'll just have the goodness to sit with your feet on the fender in the drawing-room, and give yourself a right good toasting while Miss Wickham and I are examining the house."

"Oh no," I began.

"Oh yes," said Mrs. Fanning; "don't be shy, love." She gave me another wink so broad that I did not dare to expostulate further. Had I done so, Albert would probably have gone on his knees on the spot and implored of me there and then to make him the happiest of men.

Accordingly we all entered the drawing-room which was furnished *à la* Maple. It was a large room, and there were a great many tables about, and I wondered how stout Mrs. Fanning could cross the room without knocking over one or two. She looked round her with admiration.

"It's amazing the taste you have," she said, gazing at her son as if he were a sort of demigod. He put her into a comfortable chair by the fire, and then he and I began to do the house. Was there ever such a dreadful business? We began at the attics, and we thoroughly explored room after room. I did not mind that. As long as I could keep Albert Fanning off dangerous ground I was quite ready to talk to him. I was ready to poke at the mattresses on the new beds, and to admire the chain springs, and to examine the ventilators in the walls of every single room. I said "Yes" to all his remarks, and he evidently thought he was making a most favourable impression. We took a long time going over the house, but I did not mind that, for Mr. Fanning was in his element, and was so pleased with his own consummate common sense and his own skill in getting the right things into the right corners, and in showing me what a mind he had for contriving and for making money go as far as possible, that I allowed him to talk to his heart's content. The brougham must soon be ordered again, and we must get back to town, and the awful time would be at an end. But when at last even the kitchens had been inspected, and the action of the new range explained to me, Albert said that he must now show me the grounds. There was no escaping this infliction, and accordingly into the grounds we went.

These were fairly spacious. There was a large fruit garden, and a kitchen garden behind it, and Albert Fanning told me exactly what he was going to plant in the kitchen garden in the spring—a certain bed in particular was to be devoted to spring onions. He told me that he hated salad without a good dash of onion in it, and as he spoke he looked at me as much as to say, "Don't you ever give me salad without onion," and I began to feel the queerest sensation, as if I was being mastered, creeping over me. I wondered if the man really intended to take me from the garden to the church, where the priest would be waiting to perform the ceremony which would tie us together for life. The whole proceeding was most extraordinary, but just at the crucial moment, just when I was feeling that I could bear things no longer, I heard Mrs. Fanning's cheery voice. How I loved the old lady at that moment!

"Albert! Albert!" she called out, "the tea is cooling. I don't approve of tea being drawn too long, and it has been in the teapot for ten minutes. Come in this minute, you naughty young folks, come in and enjoy your tea."

"I am coming," I answered, "I am very hungry and thirsty."

"Are you?" said Mr. Fanning, looking at me. "Coming, mother, coming."

I turned to run after the old lady, but he suddenly put out his hand and caught one of mine, I pulled it away from him.

"Don't," I said.

"Don't!" he replied; "but I certainly shall. I mean often to touch you in the future, so what does it matter my taking your hand now. I hope to have you near me all day long and every day in the future. You must have guessed why I brought you out here."

"I have guessed nothing, except that I am thirsty and want my tea," I replied. "I cannot talk to you any longer."

"Oh yes, you can," he replied, "and you don't stir from here until I have had my say. You thought to escape me that time in the drawing-room a few weeks back, but you won't now. Don't be angry; don't look so frightened. I mean well, I mean—I cannot tell you what I *quite* mean when I look at you, but there, you like the house?"

"Yes," I said, "very well."

"Very well indeed; let me tell you, Miss Wickham, there isn't a more comfortable house nor a better furnished house, nor a better paid-for house in the length and breadth of the county. And you like these gardens, eh?"

"Certainly," I said.

"I thought so. Well, now, the fruit garden, and the kitchen garden, and the pleasure garden, and the house, and the furniture, and the master of the house are all at your disposal. There! I have spoken. You are the one I am wishing to wed; you are the one I intend to wed. I am wanting you, and I mean to have you for better, for worse. I have not the slightest doubt that you have faults, but I am willing to run the risk of finding them out; and I have no doubt that I have faults too, but I do not think that they are too prominent, and, at any rate, I am a real, downright son of Britain, an honest, good-hearted, well-meaning man. I believe in the roast beef of Old England and the beer of Old England, and the ways of Old England, and I want an English girl like yourself to be my wife, and I will treat you well, my dear, and love you well—yes, I will love you right well."

Here his voice broke, and a pathetic look came into his eyes, and I turned away more embarrassed, and more distressed than ever I was in my life.

"You will have all that heart can desire, little girl, and your poor, delicate mother, shall come and live with you in this house; and she and my mother can have a sitting-room between them. We shall be a happy quartette, and you shall come to me as soon as ever you like, the sooner the better. Now you need not give me your answer yet. We know, of course, what it will be; it is a great chance for you, and I am not denying it, but come and enjoy your tea."

"But I must and will give you my answer now," I replied. "How can you for a single moment imagine that I can seriously consider your offer? It is kind of you; yes, it is kind of any man to give his whole heart to a girl; and, I believe, you are sincere, but I can only give you one answer, Mr. Fanning."

"And that?" he said.

"It is quite—quite absolutely impossible! I could never love you; I could never, never marry you. I am sorry, of course, but I have nothing—nothing more to say."

"You mean," said Albert Fanning, turning pale, and a queer, half angry, half wild look coming and going on his face, "that you *refuse* me—me, and my house, and my brougham, and my gardens, and my paid-for furniture! Is it true?"

"I refuse you, and all that you want to confer upon me," I answered. "I know you mean well, and I am—oh, yes, I *am* obliged to you. Any girl ought to be obliged to a man who offers her the best he has; but I could never under any circumstances marry you. Now, you know."

"You will rue it, and I do not think you mean it," he said. His face turned red, then purple, he turned on his heel, and allowed me to walk back to the house alone.

My head was swimming. My eyes were full of smarting tears which I dared not shed. I entered the drawing-room where Mrs. Fanning was waiting for me.

"Ah! here you are," she cried, rubbing her hands, and speaking in a very cheerful tone; "and where is Albert? Has he—has he?—why, what is the matter, my love?"

"I must tell you the truth," I answered, "for I know you will guess it. Your son has been kind enough to ask me to marry him. You knew he meant to ask me, did you not? but I—I have refused him. No, I don't want any tea; I don't want even to go back in the brougham. I can never, never marry your son, Mrs. Fanning; and you must have known it—and it was very unkind of you to bring me here without saying anything about it." And then I sank on the nearest chair, and sobbed as if my heart would break.

CHAPTER XVIII

BUTTERED BREAD

Mrs. Fanning let me cry for a moment or two without interrupting me. I think in her way she had plenty of heart; for once when I raised my head, feeling relieved from the bitter flow of those tears, I found that she was looking at me with a quizzical, but by no means unkindly glance.

"We'll say nothing about this at present," she exclaimed; "you shan't be plagued, my dear. I'll talk to Albert, and say that you are not to be worried; but whether you take him in the long run or not, you want your tea now. Come, child, drink up this nice cup of hot tea."

As she spoke she squeezed herself on to the sofa by my side; and gave me tea according to her taste, and insisted on my drinking it; and I could not refuse her, although my sobs were still coming heavily.

"Ah, you're a proud young girl," she said, "you're one of those who do not know which side their bread is buttered; but you will some day, the knowledge will come to you, and soon, I'm thinking, soon."

Here she looked intensely mysterious, and nodded her head emphatically.

"And there's not a better fellow in the length and breadth of England than my son, Albert," she continued; "there's no one who would give his wife a better time. Kind, he would be to her; firm, he would be no doubt too. He would make her obey him, but he would make her love him too. You will know all about it by-and-by, my dear, all about it by-and-by. For the present we'll say nothing more. Albert shan't drive with us back in the brougham, although I know he meant to do so. Poor fellow! could love go further; his legs cramped up on that little seat at the back, but love feels no pain, dear; no more than pride feels pain. It's a bit of a shock to you, I know. Proposals always are; that is, to modest girls. I felt terribly flustered when Albert's father asked me to marry him. I assure you, my love, I could not bear the sight of him for the next fortnight. I used to say, whenever he entered a room, 'I'm going out, Albert, if you're coming in. Get right away now, if you don't want me to hate you for ever,' but, in the end, my dear love, I was head over ears in love with him. There never was a better husband. He would be masterful as a good man should; but, dear, I worshipped the ground he trod on, and it was he who made the beginning of that fortune which Albert has turned into so big a thing. Well, my love, you have seen the house, and you have gone over the grounds, and you have done something else. You have looked into the great good heart of my son, Albert; and after a time, I have no doubt, you will creep into that heart, and take refuge; but mum's the word at present, mum's the word."

The idea of my creeping into Albert's heart as a final cave of refuge was so funny, that I could scarcely keep back my smiles; and I almost became hysterical between laughing and crying, so much so, that Mrs. Fanning had to put her arms round me and hug me, and call me her dear little girl.

I was very glad she did not say, "dear little thing." By-and-by she ordered the carriage, and we went back to town. She was most affectionate to me. She assured me many times that she quite understood; that she had gone through precisely the same phases with regard to Albert Fanning the first but that it had all come right, and that her passion for the godly man had been very strong by-and-by. I should feel just the same with regard to Albert the second. It was the way of girls; that is, nice girls.

"Don't talk to me about that Miss Marion Armstrong," she said. "The ways of that girl turn me sick. It is the contrast you make to Marion Armstrong which has done the business more than anything else, my dear Miss Wickham. But there, dear, there we'll turn the conversation."

"I earnestly wish you would," I said

"Ah," she said, "how history repeats itself. I used to feel as if I would like to box any one in the face who talked to me about my dear Albert long ago. But oh, how I loved him before all was over, how I loved him!"

She almost shed tears at the recollection. In short, I had a most unpleasant drive home. At last it was over. I got out of the brougham, with its red body and chocolate wheels, and staggered rather than walked into the house. I did not dare to see mother until all traces of emotion had left my face, but I made straight for Jane's sanctum.

"Jane," I said the moment I found myself there, "the Fannings must go away; they must, Jane, they must."

"Why so?" asked Jane.

"I will tell you what has just happened. Mother must never know, but I must tell some one. Mrs. Fanning took me into the country in their new brougham. We went to Highgate; they have a house there. Mr. Fanning was there to meet us. He called me a little thing, and he took me over the house and over the grounds, and told me, on pain of his direst displeasure, that I was never to give him salad without onions, and then he asked me to *marry him*. O Jane! what is to be done?"

"But didn't you always know that he was going to ask you?" inquired Jane in a low voice.

"Ask me to marry him! How could I suppose anything so preposterous?" I exclaimed.

"Well, dear, I know it goes very sore with you, and I hope, with all my heart and soul, that it may not be necessary."

"Necessary!" I said, "what do you mean? O Jane! don't talk in that way, you'll drive me mad. I cannot stay in the house with the Fannings any more."

"Let me think for a moment," answered Jane. She looked very careworn and distressed, her face had grown thin and haggard. She looked years older than before we had started the boarding-house. I was quite sorry to see the change in her face.

"Our life does not suit you," I said.

"Oh, it suits me well enough," she replied, "and I never leave a sinking ship."

"But why should this ship be sinking? I thought we were doing so well, the house is almost always full."

"It is just this," said Jane: "we charged too little when we started. If the house was choke-full, all the attics and the three different floors let, we could not make the thing pay, that's the awful fact, and you ought to know it, Westenra. We should have begun by charging more."

"Then why didn't we?" I said. "I left all those matters to you, Jane. I was very ignorant, and you came and——"

"I am not blaming you, my dear Westenra," said Jane; "only it is very, very hard to go on toiling, toiling all day and almost all night, and to feel at the same time that the thing cannot pay, that it can never pay."

"But why didn't we begin by charging more, and why can't we charge more now?"

"Because people who live in Bloomsbury never pay more," answered Miss Mullins, "that is it, dear. If we meant this thing to succeed we should have started our boarding-house in Mayfair, and then perhaps we might have had a chance of managing. Perhaps with a connection like yours we could have made it pay."

"Never," I said, "none of our friends would come to us, they would have been scandalised. It would never have done, Jane."

"Well, well, we have got ourselves into a trap, and we must get out the best way we can," was Jane's lugubrious answer.

"Oh, never mind about our being in money difficulties now," I cried, "do think of me, Jane, just for a moment, do make things possible for me. Remember that I am very young, and I was never accustomed to people of the Fanning type. Do, I beseech of you, ask them to go. Mr. Fanning's action to-day will make your request possible. Jane, if I went on my knees and stayed there all my life, I could not marry him, and the sooner he knows it the better."

"I will think things over," said Jane. I never saw anything like the look of despair which was creeping over her face.

"Things are coming to a crisis," she continued, "and I must confide in you fully, but not just now, we must get dinner over first. Your mother was ill while you were away, she won't come to dinner to-night."

"Mother ill! Anything serious?" I cried in alarm.

"Only a little faintness. I have got her comfortably to bed."

"Well, of course, I shan't dine to-night, I shall stay with mother."

"But you must, my love, it is absolutely necessary that you should appear at dinner, and you must be quite cheerful too in her room. She is quite herself now, and is looking over a new book, and when you go to her you will see that she has had a nice dinner, nourishing and suitable. Now go and change your dress, and make yourself look smart. Now that Mr. Randolph is gone, and your mother is too ill to be often in the drawing-room and dining-room, the affairs of the household rest upon you. You must make yourself smart; you must make yourself attractive. It must be done, Westenra, it must, and for your mother's sake."

Jane spoke with such determination that she stimulated my courage, and I went away to my own room determined to act on her advice.

At the other side of the wall I heard Mrs. Fanning's heavy steps as she walked about. She did not seem to be at all depressed at my refusal of her son Albert. On the contrary, she was in very good spirits. She had been in excellent spirits all the way back, and had kept on assuring me that I was only going on the usual tack of the modest maiden, the maiden who was worthy of such a man as her godly son Albert. Had not she herself hated Albert's father for a whole fortnight after his proposal, and had she not been glad, very glad, in the end to creep into his great heart for shelter? Did she suppose that I also would be glad to creep into Albert the second's great heart for shelter? Oh, it was all unbearable. But, nevertheless, there was a spirit of defiance in me. I had tried my ugly dresses in vain, I had tried being grave and distant in vain. I had tried everything, but nothing had availed; Mr. Fanning was determined to have me for his wife. I wondered if the man cared for me, perhaps he did after his fashion, but as no self-denials on my part had the effect of repulsing him, I would give way to my fancy and dress properly for dinner. I put on a very pretty pink dress which I had not yet worn, and ran downstairs.

At dinner I sat opposite Mr. Fanning. Mother's place was empty, and Mrs. Fanning called across the table to know what was the matter with her.

I said that she was tired and had gone to bed, whereupon Mrs. Armstrong immediately remarked, that it was a very good thing we had such an excellent housekeeper as Miss Mullins to look after things in my mother's serious state of health, otherwise the house would go to wreck and ruin, she said.

Mrs. Armstrong looked daggers at me for wearing my pink dress. She had never seen anything so stylish as that soft, graceful robe before, and between her jealousy at seeing me so attired, and her earnest wish to copy it for Marion, she scarcely knew what to do with herself. She darted angry glances at my face, and then tried to measure with her eye the amount of ribbon on the bodice, and the quantity of chiffon round the neck. But Mr. Fanning, to my great relief and delight, did not appear to take the slightest interest in me. I do not think he once glanced at my pretty evening frock. He absorbed himself altogether with Marion Armstrong. He talked to her all during dinner, and invited her in a loud voice to come and see him at his office on the following day.

"I told you, Miss Armstrong," he said, "that as a rule I am brutal to the people who come to me trying to sell their wares. Those silly folks who bring their useless manuscripts and their poor little amateur drawings to my office find that I make short work with them.

"'If you like to leave your manuscript or your drawings,' I say to them, 'you can do so, but as to the chance of their being accepted, well, look for yourselves. Do you see that pile? all that pile of manuscripts has to be read before yours. If you leave your manuscripts they go under the pile at the bottom; there will be nearly a ton of stuff on top of them. You take your chance. You had best go away at once with what you have brought, for I am not likely to require it.' They mostly do go away, Miss Armstrong, for I am brutal in my words and brutal in my tone. There is no use in buoying people up with false hopes." Here he gave a loud guffaw, which reached my ears at the further end of the table.

Captain Furlong bent across at that moment to say something to me, and I saw that he was much displeased at Mr. Fanning's loud, aggressive words. But Mr. Fanning, after all, was nothing to Mrs. Fanning. It was quite pleasant to me to see that he should turn his attentions to Miss Marion Armstrong, but Mrs.

Fanning's winks were more than I could endure. They were just as much as to say, "Listen to him now; he is only doing that to draw you on." So plainly did her speaking eyes announce this fact, that I dreaded each moment her saying the awful words aloud, but fortunately she did not go quite so far as that.

When dinner was over Mrs. Armstrong came and sat near me.

"Have you seen any of Marion's drawings lately?" she asked.

"No," I replied; "is she getting on well?"

"Is she getting on well!" retorted Mrs. Armstrong. "The girl is a genius. I told you before that her whole soul was devoted to h'Art. Well, I may as well say now that she has sold a little set of drawings to Mr. Fanning. He means to bring them out in his Christmas number of the *Lady's Handbag*. Have you ever seen the *Lady's Handbag*, Miss Wickham?"

"No," I answered; "I cannot say that I have."

"I am surprised to hear it. The *Lady's Handbag* is one of the most striking and widely read periodicals of the day. It contains information on every single thing that a lady ought to know, and there is nothing in it for those low-down common sort of people who want wild excitement and sickening adventures. But you shall see it for yourself. Marion! Come here, dear Marion."

Marion, behind whose chair Mr. Fanning was standing, rose reluctantly and crossed the room with a frown between her brows.

"You will scarcely believe it, Marion, but Miss Wickham has not seen the *Lady's Handbag*. I was just telling her that you are to illustrate an article for the Christmas number. Perhaps you could oblige me by bringing a number here. I know Miss Wickham would like to see any of Mr. Fanning's publications."

Miss Armstrong left the room and returned with a copy of the *Lady's Handbag*. It was handed to me and I turned the pages. It was exactly the sort of fifth-rate production which I should expect a man of Mr. Fanning's calibre to initiate.

I gave it back to Mrs. Armstrong.

"I am so glad that Miss Armstrong is having her first success," I said then, and I thought what a suitable and admirable wife she would make for Mr. Fanning, and hoped that he might by-and-by think so himself.

As I was entering my own room that night, Mrs. Fanning popped her head out of her own door near by.

"One word, Miss Wickham," she said. She looked very funny. She had divested herself of her gay dress and was wearing a night-cap. Her night-cap had large frills which partly encircled her wide face.

"I know you're fretted by the way Albert has gone on this evening," she said, "but he's only doing it on purpose. I am sorry for that poor girl, though. You had better be quick and make up your mind, or Marion Armstrong will fall over head and ears in love with him, but if you imagine for a single moment that he thinks sincerely of her you are greatly mistaken. It's you he wants, and you he'll have. Go to bed now, dear, and dream of him, but I understand your ways perfectly. I felt just the same about Albert the first."

CHAPTER XIX

YOU USED TO LOVE US

Mother was very ill for the next few days, and I was so much occupied with her that I had no time to think of either Mr. or Mrs. Fanning. When I was in the drawing-room my heart was full of her; when I forced myself to go to meals, I could only think of her dear face. Was she going to be taken away from me before the year was up? Oh, surely God would at least leave me my one treasure for that short time. In those days I used to go away by myself and struggle to pray to God, but my heart was heavy, and I wondered if He heard my restless and broken words. I used to creep out sometimes and go into a church alone, and try to picture what my future would be when mother was gone; but I could not picture it. It always rose before me as a great blank, and I could not see anything distinctly. It seemed to me that I could see everything when mother was present, and nothing without her. And then I would go back again to her room and rouse myself to be cheerful, and to talk in a pleasant tone. I was doing the utmost that duty required of me just then. I determined that nothing would induce me to look further afield. Life without mother I did not dare to contemplate. But there were moments when the thought of one person came to my heart with a thrill of strength and comfort. I missed Jim Randolph, and longed for him to come back.

As the winter passed away and the spring approached, I began to hope for his return. I began to feel that when once he was back things would be right, anxiety would be removed from Jane's face, the strain would be removed. Mother would have her friend near her, and I also should not be friendless when my time of terrible trouble came, for of course mother was dying. The doctor was right. It was a question perhaps of days, of months at most, but if Mr. Randolph came back I thought that I could bear it.

When mother and I were alone I noticed that she liked to talk of Jim, and I was more than willing to listen to her, and to draw her out, and to ask her questions, for it seemed to me that she knew him a great deal better than I did.

"There always seems to be a mystery surrounding him," I said on one occasion. "You know much more than I do. I like him, of course, and I am sure you like him, mother."

"Except your dear father, West," replied mother, "he is the best fellow I ever met, and he will come back again, dearest. I shall be very glad when he comes back. We ought to hear from him soon now."

The winter was now passing away and the spring coming, and the spring that year happened to be a mild and gracious one, without much east wind, and with many soft westerly breezes, and the trees in the Square garden put on their delicate fragile green clothing, and hope came back to my heart once more.

One day I had gone to do some messages for mother in Regent Street. She had asked me to buy some lace for a new fichu, and one or two other little things. I went off to fulfil my messages with my heart comparatively light.

I went to Dickins & Jones', and was turning over some delicate laces at the lace counter when a hand was laid on my shoulder. I turned with a start to encounter the kind old face of the Duchess of Wilmot.

"My dear Westenra," she said, "this is lucky. How are you? I have heard nothing of you for a long time."

Now, I had always loved the Duchess, not at all because she was a duchess, but because she was a woman with a very womanly heart and a very sweet way, and my whole heart went out to her now—to her gracious appearance, to her gentle, refined tone of voice, to the look in her eyes. I felt that I belonged to her set, and her set were delightful to me just then.

"Where are you going," inquired the Duchess, "after you have made your purchases?"

"Home again," I answered.

"My carriage is at the door; you shall come with me. You shall come and have tea with me."

"I have not time," I said. "Mother is not well, and I must hurry back to her."

"Your mother not well! Mary Wickham not well! I have heard nothing for months. I have written two or three times, but my letters have not been replied to. It is impossible to keep up a friendship of this sort, all on one side, Westenra. And you don't look as well as you did, and oh! my dear child, is that your spring hat?"

"It is; it will do very well," I answered. I spoke almost brusquely; I felt hurt at her remarking it.

"But it is not fresh. It is not the sort of hat I should like my god-daughter to wear. They have some pretty things here. I must get you a suitable hat."

"No, no," I said with passion. "It cannot be."

"You are so ridiculously proud and so ridiculously socialistic in all your ideas.

135

But if you were a true Socialist you would take a present from your old friend without making any fuss over the matter."

As the Duchess spoke she looked at me, and I saw tears in her eyes.

"And I am your godmother," she continued. "I do not like to see you looking as you do. You want a new hat and jacket; may I get them for you?"

At first I felt that I must refuse, but then I reflected that it would please mother to see me in the hat and jacket which the Duchess would purchase. I knew that the buying of such things were a mere bagatelle to her, and the little pleasure which the new smart things would give mother were not a bagatelle. My own feelings must be crushed out of sight. I said humbly, "Just as you like." So the Duchess hurried me into another room, and a hat that suited me was tried on and paid for, and then a new jacket was purchased, and the Duchess made me put on both hat and jacket immediately, and gave the address of 17 Graham Square to have my old things sent to.

The next moment we were bowling away in her carriage.

"Ah," she cried, "now you look more like yourself. Pray give that old hat to the housemaid. Don't put it on again. I mean to drive you home now, Westenra."

"Thank you," I answered.

"I mean to see your mother also. Is she seriously ill?"

"She is," I replied. I lowered my eyes and dropped my voice.

"But what is the matter, my poor child? You seem very sad."

"I have a great deal to make me sad, but I cannot tell you too much now, and you must not question me."

"And Jim has gone, really?"

"Mr. Randolph has gone."

The Duchess seemed about to speak, but she closed her lips.

"He wrote and told me he had to go, but he will come back again. When did you say he went, Westenra?"

"I did not say, Duchess."

"But give me the date, dear, please, and be quick."

I thought for a moment.

"He left England on the 30th of November," I said.

"Ah, and this is the 15th of March. What a nice genial spring we are having. He will be home soon; I am sure of that."

"Have you heard from him?" I asked abruptly.

"Just a line *en route*. I think it was dated from Colombo. Have you heard?"

"I believe mother had a letter, and I think Jane had."

"He has not written to you?"

"No." I felt the colour leap into my cheeks like an angry flame. I was ashamed of myself for blushing.

The Duchess looked at me attentively, and I saw a pleased expression in her eyes. That look made me still more uncomfortable. She bent towards me, took my hand, and pressed it.

"You like Jim, do you not?" she said.

"Yes," I answered very slowly. "I do not know Mr. Randolph well, but what little I have seen of him I like. He is courteous, and he thinks of others; he is very unselfish; he has much sympathy and tact, too. I think he is very fond of mother."

The Duchess gave the queerest, most inexplicable of smiles.

"He is a dear fellow," she said. "Westenra, when you come back to us we will all rejoice."

"I do not understand you," I answered coldly. "It is impossible for me ever to come back to you. I have stepped down."

"When you come back we will rejoice," she repeated.

"But I am not coming back. I do not even know that I want to. If you had come to see mother sometimes—mother, who is just as much a lady as she ever was, who is sweeter and more beautiful than she ever was—you might have done us a great service, and I could have loved you, oh! so dearly; but you have forsaken us, because we are no longer in your set. Duchess, I must speak the truth. I hate sets; I hate distinctions of rank. You used to love us; I did think your love was genuine. We lived in a nice house in Mayfair, and you were our great and kind friend. Now you do not love us, because—because we are poor."

"You are mistaken, Westenra. I love you still, and I have never forgotten you. I will not come in now, but I will come and see your mother to-morrow."

"That will please her," I answered, drying away the tears which had risen to my eyes. "But please do not disappoint her. I will tell her of your visit. Do not keep her waiting. She is weak; she has been very ill. At what hour will you come?"

"About twelve o'clock. But she must be very bad indeed from the way you speak."

"She is far from well."

"Are you hiding anything from me, Westenra?"

"I am," I replied stoutly. "And you cannot get my secret from me. When you see mother to-morrow perhaps you will know without my speaking. Do not say anything to agitate her."

"My poor, poor child. Westenra, you ought never to have left us. You do not look well; but never mind, spring is coming, and Jim Randolph will be home before May."

CHAPTER XX

RUINED

It was on the afternoon of that same day that Jane Mullins sent for me to go into her private sitting-room.

"Shut the door," she said, "I must talk to you."

Really Jane looked most queer. During the last month or two, ever since Mr. Randolph went away, she had been taking less and less pains with her dress; her hair was rough and thinner than ever; her little round figure had fallen away; she seemed to have aged by many years. She was never a pretty woman, never in any sense of the word, but now there was something grotesque about her, grotesque and at the same time intensely pathetic.

"I have done all I could," she said. "Lock the door, please, Westenra."

I locked the door.

"Now come and sit here, or stand by the window, or do anything you like; but listen with all your might, keep your attention alert."

"Yes," I said, "yes."

"We are ruined, Westenra," said Jane Mullins, "we are ruined."

"What!" I cried.

Jane said the words almost ponderously, and then she threw her hands to her sides and gazed at me with an expression which I cannot by any possibility describe.

"We are ruined," she repeated, "and it is time you should know it."

"But how?" I asked.

"How?" she cried with passion, "because we have debts which we cannot meet—we have debts, debts, debts on every side; debts as high as the house itself. Because we deceived our landlord, unintentionally it is true, but nevertheless we deceived him, with promises which we cannot fulfil, he can take back the lease of this house if he pleases, and take it back he will, because our paying guests don't pay, because the whole thing from first to last is a miserable failure. There, Westenra, that's about the truth. It was your thought in the first instance, child, and though I don't want to blame you, for you did it with good meaning, and in utter ignorance, yet nevertheless you must take some of the brunt of this terrible time. I cannot bear the whole weight any longer. I have kept it to myself, and it has driven me nearly mad. Yes, we are ruined."

"You must explain more fully," was my answer.

Her agitation was so great that by its very force it kept me quiet. I had never seen her absolutely without composure before; her usually brisk, confident manner had deserted her.

"You have kept me in the dark," I continued, "and you have done wrong, very wrong. Now please explain how and why we are ruined."

"Here are some of the accounts; understand them if you can," she said. She opened a drawer and pulled out a great account book. "Now look here," she said, "the house is absolutely full, there is not a single room to be let; I declined four fresh parties only this morning; Emma is perfectly tired opening the door to people who want to come here to board, the house has got a name and a good one. It is said of it that it is in Bloomsbury and yet smacks of the West End. You and your mother and Jim Randolph, bless him! have to answer for that. It's all your doing, and the people have talked. Everything has been done that could be done to make the place popular, and the place is popular, but now, you look here. Here are the takings"—she pointed to one side of the ledger—"here are the expenses"—she pointed to the other—"expenses so much, takings so much, look at the balance, Westenra. Of course you don't know much about accounts, but you can see for yourself."

I did look, and I did see, and my heart seemed to stand still, for the balance on the wrong side of the ledger represented many pounds a week.

"Then this means," I said, for I was sharp enough in my way, "that the longer we go on the heavier we get into debt. Every week we lose so much."

"We do, dear, that's just it."

"But cannot we retrench?"

"Retrench! how? Do you suppose the boarders will do without their comfortable hot coffee, and the other luxuries on the board at breakfast? Do you suppose they will do without their lunch, their afternoon tea with plenty of cakes and plenty of cream, their late dinner, at which appears all the luxuries of the season?—why, the house would be empty in a week. And we cannot have fewer servants, we have only four, very much less than most people would have for an establishment of this kind, and Emma already complains of pains in her legs, and says she is worn out going up and down stairs."

"But the place looks so thriving," I said.

"Looks! what have looks to do with it?" said Jane. "I feel nearly mad, for I always thought I could pull the thing through; but it's going on at a loss, and nothing can go on at a loss; and then, dear, there are bad debts—one or two people have shuffled off without paying, and there are the furniture bills, they are not all met yet."

"But I thought," I said, "that the seven thousand pounds——"

"Ay," cried Jane, "and that is where the bitterness comes in. That money was supposed to be all right, to be as sure and safe as the Bank of England, and it is not all right, it is all wrong. But that is James Randolph's story. When he comes back he will explain the rights of it to you, my dear. If I could only hear from him that the money was safe, we could wind up honourably in the autumn and stop the concern; but I have not heard, I have not heard; there has been nothing but silence, and the silence drives me mad. Westenra, what is to be done?"

"Give the whole thing up now," I said, "there is nothing else to be done. We must stop."

"Stop!" answered Jane. "You talk with the ignorance of a young girl. If we stop now we will have the whole house of cards about our ears; the tradespeople will sue for their money, the bailiffs will be in and will take possession of the furniture, even the very bed your mother sleeps on will be taken from under her. The awful, terrible position is, that we can neither stop nor go on. It is fearful, fearful. Oh, if I could only borrow a thousand pounds within a week, I would not care a farthing. I would not even care if your mother was strong, but to have this crash come about her in her present state of health, why, it would kill her. Westenra, poor child, you are young and unaccustomed to these things, but I must unburden my mind. There is ruin before us; I can scarcely stave it off for another week, and I have not had a line from Mr. Randolph, and I am nearly wild."

"And you think a thousand pounds would keep things going for a little longer," I answered.

"Yes, we could stay on until the end of the season if I could get that money. It would pay the quarter's rent, and the tradespeople's bills, and the big furniture bills. And long before it was out Mr. Randolph must come back and put everything straight. His return is what I am hoping for more than the rising of the sun."

"But oh, Jane, how—how am I to get the thousand pounds?"

"I was thinking that Duchess of yours might lend it."

"No," I said, "I cannot ask her; besides, I know she would not. Though she is a Duchess she has not got a lot of money to spare. The Duke manages everything, and she just has her allowance, and a great deal to do with it. I cannot ask her."

"There is one other way in which ruin could be averted," said Jane slowly, "but that I suppose is not to be thought of. Well, I have told you, and I suppose it is a sort of relief. Things may go on as they are for another week or two, but that's about all."

I felt that I trembled, but I would not let Jane see.

"You have been very brave. You have ruined yourself for our sakes," I cried impulsively. But at the same time I could not help adding, "That friend of yours who promised you seven thousand pounds ought not to have failed you at a critical moment like the present."

"I won't have him blamed," said Jane, her face turning crimson; "it is not his fault. Man could not do more."

"Jane," I said, facing her, "tell me the truth now; what is the name of your friend?"

"You won't get his name out of me," answered Jane. "Mr. Randolph has gone to Australia to put things straight with him. When I hear from Mr. James Randolph all will be well."

"Have you never heard since he left?"

"Twice during the voyage, but not since. It is wonderful why he is so silent. There, I seem to have lost hope."

"Jane," I cried, "why don't you give us up and go back to your own little house?"

"Bless you, child, I'm not the one to leave a sinking ship. Oh, we'll go on a little bit longer, and it has cheered me a little to confide in you. I will work the ship for another week or so, and there will be an extra nice dinner to-night, and spring asparagus, real English grown, and your mother shall have the greater portion of it. Oh dear, oh dear, if the house were twice its size we *might* make it pay, but as it is it's too big and it's too small; it's one of the betwixt-and-betweens, and betwixt-and-between things *never* do, never, never. Child, forgive me, I am sorry to add to your cares. If it were not for your mother I should not mind a bit."

I could do nothing to comfort Jane. I went up to her and kissed her, and held her hand for a moment, and then went slowly away to my own room. I did not attempt to shed a tear, I was not going to cry just then, it behoved me to be very brave; there was a great deal to be borne, and if I gave way it seemed to me that everything must come to an end. I felt some pride in my young strength and my courage, and was resolved that they should not fail me in my hour of need. So I put away the new hat and pretty jacket and went down to mother, and I amused mother by showing her the lace I had bought, and I told her all about the Duchess, and mother was much pleased at the thought of seeing her old friend on the following morning, and she and I sat that afternoon in the drawing-room making up the pretty lace fichu, and I resolved that mother should wear it the next day when the Duchess came.

There was the most awful trouble hanging over us all; my mother's days on earth were numbered, and my scheme, my lovely castle in the air, was falling to ruins about my head. But all the same mother and I laughed and were cheerful, and the visitors who came into the drawing-room that afternoon thought what a picturesque group mother and I made, and what a lovely room it was, and how much superior to most boarding-houses; and they inquired, more than one of them, when there would be a vacancy, and said they would write to Miss Mullins on the subject. Poor Jane Mullins! she was bearing the brunt of the storm. I pitied her from the depths of my heart.

CHAPTER XXI

MR. PATTENS

The next day the Duchess called, and mother was looking so well for her, and so pleased to see her old friend again, that I do not think at first the Duchess of Wilmot half realised how ill she was. I just saw her for a moment, and then went out. I came back again at the end of an hour. Mother's cheeks were quite bright, and her eyes shining, and her hand was in the Duchess's hand, and when she looked at me her eyes grew brighter than ever, and she said to me—

"Come here, darling," and she raised her dear lips for me to kiss her.

I did kiss those lips, and I thought them too hot, and I said to the Duchess—

"You are tiring mother, you have stayed with her long enough."

"Oh no, let her stay; I do love so much to see her," said my mother, so I could not have the heart to say any more, and I went away to a distant part of the room, and they began whispering again just like the dearest friends which they really were, and at last the Duchess came up to me and said—

"Come downstairs with, me, West."

I went with her, and wondered why she called me by mother's pet name, but I loved her very much.

"Tell me the truth about your mother," said the Duchess as soon as we got into the hall. "At first I thought her fairly well, but she is feverish, quite feverish now. Have I overtired her?"

"I cannot tell you anything except that she is not strong," I said; "that you have come so seldom to see her, that you have over-excited her now. Oh, I cannot wait, I must go back to her."

"I will come again to-morrow or next day," said the Duchess; "I don't like her appearance at all."

The Duchess went away, and I returned to mother.

"It was nice to see Victoria," said my mother. "She is just the same as ever, not the least changed. She told me about all our old friends."

"You are over-excited," I said, "you ought to stay quiet now."

"On the contrary, I am well and hungry; only I wonder when I shall see her again."

"She said she would come to-morrow or next day," I answered.

In the evening mother certainly seemed by no means worse for the Duchess's visit, and the next day she said to me, "Victoria will certainly call to-morrow." But to-morrow came and the Duchess did not arrive, nor the next day, nor the next, and mother looked rather fagged, and rather sad and disappointed, and at the end of a week or fortnight she ceased to watch anxiously for the sound of wheels in the Square, and said less and less about her dear friend Victoria.

But just then, the thoughts of every one in the house except mother (and the news was carefully kept from her), were full of a great and terrible catastrophe, and even I forgot all about the Duchess, for one of our largest Orient liners had foundered on some sunken rocks not far from Port Adelaide, off the coast of South Australia, and there had been a terrific shipwreck, and almost every one on board was drowned. The vessel was called the *Star of Hope*. The papers were all full of it, and the news was on every one's lips; but just at first I did not realise how all important, how paralysing this same news was for us. I read the trouble first in Jane's face.

"You must not let your mother know about the shipwreck," she said.

"But I cannot keep the newspapers from mother, and every newspaper is full of it," I replied; "surely, Jane, surely—oh, you cannot mean it—no person that we know was on board?"

"I have a great fear over me," she answered.

I clutched her arm, and looked into her face with wild eyes. My own brain seemed to reel, my heart beat almost to suffocation, then I became quiet. With a mighty effort I controlled myself.

"Surely," I said, "surely."

"His name is not mentioned amongst the list of passengers, that is my one comfort; but it is quite possible, on the other hand, that he may have gone on board at Adelaide," she continued, "for I know he had business close to Adelaide, he told me so. If that was the case they might not have entered his name in the ship's list of passengers, and—oh, I have a great, a terrible fear over me, his silence, and now this. Yes, child, it is true, he was, if all had gone well, to be on his way home about now; but he has never written, and now this shipwreck. I am more anxious, far more anxious than I can say."

That night I did not sleep at all. Thoughts of Jim Randolph filled my mind to the exclusion of all hope of repose. Was he really drowned? Had he left the world? Was I never to see his face again? There was a cry at my heart, and an ache there which ought to have told me the truth, and yet I would not face the truth. I said over and over to myself, "If he dies, it is terrible; if he dies, it means ruin for us;" but nevertheless I knew well, although I would not face the truth, that I was not thinking of the ruin to the house in Graham Square, nor the blow to mother, nor the loss of James Randolph simply as a friend. There was a deeper cause for my grief. It was useless for me to say to my own heart Jim Randolph was nothing to me. I knew well that he was. I knew well that he was more to me than any one else in the wide world; that I—yes, although he had never spoken of his love for me, I loved him, yes, I loved him with my full heart.

In the morning I made up my mind that I would go and see the Duchess. Perhaps, too, she might know something about Jim Randolph, as he was a friend of hers, a friend about whom she was always hinting, but about whom she said very little.

As I was leaving the house Jane called me into her sitting-room.

"Where are you going," she said.

I told her.

"Did you ever think over that idea of mine that you might ask the Duchess to lend us that thousand pounds?" she said. "You remember I mentioned it, and you said you would not do it; but things are very grave, very grave indeed; and if—if my fear about Mr. Randolph is true, why things are graver than ever, in fact everything is up. But I would like for *her* sake, poor dear, for her sake to ward off the catastrophe as long as possible. She was very ill last night, and I was up with her for a couple of hours. I wouldn't disturb you; but didn't you think yourself that she looked bad this morning?"

"Oh yes," I said, the tears starting to my eyes; "I thought mother looked terribly ill, and I am going to see the Duchess. She ought to call in order to make mother happy."

"Shut the door, Westenra," said Jane, "I have something I must say."

I shut the door, I was trembling. Jane was no longer a rock of defence, she made me more frightened than any one else in the house.

"Oh, what is it?" I said; "don't be mysterious, do speak out."

"Well, it is this," said Jane, "we want that thousand pounds just dreadfully. If we had it we could go on, we could go on at least till the end of the season, and there would be an excuse to take your mother to the country, and she might never know, never; but it wants two months to the end of the season, and the house is full, and every one is in the height of good humour, and yet they are all walking on the brink of a precipice; the earth is eaten away beneath us, and any moment the whole thing may topple through. Why, it was only yesterday——"

"What happened yesterday?" I asked.

"A man came, a Mr. Pattens."

"What has Mr. Pattens to do with us?" I said.

"You listen to me, my dear; things are so grave that I can scarcely smile, and you are so ignorant, Westenra."

"Well," I said, "do tell me about Mr. Pattens."

"He is the butcher, dear, and we owe him over a hundred pounds, and he is positively desperate. He asked to see me, and of course I saw him, and then he said he *must* see your mother."

"See mother? But mother never sees the tradespeople."

"I know, love; but it was with the utmost difficulty I could keep him from not seeing her. He said that she was responsible for his account, and that if I would not let him see her he would do the other thing."

"What?" I asked, "what?"

"Well, my dear, it is coming, and you may as well bear it. There will be a bailiff in this house in no time. Yes, there'll be a man in possession, and how is your mother to stand that? You think whether you would rather just tell your grand friend the Duchess, and save your mother from the depths of humiliation, or whether you will let things take their course. Pattens is desperate, and he is the sort of man who will have no mercy. I have had to get the meat from another butcher—we can't hold out much longer. I have paid away the last shilling of the reserve fund I had in the bank. Oh dear, oh dear! why did Mr. Randolph go away? If he has gone down in the *Star of Hope*, why truly it is black night for us."

"I will do my best, Jane, and do keep up heart; and oh, Jane, keep mother in her room, she must not know, she must not meet this terrible danger. O Jane! do your best."

"I will, love. Even at the very worst day dawns but it is black night at present, that it is," said the faithful creature.

As I was going out who did I see standing on the threshold but Mrs. Fanning. Mrs. Fanning had been away for over a fortnight, and I must say we greatly enjoyed her absence, and I in particular enjoyed it; but when I saw her comely, good-humoured, beaming face now, it seemed to me that my heart went out to her. She looked at me, and then she opened her arms wide.

"Come to me, you dear little soul," she said; "come and have a hearty hug." She clasped me tightly, and kissed me over and over again.

"I am only back an hour," she said. "And how is Albert?"

"I have not seen Mr. Fanning this morning," I answered, and I tried to disengage myself from those cheery arms.

"Dear, dear, you don't look at all the thing," she said; "there's the brougham outside, would not you like a drive, honey? You and I might go out by ourselves. Come, dearie."

"No, thank you," I answered, "I am going on some special business for mother."

"Then whatever it is, can't you make use of the brougham? It was all built and painted to suit your style, love, and why should not you make use of it? Albert would be that proud."

"Oh, indeed he would not, Mrs. Fanning; but please do not speak of it, I cannot, I really cannot."

"Well, if you won't, you won't," said the good woman. "I have come back, though, and I hope to see a good deal of you; I have got lots to tell you. I have been collecting early reminiscences."

"Of what?" I could not help asking.

"Of Albert's babyhood and childhood, they are that touching. I found a little diary he used to keep. I declare I laughed and I cried over it. We'll read it together this evening. Now then, off you go, and do get some colour back into your pale cheeks; you are quite the prettiest, most graceful, most h'aristocratic young lady I ever saw; but you are too pale now, you really are."

I did not say any more; I grasped Mrs. Fanning's hand.

"How is your dear mother?" she said.

"Mother is not at all well."

"Ah, poor dear, poor dear," said Mrs. Fanning; "then no wonder your cheeks are pale. I said to Albert the very last night I left, 'Albert, if you win her, she's worth her weight in gold, it is a gold heart she has; you watch her with her mother, Albert, and think what she'll be to you.'"

"Mrs. Fanning, you really must not talk in that way," I said. "Please let me go."

She did let me go. My contact with her had slightly braced me. I felt angry once more with the terrible Albert; but Mrs. Fanning was kindness itself. Oh, if only Albert had been a different man, and I had really cared for him, and I —but why think of the impossible.

I got into an omnibus, and gave the man directions to put me down at the nearest point to the Duchess's house. I found myself echoing Jane Mullins's words, "Why had Jim Randolph gone away?"

I arrived at the Duchess's in good time. I had made up my mind to tell her all. She must lend us a thousand pounds. Mother must be saved; mother must be kept in the dark as to the utter ruin of my mad plan. I whispered the story as I would tell it to my old friend over and over to myself, and when I mounted the steps of the house and rang the bell I was trembling, and felt very faint and tired. The footman opened the door, and I inquired for her Grace.

"Can I see her?" I said. "I am Miss Wickham; I want to see her on very special business."

"I will mention that you have called, madam," replied the man; "but her Grace is not visible, she is very ill. She has been in bed for several days, and the doctor is with her. It is influenza."

Then, indeed, I felt my last hopes tottering.

"I am sorry her Grace is ill," I said. I paused for a moment to consider. "Can I see Miss Mitford?" I inquired then. Miss Mitford was a lady who did some correspondence for the Duchess, and who was generally to be found in the house.

Miss Mitford came downstairs immediately, and I saw her in a small room to the left of the great hall.

"It is the shock about Mr. Randolph," she said at once.

"Then is it really supposed that he was drowned in the *Star of Hope*?" I cried.

"He mentioned that he was coming to England by that boat," replied Miss Mitford. "The Duchess is certain that he is amongst the passengers, although his name has not been mentioned as yet in any list. Her Grace is terribly upset, more particularly as Mr. Severn, Sir Henry Severn's only son, died a fortnight ago. There is great confusion, and Mr. Randolph ought to be back."

I did not ask any questions with regard to this latter news, nor did it interest me in the very least. Of course Mr. Randolph ought to be back, but for very very different reasons. I went sorrowfully, oh so sorrowfully, away.

When I returned home Jane was waiting for me in the hall. She was hovering about, looking very untidy and very anxious.

"Well," she said; "come in here, I must speak to you."

"But it is luncheon time," I said, "and people will wonder."

"Let them wonder. Did you see her? Did she promise to lend it? That man has been here again. He is desperate, and says that if he is not paid in two days he will put in the bailiff."

"And what will that mean?" I asked.

"Ruin—utter and complete. But tell me, did you see the Duchess?"

"I did not," I answered; "she is ill in bed; and oh, Jane, it is the shock about Mr. Randolph which has caused her illness. The Duchess is quite sure that he did sail in the *Star of Hope*. O Jane! what is to be done?"

"God only knows," answered Jane Mullins; "we are up a tree, and that's the truth."

CHAPTER XXII

THE MAN IN POSSESSION

I cannot exactly say how the next two days went by. Even in a crisis, people get more or less accustomed to the thundercloud overhead, and the feeling of insecurity below. I still found that I could eat, I could walk, I could even sleep. I still found that I could be calm in my mother's presence, and could say little funny nothings to amuse her; and I sat in such a position, that she did not see the shadow growing and growing on my face, and the guests did not suspect anything. Why should they? They were enjoying all the good things of my most miserable failure.

Jane, however, never appeared in the drawing-room now; she left the entertaining of the visitors to me. She told me boldly that I must take it on me; that it was the least I could do, and I did take it on me, and dressed my best, and talked my best, and sang songs for our visitors in the evenings when my own heart was breaking.

Captain and Mrs. Furlong were very kind. They noticed how, more and more often, mother was absent from meals, and how the colour was paling from my cheeks with anxiety for her. It was truly anxiety for her, but they did not guess what principally caused it.

On the evening of the third day I hurried into the dining-room just before dinner. I quite forgot what I had gone for. It had been a brilliant May day, but in the evening a fog had come on—a heavy sort of cloud overhead, and there was a feeling of thunder in the air, and the atmosphere was close. I remember that the windows of the dining-room were wide open, and the long table was laid in its usual dainty, and even sumptuous, manner for dinner. There were some vases of flowers, and the plate, and china, the polished glass, the snowy napery, all looked as tasteful, as fresh, as pretty, as heart could desire. The guests were accustomed to this sort of table, and would have been very angry if they had been asked to sit down at any other.

Emma was hurrying in and out, putting final touches to the preparations for the great meal. I thought she looked pale, and very anxious, and just as I was entering the room she came up to me, and said in a hurried whisper—

"If I were you, Miss Westenra, I wouldn't go in."

"Why not?" I asked, "why should not I go into the dining-room?"

She did not say any more; but as I insisted on going in, pushed past me almost rudely, at least, I thought so at the moment, and went away, shutting the door after her. Then I discovered the reason why she had wished me not to go into the room. A little short man, stout and podgy, in a greasy coat, and a greasy waistcoat, and a dirty tie, rose as I entered.

"Beg pardon, miss," he said. He was seated in a chair not far from the window. He had a dirty newspaper on his lap, and by his side was a glass which must have contained beer at one time, but was now empty.

"I'm Scofield," he said, "Josiah Scofield at your service, miss. May I ask, miss, if you're Miss Wickham?"

"I am," I answered; "what are you doing here? Does Miss Mullins know you are here?"

"Yes, miss," answered the man in quite a humble, apologetic tone, "she knows quite well I am here, and so do Emma, the servant; and so do the other servants, and the reason why too, miss. It's on account of Pattens, I'm here, miss; and I've come to stay, if you please."

"To stay!" I echoed feebly, "to stay, why?"

"You see, miss," continued the man; "this is how things is. You're the daughter of the lady who owns this house, and I have heard that you own it partly yourself; and it's this paper that justifies me, miss, and I can't go out."

As he spoke, he pulled a long, ugly, foolscap envelope out of his pocket, and taking a paper from it, opened it, and showed it to me. I saw something about *Victoria*, and *by the grace of God*, and some other words in large, staring print, and then my own name, and my mother's, and Jane Mullins'; and I thrust it back again. I could not understand it, and I did not care to read any further.

"I have heard of men like you," I said slowly; "but I have never seen one of them before."

The man was gazing at me with his queer, bloodshot eyes, full of the strangest pity.

"It must be a horrid profession for you," I said suddenly. I could not help myself; at that moment I seemed to forget my own trouble in sorrow for the man who had to do such dirty work. Was my brain going?

Scofield did not answer my last remark. He put it aside as too foolish to require a reply.

"A very pretty young lady," I heard him mutter, "and I'm that sorry for her." He looked me all over.

"Now, miss," he said, "there are two ways of taking a man of my sort."

I nodded my head.

"There's the way of succumbing like, and going into hysterics, and making no end of a scene, and the man stays on all the same, and the neighbours get wind of it, and the ruin's complete in no time, so to speak. 'Taint nothing much of a bill that's owed to Pattens, and even if half of it was to be paid, I have not the slightest doubt that Pattens would take me out and give you a bit more time; but there's no use in quarrelling with me, nor telling me to go, for go I won't, and can't. I had my orders, and I'm the man in possession. You have got to face that fact, miss."

"But you spoke of two ways," I said. "What is the way which is not—not quite so hopeless?"

"Ah!" said the man, rubbing his hands, "now, we are coming to our senses, we are. Now I can manage matters fine."

I glanced at the clock. It was already seven o'clock, and we dined at half-past. The air outside seemed to grow heavier and heavier, and the sky to grow darker, and I expected the thunder to roll, and the lightning to flash at any moment: but what did external things matter. There was a storm in my heart which kept out the sound, and the meaning of external storms.

"Mother! mother!" I kept murmuring under my breath, "this will kill you, mother. O Mother! and it has been my fault. My wild, wild scheme has come to this!"

I felt so ill, that I could scarcely keep upright, and yet I could not sit in the presence of that man. The next moment everything in the room seemed to go round, and I was obliged to totter towards a chair. I think I lost consciousness, for when I came to myself, I found the little dirty greasy man had brought me a glass of water, and was standing near.

"You pluck up heart, child," he said, "there now, you're better. This is not the first nor the second time I have been in a house as big as this, and just as grand and full of visitors, and everything seemingly as right as possible, and the house undermined. I've seen scores of times like this, and pretty misses, like you, cut to the heart. It's a nasty trade is mine, but we all must live, my dear, and I'm truly sorry for you, and now, if you'll just let me advise you?"

"What?" I asked, "what?"

"You don't want the guests to know as I'm here?"

"Of course not."

"I must stay, and the servants had better know as little about me as possible. Of course, they have seen me already, but anyhow it is a sort of disguise that is commonly managed, and I had better do it."

"What do you mean?" I cried.

"My son, Robert, will be round directly. He often comes to me when I am in possession; I expect by the same token that's his ring I hear now. If you'll give me five shillings, miss, I'll do just what you want, and nobody need guess."

"But what? what?" I asked.

"Bob is bringing me my servant's livery, miss, and I'll attend at table to-night as your new man-servant. I look extremely well in livery, and I have often attended in the houses of gentry just as grand as yourself. Have you got five shillings in your pocket, miss? I have to earn my bread, and I can't do it for less. Nobody will guess who I am, and why I am here, if you'll give me that five shillings."

"Take it, take it," I cried. I thrust two half-crowns into his palm, and fled from the room. In the hall I found that I had run almost into the arms of Mr. Fanning.

"Why, Miss Wickham," he cried. He caught my hand to keep me from falling; "why, my dear, what is the matter?" he said then; there was a world of affection and sympathy in his voice, but I hated him for speaking to me thus.

"I have been feeling ill," I said, "I cannot go down to dinner."

"But what is wrong?" he said. He backed towards the dining-room door, and I did not want him to go in. He was so sharp; he would know at once what that little greasy man meant. I knew by his manner, and by hints that his mother had dropped, that they were both of them by no means in the dark with regard to our affairs. He must not go into the dining-room.

"Don't go in; come upstairs with me," I said.

"Oh, that I will, with pleasure," he answered, delighted at my tone, "and if you are really ill we must get the doctor. We cannot allow you to be really ill, you know, that would never do. I am very fond of nice girls like you; but they must keep their health, oh yes, they must. Now you are better, that is right. It's this horrid air, and the storm coming on. You want the country. It's wonderfully fresh at Highgate; splendid air; so bracing. I have been out at my place this afternoon, and I cannot tell you what a difference there is. It is like another climate."

"Then why don't you stay in your place?" I could not help answering. "What is it for, if you do not live there?"

"I won't live in it, Miss Wickham, until I bring my wife there to bear me company. But now if you are ill, do go to your room and rest; only come down to dinner, pray. I never could do with hysterical girls; but run upstairs and rest, there's a good child."

I left him, went to my attic, shut and locked the door, and threw myself on the ground. O God! the misery of that hour, the bitter blackness of it. But I must not give way; I must appear at dinner. Whatever happened I must not give way.

I got up, arranged my hair, washed my face and hands, dressed myself in the first evening dress I came across, and went downstairs. The beautiful little silver gong sounded, and we all trooped down to the dining-room. There were pleased smiles among the guests. The room was crowded. Every seat at the long table had its occupant. Several fresh paying guests had arrived, and there was the little man in livery helping Emma to wait. How pleased the old paying guests were to see him. The new paying guests took him as a matter of course. Mrs. Armstrong, in particular, nodded to Miss Armstrong, and bent across to Mr. Fanning and said—

"I am so pleased to see that poor Emma is getting a little help at last." And Mr. Fanning looked at me and gave me a broad, perceptible wink. I almost felt as if I must go under the table, but I kept up my courage as people do sometimes when they are at the stake, for truly it was like that to me. But mother was there, looking so sweet and fragile, and a little puzzled by the new waiter's appearance.

"What is your name?" I heard her say to him as he brought her some vegetables, and he replied in a smug, comfortable voice, "Robert, ma'am." And then she asked him to do one or two things, just as she would have asked our dear little page in the old days which had receded, oh! so far, into the background of my life.

That evening, in the drawing-room, Mrs. Fanning came up to me.

"They are all talking about Robert," she said.

She sat down, shading me by her own portly figure from the gaze of any more curious people.

"You shan't sing to-night," she said; "you're not fit for it, and I for one won't allow it. I told Albert I'd look after you. We'll have to make excuses to-morrow when *he's* not here."

"When who is not here?" I asked.

"The man they call Robert, who waited at dinner to-night."

"But he'll be here to-morrow," I said; "you know he will; you know it, don't you?"

She bent a little closer, and took my hand.

"Ah, dearie, my dearie," she said. "I have been low down once. It was before Albert the first made his fortune. I have been through tight times, and I know all about it. There, my dearie, take heart, don't you be fretting; but he won't be here to-morrow, my love."

"But he will," I said.

"He won't, darling. I know what I'm talking about. We must make excuses when he goes. We must say that he wasn't *exactly* the sort of servant Jane Mullins wanted, and that she is looking out for a smarter sort of man. Don't you fret yourself over it, my darling."

"Oh! I feel very sick and very tired," I cried. "Mrs. Fanning, will you make some excuse for me to mother? I must go upstairs and lie down."

"I'll have a talk with your mother, and I'll not let out a thing to her," said Mrs. Fanning, "and I'll take you up and put you right into bed myself. I declare you do want a little bit of mothering from a woman who has got abundant strength. Your own poor, dear mother would do it if she could, but she hasn't got the strength of a fly. I am very strong, dear, owing to Dr. Williams' Pink Pills, bless the man!"

Just at that moment Mr. Fanning came up.

He bent his tall, awkward figure towards his mother, and I distinctly heard the odious word "Robert," and then Mrs. Fanning took my hand and led me out of the drawing-room. She was very kind, and she helped me to get into bed, and when I was in bed she took my hand and said she was not going to stir until I fell asleep.

"For I have been through these times, my dear, but the first time is the worst of all," said the good woman, and she held my hand tightly, and in spite of myself her presence comforted me and I did drop asleep.

The next morning when I went down to breakfast I could not see any sign of Robert. Immediately afterwards I went into Jane's room.

"Where is the man in possession?" I said bitterly.

Jane's face looked a little relieved.

"Haven't you heard?" she said; "he has gone. It was Mr. Fanning who did it. He paid the bill in full, and the man has gone. He went last night. Mr. Fanning is arranging the whole thing, and the man in possession won't come back, that is, for the present. I begin to see daylight. I am glad you have made up your mind to be sensible, Westenra."

CHAPTER XXIII

ALBERT

I was so stunned I could not speak at all for a minute, then I said, after a brief pause—

"Do you know if Mr. Fanning is in?"

"No, why should he be in?" replied Miss Mullins in an almost irritable voice, "he has got his work to do if you have not. Men who are generous on the large scale on which he is generous, cannot afford to be idle—that is, if they are going on adding to their fortunes. He is out and probably in the city, he is a great publisher, you know, and extremely successful. For my part, I respect him; he may be a rough diamond, but he is a diamond all the same."

Still I did not speak, and I am sure my silence, and the stunned subdued heavy expression on my face, vexed Jane more than any amount of words I might have uttered.

"I will go and see if he has really gone," I said. "It is sometimes quite late before he starts for the city, I want to speak to him at once."

"Now, Westenra, if you in this crisis make mischief," began Miss Mullins.

"Oh, I won't make mischief," I said, "but I must speak to Mr. Fanning."

I had almost reached the door when she called me back.

"One moment," she said.

I turned, impatiently.

"Please don't keep me, Jane, I must see Mr. Fanning before he goes to the city —I will come back afterwards."

"If I wasn't almost sure what you are going to say to Mr. Fanning, I would let you go," said Jane, "but you ought to know—your mother was very ill, worse than I have ever seen her before, last night."

"Mother ill in the night, and you never told me!" The greater trouble seemed to swallow up the lesser, and for the time I forgot Mr. Fanning, the man in possession, and everything in the world except mother herself.

"She had a sharp attack," continued Jane, "rigors and extreme weakness. I happened most fortunately to go into her room about midnight, and found her in an alarming state. Dr. Anderson was summoned. She is better, much better, but not up yet."

"But, Jane, why, why did you not wake me?"

"I should, dear, if there had been real danger, but she quickly recovered. You looked so ill yourself last night, that I had not the heart to disturb your sleep. And there is no danger at present, no fresh danger, that is. Unless something happens to cause her a sudden shock, she is comparatively well, but it behoves you, Westenra, to be careful."

"And suppose I am not careful," I said, a sudden defiance coming into my voice.

"In that case——" said Miss Mullins. She did not finish her sentence. She looked full at me, raised her hands expressively, and let them fall to her sides.

Nothing could be more full of meaning than her broken sentence, her action, and the expression of her face.

"But you could not deliberately do it," she said slowly, "you could not expose a mother like yours to——"

"Of course I could do nothing to injure mother," I said, "I will try and be patient; but Jane, Jane, do you know really what this means? Can you not guess that there are things that even for a mother, a dying mother, a girl ought not to do?"

"I do not see that," answered Jane deliberately; "no, I do not, not from your point of view. You can do what is required, and you can bear it."

I knew quite well what she meant. She did not call me back this time when I left the room. I heard her mutter to herself—her words startled me—putting a new sort of sudden light on all our miserable affairs.

"My little home gone too," I heard her mutter, "ruin for me too, for me too."

I stood for a moment in the dark passage outside Jane's room. There was no one there, and I could think. I did not want to go into the big hall, nor to run up the staircase. I might meet some of those smiling, well satisfied, delighted and delightful paying guests, those paying guests who were ruining us all the time. Yes, I knew at last what Jane meant, what Mrs. Fanning meant, what Albert Fanning meant. We would be relieved from our embarrassments, mother would receive no shock *if I promised to marry Albert Fanning*. Albert Fanning would save the position, he would pay the necessary debts; he was rich, and for love of me he would not mind what he did. Yes, I supposed it was love for me. I did not know, of course. I could not fancy for a moment that a girl like myself could excite any feeling of worship in a man like Albert

Fanning, but anyhow, for whatever reason, he wanted me (and he did want me), he was willing to pay this big price for me. My heart trembled, my spirit quaked. I stood in the luxury of the dark passage, clasped my hands to my brow, and then determined not to give way, to be brave to the very end.

I ran upstairs and entered the drawing-room. It was tidy, in perfect order. I was glad to find no one there. I went and stood under father's picture. I gazed full up at the resolute, brave, handsome face.

"You died to win your V.C.," I said to myself, and then I turned to leave the room. I met Mrs. Furlong coming in.

"Ah, dear child," she said, "I am so glad to see you. But what is the matter? You don't look well."

"I am anxious," I answered; "mother had a very serious attack last night."

"We are all full of concern about her," replied Mrs. Furlong. "Won't you sit down for a moment? I wish to talk to you. Ah, here comes my husband. Philip, we have bad news about dear Mrs. Wickham, she was very ill last night."

"Your mother, Miss Wickham, is very far from strong," said Captain Furlong. He came and stood near me; he looked full of sympathy. He was very nice and kind and gentlemanly. He had been kind and courteous, and unselfish, ever since he came to the house.

"You are very good, both of you," I said. "I am going to mother now; please, don't keep me."

"But is there anything we can do? Would change be of service to her?" said Mrs. Furlong. "I know it is a little early in the year, but the spring is coming on nicely, and she must weary so of London, particularly this part of London; she has been accustomed to such a different life."

"I do not think our present life has injured her," I said. "She has not had any of the roughing. Things have been made smooth and pleasant and bright for her."

"All the same, it has been a very, very great change for her," said Mrs. Furlong. "It has been good neither for her nor for you. Yes, Philip," she continued, noticing a warning expression on her husband's face, "I have got my opportunity, and I will speak out. I am quite certain the sooner Westenra Wickham, and her dear mother, leave this boarding-house the better it will be for both of them. What has a young, innocent girl, like Westenra, to do with paying guests? Oh, if they were all like you and me, dear, it would be different; but they are not all like us, and there's that"—she dropped her voice. Captain Furlong shook his head.

"Miss Wickham has accepted the position, and I do not see how she can desert her post," he said.

"Never fear, be sure I will not," I answered; "but please—please, kind friends, don't keep me now."

"There is just one thing I should like to say before you go, Miss Wickham," said Captain Furlong; "if you find yourself in trouble of any sort whatever, pray command both my wife and myself. I have seen a good deal of life in my day. My wife and I are much interested, both in you and your mother. Now, for instance," he added, dropping his voice, "I know about tight times; we all of us get more or less into a tight corner, now and then—if a fifty pound note would——"

"Oh no, it would not do anything," I cried. My face was crimson; my heart seemed cut in two.

"Oh! how can I thank you enough?" I added; and I ran up to the kind man and seized his hands. I could almost have kissed them in my pain and gratitude. "It would be useless, quite useless, but I shall never forget your kindness."

I saw the good-natured pair look at one another, and Mrs. Furlong shook her head wisely; and I am sure a dewy moisture came to her eyes, but I did not wait to say anything more, but ran off in the direction of mother's room. A softened light filled that chamber, where all that refinement and love could give surrounded the most treasured possession of my life. Mother was lying in bed propped up by pillows. She looked quite as well as usual, and almost sweeter than I had ever seen her look, and she smiled when I came in.

"Well, little girl," she said, "you are late in paying me your visit this morning?"

"It was very wrong of you, mother, not to send for me when you were so ill last night," I answered.

"Oh, that time," said mother, "it seems ages off already, and I am quite as well as usual. I have got a kind nurse to look after me now. Nurse Marion, come here."

I could not help giving a visible start. Were things so bad with mother that she required the services of a trained nurse? A comely, sweet-faced, young woman of about thirty years of age, now approached from her seat behind the curtain.

"The doctor sent me in, Miss Wickham; he thought your mother would be the better for constant care for two or three days."

161

"I am very glad you have come," I answered.

"Oh, it is so nice," said mother; "Nurse Marion has made me delightfully comfortable; and is not the room sweet with that delicious old-fashioned lavender she uses, and with all those spring flowers?"

"I have opened the window, too," said the nurse, "the more air the dear lady gets the better for her; but now, Miss Wickham, I cannot allow your mother to talk. Will you come back again; or, if you stay, will you be very quiet?"

"As you are here to look after mother I will come back again," I said. I bent down, kissed the lily white hand which lay on the counterpane, and rushed from the room. Stabs of agony were going through my heart, and yet I must not give way!

I ran upstairs, and knocked at Mrs. Fanning's door. As Albert Fanning was out, I was determined to see her. There was no reply to my summons, and after a moment I opened the door and looked in. The room was empty. I went to my own room, sat down for a moment, and tried to consider how things were tending with me, and what the end would be. Rather than mother should suffer another pang, I would marry Albert Fanning. But must it come to this!

I put on my outdoor things, and ran downstairs. The closeness and oppression of the day before had changed into a most balmy and delicious spring morning; a sort of foretaste day of early summer. I was reckless, my purse was very light, but what did that matter. I stopped a hansom, got into it, and gave the man Albert Fanning's address in Paternoster Row. Was I mad to go to him—to beard the lion in his den? I did not know; I only knew that sane or mad, I must do what I had made up my mind to do.

The hansom bowled smoothly along, and I sat back in the farthest corner, and tried to hope that no one saw me. A pale, very slender, very miserable girl was all that they would have seen; the grace gone from her, the beauty all departed; a sort of wreck of a girl, who had made a great failure of her life, and of the happiness of those belonging to her. Oh, if only the past six or eight months could be lived over again, how differently would I have spent them! The cottage in the country seemed now to be a sort of paradise. If only I could take mother to it, I would be content to be buried away from the eyes of the world for evermore. But mother was dying; there would be no need soon for any of us to trouble about her future, for God Himself was taking it into His own hands, and had prepared for her a mansion, and an unfading habitation.

I scarcely dared think of this. Be the end long, or be the end short, during the remaining days or weeks of her existence, she must not be worried, she must go happily, securely, confidently, down to the Valley. That was the thought, the only thought which stayed with me, as I drove as fast as I could in the direction of Mr. Fanning's place of business.

The cab was not allowed to go up the Row, so I paid my fare at the entrance, and then walked to my destination. I knew the number well, for Albert had mentioned it two or three times in my hearing, having indeed often urged me to go and see him. I stopped therefore at the right place, looked up, saw the name of Albert Fanning in huge letters across the window, opened the door and entered. I found myself in a big, book saloon, and going up to a man asked if Mr. Fanning were in. The man was one of those smart sort of clerks, who generally know everybody's business but their own. He looked me all over in a somewhat quizzical way, and then said—

"Have you an appointment, miss?"

"I have not," I replied.

"Our chief, Mr. Fanning, never sees ladies without appointments."

"I think he will see me," I answered, "he happens to know me. Please say that Miss Westenra Wickham has called to see him."

The clerk stared at me for a moment.

"Miss West! what Wickham Miss? Perhaps you wouldn't mind writing it down."

I did not want to write down my name, but I did so; I gave it to the clerk, who withdrew, smiling to a brother clerk as he did so. He came back in a minute or two, looking rather red about the face, and went back to his seat without approaching me, and at the same time I heard heavy, ungainly steps rushing downstairs, and Mr. Fanning, in his office coat, which was decidedly shabby, and almost as greasy as the one which belonged to the "Man in Possession" on the previous evening, entered the saloon. His hair stood wildly up on his head, and his blue eyes were full of excitement. He came straight up to me.

"I say, this is a pleasure," he exclaimed, "and quite unlooked for. Pray, come upstairs at once, Miss Wickham. I am delighted to see you—delighted. Understand, Parkins," he said, addressing the clerk who had brought my message, "that I am engaged for the present, absolutely engaged, and can see *no one*. Now, Miss Wickham, now."

He ushered me as if I were a queen through the saloon, past the wondering and almost tittering clerks, and up some winding stairs to his own sanctum on the first floor.

"Cosy, eh?" he said, as he opened the door, and showed me a big apartment crowded with books of every shape and size, and heavily, and at the same time, handsomely furnished. "Not bad for a city man's office, eh?" he continued, "all the books are amusing; you might like to dip into 'em by-and-by, nothing deep or dull, or stodgy here, all light, frothy, and merry. Nothing improving, all entertaining. That is how my father made his fortune; and that is how I, Albert the second, as the mater calls me, intend to go on adding to my fortune. It is on light, frothy, palatable morsels that I and my wife will live in the future, eh, eh? You're pleased with the look of the place, ain't you. Now then, sit right down here facing the light, so that I can have a good view of you. You're so young; you have not a wrinkle on you. It's the first sign of age coming on when a girl wishes to sit with her back to the light, but you are young, and you can stand the full glare. Here, you take the office chair. Isn't it comfortable? That's where I have sat for hours and hours, and days and days; and where my father sat before me. How well you'd look interviewing authors and artists when they come here with their manuscripts. But there! I expect you'd be a great deal too kind to them. A lot of rubbish you would buy for the firm of Fanning & Co., wouldn't you now, eh? Ah, it's you that has got a tender little heart, and Albert Fanning has been one of the first to find it out."

I could not interrupt this rapid flow of words, and sat in the chair indicated, feeling almost stunned. At last he stopped, and gazing at me, said—

"Well, and how *is* Miss Westenra Wickham, and what has brought her to visit her humble servant? Out with it now, the truth, please."

Still I could find no words. At last, however, I said almost shyly—

"You have been kind, more than kind, but I came here to tell you, you must not do it."

"Now that's a pretty sort of thing to bring you here," said Mr. Fanning. "Upon my soul, that's a queer errand. I have been kind, forsooth! and I am not to be kind in the future. And pray why should I turn into an evil, cruel sort of man at your suggestion, Miss Wickham? Why should I, eh? Am I to spoil my fine character because you, a little slip of a girl, wish it so?"

"You must listen to me," I said; "you do not take me seriously, but you must. This is no laughing matter."

"Oh, I am to talk sense, am I? What a little chit it is! but it is a dear little thing in its way, although saucy. It's trying to come round me and to teach me. Well, well, I don't mind owning that you can turn me with a twist of your little finger wherever you please. You have the most bewitching way with you I ever saw with any girl. It has bowled Albert Fanning over, that it has. Now, then, what have you really come for?"

"You paid the bill of Pattens the butcher either this morning or last night, why did you do it?"

Mr. Fanning had the grace to turn red when I said this. He gave me even for a moment an uncomfortable glance, then said loudly—

"But you didn't surely want that fellow Robert to stay on?"

"That is quite true," I replied, "but I still less want you, Mr. Fanning, to pay our debts. You did very wrong to take such a liberty without my permission, very, very wrong."

"To tell you the honest truth, I never wished you to know about it," said Mr. Fanning. "Who blurted it out?"

"Jane Mullins, of course, told me."

"Ah, I mentioned to the mater that it would be very silly to confide in that woman, and now the little mater has done no end of mischief. She has set your back up and—but there, you were bound to know of it sooner or later. Of course the butcher's is not the only bill I must pay, and you were bound to know, of course. I don't really mind that you do know. It's a great relief to you, ain't it now?"

"It is not a great relief, and what is more I cannot allow it."

"You cannot allow it?"

"No."

Mr. Fanning now pulled his chair up so close to mine that his knees nearly touched me. I drew back.

"You needn't be afraid that I'll come closer," he said almost sulkily, "you know quite well what I feel about you, Miss Wickham, for I have said it already. I may have a few more words to deliver on that point by-and-by, but now what I want to say is this, that I won't force any one to come to me except with a free heart. Nobody, not even you—not even *you*—although, God knows, you are like no one else on earth, shall come to me except willingly. I never met any one like you before, so dainty, so fair so pretty— oh, so very pretty, and such a sweet girl and, upon my word, you can make just anything of me. But there, the time for love-making has not yet come, and you have something ugly to say in the back of your head, I see the thought shining out of your eyes. Oh, however hard you may feel, and however much pain you mean to give me, you cannot make those eyes of yours look ugly and forbidding. Now I am prepared to listen."

He folded his arms across his chest and looked full at me. He was in such great and desperate earnest that he was not quite so repellant as usual. I could not but respect him, and I found it no longer difficult to speak freely to him.

"I come as a woman to appeal to a man," I said. "You are a man and I am a woman, we stand on equal ground. You would not like your sister, had you a sister, to do what you want me to do. I appeal to you on behalf of that sister who does not exist."

He tried to give a laugh, but it would not rise to his lips.

"As you justly remarked," he said, "I have not got a sister."

"But you know, you must know, Mr. Fanning, what you would feel if you had a sister, and she allowed a man who was no relation, no relation whatever, to take her debts and pay them. What would you think of your sister?"

"I'd say the sooner she and that chap married the better," was Mr. Fanning's blunt response; "they'd be relations then fast enough, eh, eh? I think I have about answered you, Miss Wickham."

"But suppose she did not want to marry that man; suppose she had told him that she never would marry him; suppose he knew perfectly well in his heart that she could not marry him, because she had not a spark of love to give him?"

"But I don't suppose anything of the sort," said Mr. Fanning, and now his face grew white, uncomfortably white, and I saw his lips trembling.

"There now," he said, "you have had your say, and it is my turn. I see perfectly well what you are driving at. You think I have taken an unfair advantage of you, but this was the position. I knew all about it, I had seen it coming for some time. Jane Mullins had dropped hints to mother, and mother had dropped hints to me, and, good gracious! I could tell for myself. I am a man of business; I knew exactly what each of the boarders paid. I knew exactly or nearly to a nicety, and if I didn't my mother did, what the dinners cost which we ate night after night in your dining-room, and what the furniture must have cost, and what the breakfast cost, and the hundred and one things which were necessary to keep up an establishment of that kind, and I said to the mater, 'Look you here, mater, the incomings are so and so, and the outgoings are so and so, and a smash is *inevitable*. It will come sooner or later, and it is my opinion it will come sooner, not later.' The mater agreed with me, for she is shrewd enough, and we both thought a great deal of you, and a great deal of your mother. We knew that although you were dainty in your ways, and belonged to a higher social class than we did (we are never going, either of us, to deny that), we knew that you were ignorant of these things, and had not our wisdom, and we thought Jane Mullins was a bit of a goose to have launched in such a hopeless undertaking. But, of course, as the mater said, she said it many, many times, 'There may be money at the back of this thing, Albert, and if there is they may pull through.' But when Mr. Randolph went off in that fine hurry last winter, we found out all too quickly that there was no money at the back, and then, of course, the result was inevitable.

"I expected Pattens to send a man in, for I had met him once or twice, and he told me that his bill was not paid, and that he did not mean to supply any more meat, and what Pattens said the baker and greengrocer said too, and so did Allthorp the grocer, and so did the fishmonger, Merriman, and so did all the other tradespeople, and if one spoke to me, so did they all. I have paid Pattens, but that is not enough. Pattens won't trouble you any more, his man has gone, but there is Merriman's man to come on, and there is Allthorp's man, and there are all the others, and then, above and beyond all, there's the landlord, Mr. Hardcastle. Why, the March quarter's rent has not been paid yet, and that is a pretty big sum. So, my dear young lady, things *cannot* go on, and what is to be done? Now there's the question—what is to be done?"

I stared at him with frightened eyes. It was perfectly true that I knew nothing whatever about business. I had imagined myself business-like, and full of common sense, but I found in this extreme moment that my business qualities were nowhere, and that this hard-headed and yet honest man of the world was facing the position for me, and seeing things as I ought to see them.

"What is to be done?" he repeated. "Are you going to have the bed on which your mother sleeps sold under her, and she dying, or are you not? I can help you, I have plenty of money, I have a lot of loose cash in the bank which may as well go in your direction as any other. Shall I spend it for you, or shall I not?"

"But if you do—if you do," I faltered, "what does it mean?"

"Mean!" he said, and now a queer light came into his eyes, and he drew nearer again, and bending forward tried to take my hand. I put it hastily behind me.

"I'll be frank," he said, "I'll be plain, *it means you.*"

"I cannot, oh! I cannot," I said. I covered my face with both my hands; I was trembling all over.

"Give me your promise," he said, dropping his voice very low, "just give me your promise. I'll not hurry you a bit. Give me your promise that in the future, say in a year (I'll give you a whole year, yes I will, although it goes hard with me)—say in a year, you will be mine, you'll come to me as my little wife, and I won't bother you, upon my soul I won't, before the time. I'll go away from 17 Graham Square, I will, yes I will. The mater can stay, she likes looking after people, and she is downright fond of you, but I won't worry you. Say you'll be my little wife, and you need not have another care. The bills shall be paid, and we'll close the place gradually. The boarding-house, on its present terms, cannot go on, but we will close up gradually, and poor old Miss Mullins need not be a pauper for the rest of her days. She's a right down good sort, and I'll tell you what I'll do. I'll start her in a little boarding-house of a humble kind on my own hook. Yes, I will, and she shall make a tidy fortune out of it. I'll do all that, and for you, for *you*, and you have only got to promise."

"But I cannot," I said, and now I began to sob. "Oh, I cannot. You don't want a wife who doesn't love you at all."

"Not even a little bit?" he said, and there was a pathetic ring in his voice. "Aren't you sure that you love me just a very little bit? Well, well, you will some day; you will when you know me better. I am a very rough sort of diamond, Miss Wickham, but I am a diamond all the same, if being true and honourable and honest and straightforward means anything at all. I don't want to speak too well of myself, but I do know that in my entire life I have never done a real mean or shabby thing. I am an honest fellow out and out, Miss Wickham, and I offer you all I have, and I will get you out of this scrape in a twinkling, that I will. You thought, perhaps, your fine friend Mr. Randolph would do it, but when he guessed how things were going he cut off fast enough to the other side of the world."

"I won't let you speak of him like that," I cried, and my voice rose again with anger, and the pity I had felt for Mr. Fanning a moment ago vanished as if it had never existed. "Mr. Randolph has been our true, true friend, and he may be dead now. Oh, you are cruel to speak of him like that!"

"Very well, we won't talk of him. It is unkind to abuse the dead," said Mr. Fanning in a low, considerate sort of voice. "He sailed, poor chap, in the *Star of Hope*, and the *Star of Hope* has been wrecked. He will never come back to bother anybody again, so we won't talk of him."

I was silent. A cold, faint feeling was stealing over me.

"Well, now, you listen to me," continued Mr. Fanning. "You think that it is very hard on you that a man of my sort should want you to be his wife, but men of my sort, when they make fortunes, often do marry girls like you. I have a lot of money, Miss Wickham, plenty and plenty, thousands upon thousands, and it's piling up every day. It is the froth and the light literature that has done it—all those picture-books, coloured, most of 'em, and those children's books, and those nonsense rhymes, and all that sort of thing. We have huge sales all over the world, and the money rolls in for Albert Fanning, and Albert Fanning can marry about any girl he chooses. Why shouldn't he take a wife a peg above him? It's done every day, and why should not his wife be happy? What is there against that house at Highgate, for instance, and what is there against the old woman? Is there an honester or a better heart than hers?"

"That is quite true; I really love your mother," I said.

"Ah, that's a good girl, now." He laid his big hand on mine and gave it a little pat. "And you'll be all right when you come to me; you'll be as comfortable as possible. You'll soon get accustomed to me and my ways."

"But I can never, never come to you," I cried, shrinking away. "I cannot make you that promise."

"I won't take your answer now, and I have not done speaking yet. Do you know that I have cared for you for a long time? I'll tell you how it happened. I was in the Park one day, more than two years ago. I had been in Germany, learning book-binding. There was nothing I did not go into as far as my trade was concerned, and I had come back again, and I was in the Park watching the fine folks. My pockets were comfortably lined, and I had not a debt in the world, and I was feeling pretty spry, you may be sure, and thinking, 'Albert Fanning, the time has come for you to take a mate; the time has come for you and your sweetheart to meet, and to have a right good time, and a happy life afterwards.' And I was thinking which of the suburbs I'd live in, and what sort of girl I'd have. Oh, there were plenty ready to come to me for the asking, young girls, too, with rosy cheeks and bright eyes. There was one, I never saw blacker eyes than hers; they were as black as sloes, and I always admired black eyes, because I am fair, you know, and the mater is fair. You always like your opposite as a rule, and as these thoughts were coming to me, and I was thinking of Susan Martin and her black eyes, and the merry laugh she had, and her white teeth, who should come driving slowly by, in the midst of all the other grand folks, but your little self. You were bending forward, doing something for your mother, putting a shawl about her or something, and you just gave the tiniest bit of a smile, and I saw a gleam of your teeth, and I looked at your grey eyes; and, upon my word, it was all over with me. I never knew there were girls like you in existence before. I found myself turning at first white and then red, and at first hot and then cold, and I followed that carriage as fast as I could, and whenever I had a chance I took a glance at you. Oh, you were high above me, far away from me, with people that I could never have anything to do with; but I lost my heart to you, and Susan Martin hadn't a chance. I found out from the mater that you were Miss Wickham, and that your father had been a general officer in the army, and you lived in Mayfair, and went into society; and often and often I went into the Park to catch a glimpse of you, and I got the number of your house, and sometimes I passed it by and looked up at the windows, and once I saw you there; you were arranging some flowers. I just caught the bend of your head, and I saw the shape of your throat, and your straight profile, and the whole look of you, and my heart went pitter-pat. I wasn't myself after I had caught a glimpse of you. You filled all my world, and the old mater found out there was something wrong. I am reserved about some things, and I didn't let it out to her, but at last I did, and she said, 'Courage, Albert, courage. If you want her, why shouldn't you have her? You have plenty of money, and you're a right good sort.' And then all of a sudden one day the mater came to me with news, no less news than this, that you, you plucky little darling, were going to start a boarding-house on your own account. After that, it was plain sailing."

"She is poor," said the mother. "She and her mother have lost all their money; they are down in the world, down on their luck, and they are going to do this. So then we arranged that we'd come and live in the boarding-house, and I began my courting in hot earnest, and fortune has favoured me, Miss Wickham; fortune has favoured me, Westenra, and oh! I love you, God knows how much, and I'd be a good husband to you, and you should have your own way in everything. Won't you think of it, Miss Wickham? Won't you?"

I was silent. The tears were running down my cheeks, and I had no voice to speak. I got up at last slowly.

"Won't you think of it?" he said again.

I shook my head.

"Well, I tell you what," he said, turning very pale. "Don't give me your answer now. Wait until this evening or to-morrow. I won't worry you in the drawing-room to-night. I'll keep far away, and I'll try if I can to keep everybody at bay—all those wolves, I mean, that are surrounding you—and maybe you'll think better of it, for the position is a very serious one; maybe you'll think better of it. And remember, whatever happens, there ain't a fellow on earth would make you a better husband than I shall, if you'll let me."

CHAPTER XXIV

THE BOND

I went slowly home. I walked all the way, I was glad of the exercise, I wanted to tire my body in order that my mind should not think too acutely. When I got in, it was lunch time. I went into the dining-room without taking off my hat. Jane Mullins was there, as usual she was at the foot of the table, she was busy carving, and she was chatting to Mrs. Armstrong, and Mrs. Armstrong was looking somewhat mysterious, and when she saw me she gave me a kindly nod, but I perceived the curiosity in her eyes and turned my face away.

Marion Armstrong was seldom in to lunch, she was at her School of Art doing those drawings by which she hoped to win the hand of Albert Fanning. But what chance had she of Albert Fanning?

Mrs. Fanning was present, and she looked very stout and prosperous, and mysterious and happy, and as I sat down, not far away from her, she suddenly stretched her fat hand across the table and grasped mine and said—

"How are you, dear, and how is your mother?"

I answered that I hoped mother was better, and Captain and Mrs. Furlong looked at me also with pity. I had never greater difficulty in keeping my composure than I had during that awful meal, but I did eat a cutlet when it was put on my plate, and I did manage to talk to my neighbour, a new boarder who had come up from the country, and did not know her way about anywhere. She was an excitable middle-aged lady of between forty and fifty, and she asked questions which I was able to answer, and helped me more than she knew to get through that terrible meal.

At last it was over and I went up to mother's room. To my great astonishment it was empty. Where was mother? Was she better? What could have happened? With a mingling of alarm and anticipation I ran into the drawing-room. She was there in her old accustomed seat by the window. She looked very much as usual. When she saw me she called me over to her.

"Are you surprised, West?" she said.

"I am greatly surprised," I answered; "are you better, Mummy?" I bent over her, calling her by the old childish, very childish name. She laid her thin hand on mine, her hand was hot, but her face looked, with the colour in her cheeks, and her eyes so feverishly bright, more beautiful than I had ever seen it. I sat down near her.

"You don't know how nice Nurse Marion has been," she said. "When she found I really wished to get up, she did not oppose me, and she dressed me so carefully, and I am not the least bit tired. I longed to come into the drawing-room, I seem to have quite got over that attack; you need not be anxious, West."

"Very well, I won't be anxious," I answered; "I will sit close to you here and read to you if you will let me."

"I should love to hear you, darling. Read Whittier's poem, 'My Psalm.' Some of the lines have been ringing in my head all day, and I always like the sort of cadence in your voice when you read poetry aloud."

I knew Whittier's "Psalm" well, and without troubling to get the book, I began to repeat the well-known words—

I mourn no more my vanished years:

    Beneath a tender rain,

An April rain of smiles and tears,

    My heart is young again.

The west-winds blow, and singing low,

    I hear the glad streams run;

The windows of my soul I throw

    Wide open to the sun.

No longer forward nor behind,

    I look in hope and fear:

But grateful, take the good I find,

    The best of now and here."

As I slowly repeated the words, I noticed that mother's gentle soft eyes were fixed on my face. She raised her hand now and then as if to beat time to the rhythm of the poetry. At last I reached the final verses.

"Say them slowly, West," whispered mother; "I know them so well, and they have comforted me so often. Say them very slowly, in particular that verse which speaks about death as 'but a covered way,'"

I continued—

That more and more a Providence

Of Love is understood,

Making the springs of time and sense

    Sweet with eternal good;

That death seems but a covered way,

    Which opens into light,

Wherein no blinded child can stray

    Beyond the Father's sight;

That care and trial seem at last,

    Through Memory's sunset air,

Like mountain-ranges overpast

    In purple distance fair;

That all the jarring notes of life

    Seem blending in a psalm,

And all the angles of its strife

    Slow rounding into calm.

And so the shadows fall apart,

    And so the west-winds play;

And all the windows of my heart

    I open to the day."

"Ah," said mother, when my voice finally ceased, it had very nearly failed me towards the end, "that is just how I am. I sit by the open window, I look out and beyond, I see no trouble anywhere. The peace is wonderful, wonderful. It is all my Father's doing, my heavenly Father's doing. I am so strangely happy that I cannot quite understand myself. Last night something strange happened, West. Your dear father, my beloved husband, came back to me."

"Mother!" I cried.

"Yes," she said very gently, "he did; you will understand some day, I cannot explain what happened. He came to my room. He looked at me with your eyes, my darling, only older and more grave; eyes with the weight of the knowledge of life in them, and the understanding of the Life beyond in them. He looked at me, and there was both joy and sorrow in his eyes, and the joy seemed greater than the sorrow. He even took my hand in his, and I fancied I heard him say something about our going away together, but I am not quite sure on that point. I only know that he was with me, and that now I feel no pain. Nothing can trouble me again. Even dying cannot trouble me. West, my child, what are you crying for?"

"Oh, I am not crying at all, mother, only, somehow, there is a pathos in your words, but I am not crying."

She took my hand and patted it softly.

"You have no cause for tears, as far as I am concerned," she said. "I am the happiest woman in the world, I have had a happy life, such a husband, so dear a daughter, and now this wonderful, wonderful peace, this joy, and there is no death, dear West, for those who really love; there is no real parting for those who love."

From where we sat we could see the trees in the Square garden. They had put on their spring green, and most lovely was the mantle they wore. The dust of London had not yet had time to spoil them. The freshness of their appearance on that May morning was as vivid, as perfect, as though those trees lived themselves in the heart of the country; they seemed to be a little bit of God in the middle of that town Square. I kept watching them, and glancing from time to time at mother, but all through there was in my mind another thought, the thought of Mr. Fanning and what he wanted me to do. After all, if the end of life was so full of bliss, what mattered any cross on the journey. I felt ready for sacrifice. I rose very slowly, and softly left the drawing-room.

By a sort of common consent, the boarders had all gone out on this exquisite early summer's afternoon, and mother and I had the room to ourselves. Even Mrs. Fanning had gone out. I crossed the landing, and went into mother's bedroom. Nurse Marion was there. I shut the door behind me.

"How long will mother live?" I said abruptly. I was in the humour not to walk round anything that day; I wanted to hear the truth, the whole truth, and nothing but the truth.

Nurse Marion looked at me in astonishment.

"You don't look well yourself, Miss Wickham," she answered.

"Never mind about me," I replied, "answer my question. If nothing harms her, if she gets no shock, how long will my mother live?"

"She may live for months and months," replied the nurse.

"And if she gets a shock, a sudden shock?"

"Ah!" the woman held up her hands ominously, "we must keep her from any thing of that sort, even a very little agitation would be bad for her; but I never saw a calmer, sweeter lady. She does not know she is dying, but why should

174

she be troubled, she is close to God Himself, she lives in a sort of Paradise."

"Thank you," I answered. The tears were pressing hard on my eyes, but I would not let them fall.

"She thinks all the world of you, Miss Wickham," continued the nurse. "If she has an anxiety, it is about you; but even for you I do not think she feels real fear now. You will forgive me for speaking so frankly, but I can tell, miss, for I have seen much sorrow myself, that you are perplexed and puzzled and miserable just now, but I assure you you need not be sorry on your mother's account. She lives in the Land of Beulah. Have you ever read the 'Pilgrim's Progress'? You know, of course, to what I allude?"

"I know to what you allude," I answered; "the Land of Beulah is a beautiful country, but I am too young to understand about it."

"We are none of us too young to understand about that," replied the nurse. "I have been with many people suffering as your mother suffers, but I never before came across any one quite so gentle, so resigned, so happy, so peaceful,—*it is the peace of God.*"

"We must keep her as long as we can," I said; "she is the most precious thing in all the world; we must keep her as long as we ever can. She must not have a shock nor a care."

"Of course not," answered the nurse.

I returned again to the drawing-room, taking some needlework with me. I sat near mother plying my needle, weaving a pattern with coloured silks into my embroidery.

"How lovely the day is!" said mother. She made little remarks of this sort from time to time, but she did not do what was her invariable habit, and the fact of her omitting to do this caused me some surprise. As a rule, whenever she looked at any one, she generally ended by glancing at father's picture, but to-day she did not once look at it. This impressed me as so very strange and so unlike her, that I said—

"Can't you see the picture from where you sit?" We always called it *the* picture; it was the one picture for us both.

"I can see it perfectly if I want to," she answered, "but I do not care to look at it to-day. I see his own face wherever I turn, that is much more lifelike, and more interesting, and has more varied expressions than the dear picture can have. He was with me last night, and he is here now. You cannot see him, West, but I can."

"Mother," I said, "you talk as if you were ill. Do you think you are ill?"

"Oh no, darling, just a little weak, but that soon passes. There is nothing to be alarmed about, Westenra. The fact of a person being thoroughly happy does not surely mean that that person is in danger."

"I am so glad you are happy," I said.

"I am wonderfully so; it is the glad presence of God Himself, and also of your dear father. If I have a wish in the world," continued mother then slowly, and she looked at me as she spoke, "it is to see James Randolph. I cannot imagine why he does not write. He has been very good to me, and I like him much. He is a dear fellow, full of courtesy and chivalry; he has a gentle, tender, brave heart; he would make the girl he loves happy, very happy. I should like to see him again, and to thank him."

I did not dare to tell mother what we all now firmly believed with regard to Mr. Randolph. I tried to thread my needle, but there was a mist before my eyes. The needlework nearly fell from my hand. Suddenly, in the midst of our conversation in the quiet drawing-room, I heard a commotion. Some one— two people were coming upstairs—the steps of one were heavy, there was an altercation in the landing, a voice pleaded with another voice, and the strange voice got loud and angry.

I half rose from my seat, and then sat down again.

"What is the matter?" asked mother; "you look very white, Westenra. Is there anything wrong?"

"I don't want strangers to come here just now," I said.

"But you forget, my dear child, that this is everybody's drawing-room. This cosy corner is my special seat, but we cannot possibly keep our boarders out —it is impossible, my darling."

She had scarcely said the words before the door burst open, and a man with red hair and red whiskers, in a loud check suit, entered.

"Ah," he said, "I thought as much; I thought I'd get to headquarters if I came here. Now, is this lady Mrs. Wickham, and is this young lady Miss Wickham? Now, Miss Mullins, I will see them for myself, please; you cannot keep me back; I am determined to have my rights, and——"

I rushed towards the door. One glance at mother's face was enough. It had turned white, the blue look came round her lips, there was a startled gleam in her eyes.

"What is it?" she said, and she looked at Jane.

"Go to her, Jane; stay with her," I said; "I will manage this man. Go to her, and stay with her."

Jane went to mother, and I rushed up to the man.

"I am Miss Wickham," I said; "I know what you want. Come with me into the next room."

He followed me, muttering and grumbling.

"Why shouldn't I see Mrs. Wickham—she is at the head of this establishment? My name is Allthorp; you are all heavily in my debt, and I want to know the reason why I don't see the colour of my money."

"Oh! please do not speak so loud," I implored.

"Why?" he asked. "I am not mealy-mouthed. I want my money, and I am not afraid to ask for it."

"I tell you, you shall have your money, but do not speak so loud. Mrs. Wickham is ill."

"Ah, that's a fine excuse. That's what Miss Mullins tried to put me off with. Miss Mullins seems to be a sort of frost, but I was determined either to see you or Mrs. Wickham."

"I am Miss Wickham."

"And the house belongs to you? I can sue you if I like for my money."

"Certainly you can, and I hope if you sue any one it will be me. How much is owed to you?"

"Eighty-nine pounds, and I tell you what it is, Miss Wickham. It's a shame when a man works hard from early morning to late at night, a black shame that he should not be paid what is due to him. I'd like to know what right you have to take my tea and my coffee, and to eat my preserved fruits, and to make your table comfortable with my groceries, when you never pay me one farthing."

"It is not right," I answered; "it is wrong, and you shall be paid in full." I took a little note-book and entered the amount.

"Give me your address," I said; "you shall be paid."

He did so.

"I'll give you twenty-four hours," he said. "If at the end of that time I do not receive my money in *full*, yes, in *full*, mark you, I'll have a man in. I hear it answered very well in the case of Pattens, and it shall answer well in my case. So now you have had my last word."

He left the room noisily and went downstairs. I waited until I heard the hall-door slam behind him, and then I went back to mother. She was leaning back in her chair; her eyes were closed. I bent over her and kissed her.

"What is it, West? What did that horrid man want?"

"He has gone, darling; he won't trouble us any more."

"But I heard him say something about a *debt*. Is he owed any money?"

"He was very troublesome because his account was not paid quite as soon as he wished," I said; "but that is nothing. He shall have a cheque immediately."

"But I do hope, dear Miss Mullins," said mother, turning to her and looking at her fixedly, "that you pay the tradespeople weekly. It is so much the best plan."

"Quite so," she answered.

"This house is doing splendidly, is it not?" said mother. "We shall make a fortune if we stay on here long enough?"

"Oh, quite so," answered Miss Mullins.

I stole out of the room again. Mother looked satisfied, and although her cheeks were a little too bright in colour, I hoped no grave mischief was done.

I ran downstairs. It was nearly four o'clock. I determined to wait in the hall or in the dining-room, in case any more of those awful men—wolves, Albert Fanning had called them—should arrive. Mother must not be troubled: mother must not run such an awful risk again. Just then I heard steps approaching, and there was the sound of a latch-key in the hall door. Most of our guests had latch-keys. I do not know what I noticed in that sound, but I knew who was there. I entered the hall. Mr. Fanning had come in. He did not expect to see me, and he started when he saw my face. I had never cared for Mr. Fanning—never, never. I had almost hated him rather than otherwise; but at that moment I looked at him as a deliverer. There was no one there, and I ran up to him.

"Come into the dining-room," I said. "I must speak to you," and I caught his hand. His great hand closed round mine, and we went into the dining-room, and I shut the door.

"One of them came," I said, "and—and nearly killed mother, and I promised that he—that he should be paid. His name is Allthorp. He has nearly killed mother, and he nearly killed me, and—and will you pay him, and will you pay the others?"

"Do you mean it?" said Albert Fanning. "Do you mean it? Are you asking me to do this, clearly understanding?"

"Clearly, clearly," I said.

"And may I kiss you, just to make the bond all sure?"

"You may," I said faintly. He bent forward, and I felt his kiss on my forehead.

CHAPTER XXV

YOU ARE A GOOD MAN

Within a week every debt was paid absolutely and in full. Even the landlord was abundantly satisfied. Jane Mullins lost her look of care, and became cheerful and fat and good-tempered once more. The boarders, who had been merry enough and careless enough all through, suspecting nothing, of course, seemed now to be beside themselves with merriment. The weather was so fine and the house was so pleasant. Jane Mullins quite came out of her shell. She told stories of her early life, and made those boarders who sat near her at dinner quite roar with laughter, and Captain and Mrs. Furlong also came out of their shells, and were most agreeable and kind and chatty; and mother came down to dinner as usual, and sat in the drawing-room as usual, and in the evenings there was music, and I sang my songs and played my pieces and wore my very prettiest dresses, and Albert Fanning looked at me, and looked at me, and Mrs. Fanning nodded approval at me.

Mrs. Armstrong, too, became strangely mysterious, wreathing her face in smiles now and then, and now and then looking strangely sour and disappointed, and Marion Armstrong began to flirt with a young German who had arrived. We never did want to have foreigners in the establishment, but he offered to pay a big sum for a certain room, and Jane said it would be the worst policy to leave him out. He satisfied Marion Armstrong too, which was another thing to be considered, for Marion and her mother were the sort of boarders who are always more or less the backbone of a house like ours. They stay on and on; they pay their money weekly. They speak of their aristocratic neighbours, and are mostly advertisements themselves.

Now that the German, Herr Tiegel, had come, there was certainly very little chance of Mrs. and Miss Armstrong taking their departure until the end of the season.

Jane used to go and have long talks with mother, and spoke about the future, and the extensions we should make, and Albert and his mother too talked about possible extensions. Mrs. Fanning whispered darkly to me that Albert had large ideas now with regard to the boarding-house.

"It's wonderful, my love, the interest he takes in it," she said; "I never saw anything like it in the whole course of my life, and for a publisher too! But his idea is no less than this: When the lease of the next house falls in, we take it too, and break open doors, and have the two houses instead of one. He says the two houses will pay, whereas the one don't, and never could. The boarders, poor things! think that they are doing us a splendid good turn, but this house ain't paying, and it never will, my love."

To these sort of remarks I never made any answer. I was quite cheerful; I had to be cheerful for mother's sake, and it was only at night I let myself go. Even then I tried hard to sleep well and to shut away the future.

Albert Fanning and I, by tacit consent, hardly ever met alone, and that future life which we were to lead together, when a year had expired, was not spoken of between us. A fortnight, however, after all the debts had been paid, and the house had been put upon a very sure and very firm foundation once more, Mrs. Fanning came softly to me where I was sitting in the drawing-room.

"Do you mind going into the little room for a moment," she said.

The little room was on the same floor, it was the room where I had seen Althorp on that dreadful day when I had bound myself in a bondage in many ways worse than death.

"Why?" I asked, looking at her with frightened eyes. She took my hand and patted it softly.

"You are a very good girl and a very brave one," she said, "and there's nothing Albert and I wouldn't do for you. Albert wants to have a chat with you, he's waiting in the other room; you go along, dear. Oh, after the first blush you won't mind a bit; go, dear, go."

I looked at mother, who was talking with Mrs. Furlong. The whole room was peaceful and quiet, a good many of the boarders were out, for it was now the height of the season and almost midsummer. The windows were wide open. I caught mother's eye for an instant; mother smiled at me. Of late she used to wear a very far away look. There was often an expression in her eyes which seemed to say that she and father were holding converse. I caught that glance now, and it steadied my own nerves, and stilled the rebellion at my heart. I got up steadily. Had my stepping down—oh, had my stepping down led to this? It was a bitter thought, and yet when I looked at mother, and felt that I had saved her from intolerable anguish and perhaps sudden death, I felt that it was worth while. I went into the next room.

Albert Fanning, before our engagement—(oh yes, of course, we were engaged, I must use the hated word)—Albert before our engagement had thought little or nothing of his dress, but now he was extremely particular. An evening suit had been made to fit his tall ungainly person by one of the best tailors in the West End. He was wearing it now, and his light flaxen hair was standing up straighter than ever, and he had a kind of nervous smile round his lips. When he saw me enter he came forward and held out his hand.

"Well," he said, "and how is Westenra? Sit down, won't you?"

I did sit down; I sat where some of the summer breeze coming in from across the Square garden could fan my hot cheeks. I sat down trembling. He stood perfectly still an inch or two away from me. He did not attempt to take my hand again. After a pause, being surprised at his stillness, I looked up at him; I saw his blue eyes fixed on my face, with a very hungry expression. I sighed heavily.

"Oh," I said, "you have been so very good, and I have never even thanked you."

"You never have after, just the first day," he said; "but I did not expect thanks. Thanks were not in the bond, *you* were in the bond, you know. That is all I want."

He sat down then near me, and we both must have felt the same summer breeze blowing on our faces.

"I am picturing the time when the year is out," he said slowly, "when you and I are away together in the country. I never cared much for the country, nor for nature, nor for anything of that sort, but I think I should like those things if you were with me. You embody a great deal to me, you make poetry for me. I never knew what poetry was before. I never cared for anything but nonsense rhymes and matters of that sort, until I met you, but you make poetry and beauty for me and all the best things of life. There is nothing I won't promise to do for you when you come to me, and in the meantime——"

"Yes," I said, "in the meantime."

"If you are certain sure, Westenra, that you are going to keep your bond, why, I—I won't worry you more than I can help just at present."

"Certain sure that I am going to keep my bond? Yes, I am sure," I said. "Would I take your money and, and deceive you? Would I have asked you to save us and deceive you? No, no; you think I am good. I am not specially good, but I am not so low as that."

"Dear child," he said, and now he took my hand and stroked it softly. He did not squeeze it, or draw it near to him, but he laid it on one of his own huge palms and kept on stroking it.

"The very prettiest little paw I ever saw in my life," he said then; "it's wonderful how slim it is, and how long, and how white, and what little taper fingers; it's wonderful. I never saw anything like it. You are a poem to me, that's just what you are, Westenra, you are a poem to me, and you will make a new man of me, and you will keep the bond, won't you, dear?"

"I will," I said.

"I have put down the date," he said; "I put it down in my note-book; I am going to keep it *always* by me; it is writ in my heart too. I declare I am getting poetical myself when I look at you. It's writ in my heart in gold letters. It was the 18th of May when you promised yourself to me, dear. May is not a lucky month to marry in, so we will marry on the first of June of next year. You'll promise me that, won't you?"

"Yes," I said.

"And in the meantime very likely you would rather not have it known."

"It has been most kind and generous of you and Mrs. Fanning not to speak of it," I answered.

"Just as you like about that; but I can see that, with the care of your mother and one thing or another you find me rather in the way, so I thought I would tell you that I am going off, I am going to Germany to begin with for a fortnight, and then I shall take lodgings in town. Oh, the house at Highgate won't hold me until it holds my little wife as well, but I won't live in this house to be a worry to you morning, noon, and night. And when I am not always there perhaps you'll think of me, and how faithful I am to you, and how truly, truly I love you; and you will think, too, of what you are to me, a poem, yes, that's the right word, a beautiful poem, something holy, something that makes a new man of me, the most lovely bit of a thing I ever saw. Sèvres china is nothing to you. I have seen dainty bits of art sold at Christy's before now, but there never was anything daintier than you before in the world, and I love you, there! I have said it. It means a good deal when a man gives all his love to a woman, and I give it all to you; and when everything is said and done, Westenra, bonny as you are, and lovely, and dainty as you are, you are only a woman and I am only a man."

"I think," I said suddenly, and I found the tears coming into my eyes and stealing down my cheeks, "that you are one of the best men I ever met. I did not think it. I will tell you frankly that I used to regard you as commonplace, and—as vulgar. I saw nothing but the commonplace and the vulgar in you, but now I do see something else, something which is high, and generous, and even beautiful. I know that you are a good man, a very good man. I don't love you yet, but I will try; I will try at least to like you, and on the first of June next year I will be your wife."

"Thank you, dear," he replied, "you could not have spoken clearer and plainer and more straight if you were to study the matter for ever and ever. Now I know where I am, and I am contented. With your sweet little self to take pattern by, I have not the slightest doubt that I'll win that golden heart of yours yet. I mean to have a right good try for it anyhow. The mater will be so pleased when I tell her how nicely you spoke to me to-night. I am off to Germany first thing in the morning; you won't see me for a fortnight, and I won't write to you, Westenra; you'd be worried by my letters, and I cannot express what I feel except when you are there. I won't even kiss you now, for I know you would rather not, but perhaps I may kiss your hand."

He raised my hand to his lips; I did not look at him, I slowly left the room. He was very good, and I was very fortunate. Oh yes, although my heart kept bleeding.

CHAPTER XXVI

HAND IN HAND

Mr. Fanning went away and Mrs. Fanning took care of me. She openly did this; she made a tremendous fuss about me, but she never by word or deed alluded to my engagement to her son Albert. She did not talk nearly so much as in former times of her son; perhaps he had told her that I was not to be worried, but she was very good and very nice, and I got sincerely attached to her: and I never saw the Duchess nor Lady Thesiger nor my old friends, although I heard that the Duchess was fairly well again, and was out and going into society; and every one now seemed certain that Jim Randolph had gone to the bottom in the *Star of Hope*, but by universal consent the boarders decided that the news should be kept from mother, and mother grew much better. The weather was so fine she was able to go out. We got a bath chair for her and took her out every day; and the boarding-house was thronged, absolutely thronged with guests; and by Mrs. Fanning's suggestion Miss Mullins put up the prices, and very considerably too, for the London season, but the boarders paid what they were asked willingly, for the house was so sweet and so bright and so comfortable; and Jane had her moment of triumph when she saw that No. 14 in the next street was beginning to imitate us, to put up sun blinds, and even to fix balconies on to the windows, and to have the same hours for meals; and the ladies who kept No. 14 called one day and asked to see Jane Mullins. Jane did give them a spice of her mind, and sent them away without any information whatever with regard to her plans.

"I could not tell them to their faces," said Jane to me that day, "that it wasn't I. I am just a homely body, and can only do the rough homely work; I didn't tell them that it was because I had a lady who had the face of an angel and the ways of a queen in the drawing-room, and a young lady, the princess, her daughter, that the boarding-house prospered. I never let out to them that because you two are real ladies, and know how to be courteous and sympathetic and sweet, and yet to uphold your own dignity through everything, that the place was always full. No, I never told them that. What cheek those Miss Simpsons had to try to pick my brains!"

Yes, undoubtedly, whether we were the cause or not, things seemed to be flourishing, and mother enjoyed her life; but one evening towards the end of June she began to talk of old times, of the Duchess, and the friends she knew in Mayfair, and then quite quietly her conversation turned to a subject ever I believe near her heart, James Randolph and his friendship for her.

"He ought to be back now," she said. "I have counted the months, and he ought to be in England many weeks ago. I cannot understand his silence and his absence."

I did not answer. Mother looked at me.

"He was fond of you, West," she said.

My heart gave a great throb and then stood still. I bent my head, but did not reply.

"He never wished me to tell you," said mother. "He felt, and I agreed with him, that it would be best for him to speak to you himself. He said that he would be back in England early in April at the latest, and then he would speak to you. But he gave me to understand that if for any reason his return was delayed I might act on my own discretion, and tell you what comforts me beyond all possible words, and what may also cheer you, for I can scarcely think, my darling, that the love of a man like that would be unreturned by a girl like you, when once you knew, Westenra, when once you surely knew. Yes, he loves you with all his great heart, and when he comes back you will tell him——"

"Oh don't, mother," I interrupted, "oh don't say any more."

My face, which had been flushed, felt white and cold now, my heart after its one wild bound was beating low and feebly in my breast.

"What is it, West?" said mother.

"I would rather——" I began.

"That he told you himself? Yes, yes, that I understand. Whenever he comes, West, take your mother's blessing with the gift of a good man's heart. He has relieved my anxieties about you, and his friendship has sweetened the end of a pilgrimage full—oh, full to overflowing—of many blessings."

Mother lay quite quiet after these last words, and I did not dare to interrupt her, nor did I dare to speak. After a time she said gently—

"Your father came to me again last night. He sat down by me and held my hand. He looked very happy, almost eager. He did not say much about the life he now leads, but his eyes spoke volumes. I think he will come back to-night. It is quite as though we had resumed our old happy life together."

Mother looked rather sleepy as she spoke, and I bent down and kissed her, and sat with her for some little time. I saw that she was in a sound sleep, and her lips were breaking into smiles every now and then. She had been so well lately that we had sent Nurse Marion away, for her services seemed to be no longer required.

After sitting with mother until nearly midnight I went up to my own room. I sat down then and faced the news that mother had given me.

"I always knew it," I said to myself, "but I would not put it into words before; I always guessed it, and I was happy, although I scarcely knew why. Yes, I have put it into words at last, but I must never do so again, for on the 1st of June next year I am to marry Albert Fanning, and he is a good man, and he loves me."

I stayed awake all night, and early in the morning went downstairs. I entered mother's room. I felt anxious about her, and yet not anxious. The room was very still, and very cool and fresh. The windows were open and the blinds were up; mother always liked to sleep so, and the lovely summer air was filling the room, and there was a scent of heliotrope and roses from the flowering plants on the verandah. Mother herself was lying still as still could be on her bed. Her eyes were shut, and one of her dear white hands was lying outside the coverlet. It was partly open, as though some one had recently clasped it and then let it go.

I went up to the bedside and looked down at mother. One glance at her face told me all. Some one *had* clasped her hand, but he had not let it go. Hand in hand my father and mother had gone away, out through that open window, away and away, upward where the stars are and the Golden Gates stand open, and they had gone in together to the Land where there is no Death.

CHAPTER XXVII

TOO LATE

On the evening of mother's funeral, I was sitting in the little room. I had the little room quite to myself, Jane had arranged that. I had gone through, I thought, every phase of emotion, and I was not feeling anything just then; I was sitting quiet, in a sort of stupor. The days which had intervened between mother's death and her funeral had been packed full of events. People had come and gone. Many kind words had been said to me. Mr. Fanning had arrived, and had taken my hand once again and kissed it, and looked with unutterable sorrow into my eyes; and then, seeing that I could not bear his presence, had gone away, and Mrs. Fanning had opened her arms, and taken me to her heart, and sobbed on my neck, but I could not shed a tear in return; and Captain and Mrs. Furlong had been more than kind, and more than good; and the Duchess had arrived one morning and gone into the room where mother lay (that is, what was left of mother), and had sobbed, oh, so bitterly, holding mother's cold hand, and kissing her cheek; and then she had turned to me, and said—

"You must come home with me, Westenra, you must come away from here, you are my charge now."

But I refused to leave mother, and I even said—

"You neglected her while she was alive, and now you want to take me away from her, from the last I shall ever see of her beloved face."

"I could not come; I did not dare to," said the Duchess, "it was on account of Jim. I have been grieving for Jim, and I thought I should have let his death out to her; so I had to stay away, but my heart was aching, and when I heard that she—that she had gone—I"—and then the Duchess buried her face in her hands, and sobbed, oh, so bitterly. But I could not shed a tear.

The Duchess and the Duke both went to the funeral, which made a great impression on all the guests in the boarding-house; and Lady Thesiger went; I saw her at a little distance, as I stood close to mother's grave; but all these things were over, and father and mother were together again. That was my only comfort, and I sat in the little room, and was glad that I could not suffer much more.

Into the midst of my meditations there came a brisk voice, the door was opened suddenly, there was a waft of fresh air, and Lady Thesiger stood near me.

"You are to come with me at once, Westenra," she said, "the carriage is at the door, and Miss Mullins, and that good soul, Mrs. Fanning, are packing your things. You are to come right away from here to-night."

I did not want to go.

I said, "Please leave me, Jasmine, I cannot talk to you now."

"You need not talk," said Jasmine Thesiger, "but come you must."

I opposed her as best I could; but I was weak and tired, and half stunned, and she was all life and energy; and so it came to pass, that in less than an hour, I found myself driving away in her luxurious little brougham to her house in Mayfair. She gave me a pretty room, and was very kind to me.

"I'll leave you alone, you know," she said; "I don't want to worry you in any way, but you must not stay at the boarding-house any longer. Your mother is dead, and you must come back to your own set."

"I can never come back to my own set," I answered; "or rather, my set is no longer yours, Jasmine; I have stepped down for ever."

"That is folly, and worse than folly," she replied.

She came and sat with me constantly and talked. She talked very well. She did her utmost, all that woman could possibly do, to soothe my trouble, and to draw me out, and be good to me; but I was in a queer state, and I did not respond to any of her caresses. I was quite dazed and stupid. After a fortnight I came downstairs to meals just as usual, and I tried to speak when I was spoken to, but the cloud on my spirit never lifted for a single moment.

It was now the middle of July, and Jasmine and her husband were talking of their summer trip. They would go away to Scotland, and they wanted me to go with them. I said I would rather not, but that fact did not seem to matter in the very least. They wanted me to go; they had it all arranged. I declared that I must go back to Jane to the boarding-house, but they said that for the present I belonged to them. I thought to myself with a dull ache, which never rose to absolute pain, how soon they would give me up, when they knew that I was engaged to Albert Fanning. I had not mentioned this fact yet, though it was on the tip of my tongue often and often. Still I kept it to myself. No one knew of our engagement but Jane Mullins, who, of course, guessed it, and Mrs. Fanning and Albert himself. I respected the Fannings very much for keeping my secret so faithfully, and I respected them still more for not coming to see me.

On a certain evening, I think it was the 15th of July—I remember all the dates of that important and most terrible time; oh, so well—I was alone in Jasmine's drawing-room. Jasmine and her husband had gone to the theatre; they had expressed regret at leaving me, but I was glad, very glad, to be alone. I sat behind one of the silk curtains, and looked with a dull gaze out into the street. It was between eight and nine o'clock, and the first twilight was over everything. I sat quite still, my hand lying on my black dress, and my thoughts with mother and father, and in a sort of way also with Mr. Fanning and my future. I wished that I could shut away my future, but I could not. I had done what I had done almost for nothing. Mother's life had only been prolonged a few weeks. My one comfort was, that she had gone to her rest in peace, quite sure with regard to my future, and quite happy about me and my prospects. She was certain, which indeed was the case, that I loved James Randolph, and that whenever he returned, we would marry; and if by any chance his return was delayed the boarding-house was doing well, and my temporal needs were provided for. Yes, she had all this comfort in her dying moments, so I could scarcely regret what I had done.

I sat on by the window, and thought vaguely of mother, and not at all vaguely of Albert Fanning; he was a good man, but to be his wife! my heart failed me at the terrible thought.

Just then I heard the door of the room softly open, and close as softly; there came a quick step across the floor, a hand pushed aside my curtain, and raising my eyes I saw James Randolph. He looked just as I had seen him before he went away; his eyes were full of that indescribable tenderness, and yet suppressed fun, which they so often wore; his cheeks were bronzed, he had the alert look of a man who had gone through life, and seen many adventures. And yet with all that, he was just as he always was. It seemed the most natural thing in the world to have him close to me, and I scarcely changed colour; and, after a moment's pause, said quietly—

"Then you did not die, after all?"

"No," he replied. He spoke in a cheerful, matter-of-fact, everyday voice.

"I was delayed," he said, "but I have come back at last." Then he dropped into a chair near me. "I went to 17 Graham Square," he said, "and they said you were here. I did not ask a single question. I came straight on here. Am I too late? Don't tell me I am too late."

"Oh, you know it," I answered, "you must know it, you are quite, quite too late—too late for everything, for everything!"

There was a sob in my voice, but I would not let it rise. I saw his brow darkening to a frown of perplexity and alarm, and I turned my eyes away. Had he interpreted a double meaning in my words? Did he really even now guess that he was too late for everything?

"Tell me about your mother," he said, in a choking voice; "is she——?"

He looked at me, and I pointed to my black dress. He uttered a sharp exclamation of pain, and then said slowly—

"I understand, Westenra, I am too late; but, thank God, not too late for everything."

As he said this I think the bitterness of death passed over me; for was he not now quite too late for everything—for the love which I could have given him, for the joy which we might both have shared, had he only come back a little sooner. I almost wished at that bitter moment that he had never returned, that he had really died. The next instant, however, a revulsion came over me, and I found that I was glad, very glad, that he was alive, that he was in the land of the living, that I had a chance of seeing him from time to time.

"To-night," I said to myself, "I will not allow anything to temper my joy. He has come back, he is alive. No matter though I must never be his wife, I am glad, glad to see him again."

"I will tell you all about what kept me," he continued, for he half read my thoughts. "We were wrecked, as of course you saw in the papers, off Port Adelaide, and nearly every soul on board perished."

"But your name was not in the lists," I answered.

"That can be accounted for," he said, "by the fact that I had only come on board a couple of hours before at Adelaide, and doubtless the purser had not time to enter my name. I had no intention of taking passage in that special liner until the morning of the day when the wreck occurred. Well, the captain went down with the ship, and only one woman, two children, myself, and some of the sailors wore rescued. As the ship went down I was struck by a spar on my head and badly injured. When I was finally picked up I was quite unconscious, and for six weeks and more I was in hospital at Adelaide. As soon as ever I was well enough I took the first boat home; and here I am, Westenra, in time—oh, I hope in time—for the best of all. But tell me, how have things been going? I have been more anxious than I can say. There must have been money difficulties. You can little imagine what I went through. Can you bear just to speak of your mother? And can you bear to tell me how 17 Graham Square has been going?"

"We had hard times, but we pulled through," I answered briefly.

"Did you?" he cried, with a sigh of relief; "what a wonderful creature Jane

Mullins is! What an extraordinary head for business she possesses! I must go and see her to-morrow, or—or to-night."

"Don't go to-night," I said, and I stretched out my hand a very little and then drew it in again; but he saw the gesture, and suddenly his strong brown hand took mine and closed over it and held it firmly.

"Then I am in time, in time for the best of all," he said, and he gave a sigh straight from the bottom of his heart. "Now, I must tell you something. Will you listen?"

I drew my hand away, he dropped it, looked at me with a hurt expression, and then went on hurriedly, "I have got something to confess to you."

"I am listening," I said.

"Perhaps you have guessed the truth. I have a great deal to answer for. I cannot tell you how I have reproached myself. I have always taken an interest in you and in your mother. Even as a schoolboy at Eton this has been the case."

"But why?" I asked.

"Did you never know—I hoped not, but your mother knew, only I begged of her not to tell you—I am the son of the man whose life your father saved? His name was Chaloner then, but with some property he changed it to the one which I now bear, and I have been called Randolph almost the whole of my life. When my father died he gave me a charge. He said if ever the time came when you or your mother were in difficulties or peril or danger, I was to remember what your gallant father had done for him. He need not have told me, for the deed had always excited my keenest admiration; but I never came across you until that day when, by the merest chance, I was at the house-agents when you came in. I heard your name and I guessed who you were, but I did not dare to look at you then. I felt strangely overpowered.

"I went away, but I came back again shortly afterwards, and, forgive me, child, I overheard a great deal of your scheme, and I remembered my father's words and determined to help you. It was I who sought Jane Mullins. Her people had been old retainers of ours, and she had always worshipped the ground on which I walked. I told her exactly what I meant to do, and she helped me straight through at once. The money which smoothed matters with the landlord and enabled you to take the house, was really my money, money which I had inherited from my mother, but which was invested in Australian stocks. At that time these stocks were paying a high dividend, and everything seemed to be going well; but you had not been three months in the boarding-house before the bank in Melbourne which held such a large amount of my

192

money went smash, and I was obliged to go over to secure what was left. The blow was most sudden, and I had no one to help me. I gave Jane Mullins what little money I had left, and went to Australia. I quite hoped I should be back before—before any great trouble came to you. I rescued a large portion of my money, and hoped that everything was all right. Then came the shipwreck, the danger, the awful fight with death in the hospital, the final home-coming, and now—now I find that I shall never see your mother again. What did she think of my long absence, my enforced silence, Westenra? What did she feel about me?"

"She always hoped you would come back, and she always loved you," I said slowly.

"Did she tell you nothing more?"

No colour could come to my face; my heart was too cold, too bitterly cold, too despairing.

"She told me something more," I said in a whisper. He bent close to me.

"That I love you, darling—that I have loved you from the first moment I saw your face—that I love your courage, and your dear, dear self? I am a wealthy man now, Westenra. Money has come to me while I have been away, and I am a wealthy man and in your set, and—and will you come to me, darling? Will you make me happy—will you? Oh! I know you love me—I feel you do. You will come to me?"

But I started up.

"I cannot," I said.

"You cannot! Then you do not love me?"

I made a great struggle. Never in the whole course of my life did I make a struggle like that. My struggle was to keep my lips closed; but I looked wildly up at Jim, and Jim looked at me, and the next moment, against my will, perhaps against his will, I was in his arms, and my head was on his breast.

"You love me; there is your answer," he said. "You need not say any more. You have gone through much. Oh! I am happy, and I will take such care of you, little West. I have loved you for so long, and so deeply."

But I managed to wrest myself away.

"I cannot go to you," I said, "and I have never said——"

"You must say it now," he answered. "You do love me?"

"Yes, but I cannot marry you; it is too late. Oh! you have been good, but there is nothing to be said; it is too late. It is as much too late as if I were dead—

dead, as mother is dead. Oh! I can say no more."

CHAPTER XXVIII

THIS DEAR GIRL BELONGS TO US

I forget all about the night that followed. I also forget the next day. I think I stayed in my room most of the time, but the day following I went down to the drawing-room. London was already emptying fast. Jim had not come back. I sat in the drawing-room wondering what was going to happen, feeling that something must happen soon—a great catastrophe—a great shattering of that castle in the air which I had built so proudly a few months ago. While I was sitting there Jasmine bustled in.

"Now that is good, West," she said. "You are better. I want to have a little chat with you."

I raised my eyes. I knew very well what she was going to talk about, but I was not prepared to tell the whole truth yet. There was one matter I kept in reserve —my engagement to Albert Fanning. Whether I did right or wrong, the announcement of that extreme news could not pass my lips. I often struggled to tell it, but never yet had I been able. I knew, of course, that if Jim came to see me again I must tell him everything, but I hoped in my mad misery that he would not come again. Then the next hour I hoped the other way. I longed most passionately to see him, and so I was torn from hour to hour and from minute to minute with longings and doubts and despairs; but all through everything, I kept my secret untold within my breast.

"It is so nice about Jim Randolph," said Jasmine, sitting down near me. "Do you know that when Sir Henry Severn dies, Jim will be the successor to the baronetcy. While Jim was away in Australia, Sir Henry's son Theodore died quite suddenly. It was awfully sad, and now James is the next in succession. Sir Henry wishes him to live either with him at Severn Towers, in Somersetshire, or to have a house close by. James went down yesterday to see the old man, and will probably be coming back to-morrow. He was very sorry to leave you, but he had to go. He will be a rich man in the future, for Sir Henry Severn is very wealthy. It is a grand chance for Jim. He never for a moment supposed that the title would come to him."

I sat silent. I had a little ring on my finger—a very plain ring, with one tiny diamond in it. It had been given to me by Albert Fanning. I would not allow him to give me a flashy or showy ring, as he wanted to do, and I think he would gladly have spent a couple of hundred pounds on my engagement-ring, but I would not have it, not until the whole thing was known, then he might lavish jewellery on me as much as he pleased for all I cared. I twisted the little ring round and thought of my bond, and said after a pause—

"I do grieve about one thing, and that is that mother did not see Mr. Randolph before she died."

"But she always knew about everything. It is an open secret," said Jasmine. "I cannot imagine, Westenra, why you are so reserved with me. Every one knows. The Duchess knows, your mother knew, I know that James loves you, that he has loved you for months and months. What else would have taken a young man like James, a man of the world, so polished, so distinguished, so charming, to live in a place like Graham Square? Besides, dear, he has told you himself, has he not?"

I felt myself turning white.

"He has told you, has he not?" repeated Jasmine.

"I would rather not say," I replied.

"Your face tells me; besides, I saw the Duchess yesterday, and she said that she was so happy, for now you would be back again in your own set. You will make a very pretty and graceful Lady Severn."

"I care nothing whatever about that," I said, and I jumped up and walked to the window. "I hate titles," I continued. "I hate rank; I hate the whole thing. It is humbug, Jasmine; humbug. Why is it necessary for us all to class together in Mayfair, or to live in large houses in the country, in order to love each other? Why should we not go on loving, whatever our worldly position? Oh! it is cruel; the whole thing is cruel."

"But you ought to be rejoiced about James," continued Jasmine, who did not evidently think it worth her while even to answer my last words. "He has come back; he is quite well. In a few years at latest he will be Sir James Severn, for of course he must take the name with the baronetcy, and you will be his pretty wife. Doubtless he will want to marry you very soon—as soon, I mean, darling, as you can bring yourself to go to him after your dear mother's death; but I knew your mother quite well enough, Westenra, to be sure that the sooner you made yourself happy the better pleased she would be, and you will be happy with such a good man. Why, he is a catch in a thousand. I cannot tell you how many girls are in love with him, and I never saw him talk to any one or flirt the least bit in the world except with your charming self. You are lucky, Westenra; very lucky."

I went now and stood by the window, and as I stood there I felt my heart give a great thump, and then go low down in my breast. I turned impulsively.

"I—I am not quite well," I began; but then I hastily thought that I must see it out. The moment had come when Jasmine Thesiger was to have all her doubts answered, her questions replied to, and my future would be clear in her eyes, for I had seen the chocolate-coloured brougham draw up at the door, and Mrs. and Mr. Fanning get out.

"What is the matter? Are you ill?" said Jasmine.

"No, no; I am quite well," I replied. I sank down on a chair. "I only saw some visitors just arrive," I continued.

"Visitors at this hour! I will tell Tomkins we are not at home."

"It is too late," I answered; "they are coming up. They are friends of mine."

"All right, child; but how queer you look," Jasmine gazed at me in great astonishment.

I hoped earnestly that I did not show my emotion too plainly, when the next moment the door was thrown open by Lady Thesiger's smart servant, and Mrs. and Mr. Fanning walked in.

Mrs. Fanning had put on black on my account. She had told me that she meant to go into mourning, as we were practically relations already. I had begged of her not, but she had not regarded my wishes in the least. She was in a heavy black serge dress, and a voluminous cape which came down nearly to her knees, and she had a black bonnet on, and her face was all beaming and twinkling with affection and sympathy and suppressed happiness. And Albert Fanning, also in a most melancholy suit of black, with his hair as upright as ever, came up to my side. I heard his usual formula—

"How is Westenra?" and then I found myself introducing him and his mother to Lady Thesiger, and Lady Thesiger gave a haughty little bow, and then sat down, with her eyes very bright, to watch events. Perhaps already she had an inkling of what was about to follow.

"We have come," said Mrs. Fanning, looking at her son and then glancing at me, "to tell you, Westenra, that we think you had better arrange to spend your holidays with us. Considering all things, it seems most fitting."

"What I say is this," interrupted Albert Fanning. "Westenra must do as she pleases. If she likes to come with us to Switzerland we shall be, I need not say, charmed; but if she prefers to stay with her ladyship"—here he gave a profound bow in the direction of Lady Thesiger—"we must submit. It is not in the bond, you know, mother, and anything outside the bond I for one debar."

"You always were so queer, my son Albert," said Mrs. Fanning, who had lost her shyness, and now was determined to speak out her mind fully.

"It's this way, your ladyship," she continued, turning to Lady Thesiger. "I may as well be plain, and I may as well out with the truth. This pretty young girl, this dear girl, belongs to us. She does not belong to you—she belongs to us."

"No, no, mother; you are wrong there," cried Mr. Fanning; "she does not belong to us at present."

"It's all the same," said Mrs. Fanning; "don't talk nonsense to me. When a girl is engaged to a man—"

"Engaged! Good heavens!" I heard Lady Thesiger mutter, and then she sat very still, and fixed her eyes for a moment on my face, with a sort of glance which seemed to say, "Are you quite absolutely mad?"

"Yes, engaged," continued Mrs. Fanning. "It is a very queer engagement, it seems to me, but it is a *bonâ fide* one for all that."

"As *bonâ fide*," said Mr. Fanning, with a profound sigh, "as there is a sky in the heavens. As *bonâ fide* as there is a day and a night; as *bonâ fide* as that I am in existence; but the marriage is not to be consummated until the 1st of June next year. That is in the bond, and we have nothing to complain of if —if Westenra"—here his voice dropped to a sound of absolute tenderness —"if Westenra would rather not come with us now."

"Please explain," said Lady Thesiger. "I knew nothing of this. Do you mean to tell me, madam, that my friend Westenra Wickham is engaged to—to whom?"

"To my son Albert," said Mrs. Fanning, with great emphasis and with quite as much pride as Lady Thesiger's own.

"Is that the case, Westenra?" continued Jasmine, looking at me.

I bowed my head. I was silent for a moment; then I said, "I am engaged to Albert Fanning. I mean to marry him on the 1st of June next year."

"Then, of course, I have nothing to say. Do you wish to go away with the Fannings, Westenra? You must do what you wish."

I looked at her and then I looked at Mrs. Fanning, and then I looked at Albert, whose blue eyes were fixed on my face with all the soul he possessed shining out of them. He came close to me, took my hand, and patted it.

"You must do just as you please, little girl," he said; "just exactly as you please."

"Then I will write and let you know," I answered. "I cannot tell you to-day."

"That is all right—that is coming to business," said Mrs. Fanning; "that is as it should be. Albert, we are not wanted here, and we'll go. You'll let us know to-morrow, my dearie dear. Don't keep us waiting long, for we have to order rooms in advance at the big hotels in Switzerland at this time of year. Your ladyship, we will be wishing you good morning, and please understand one thing, that though we may not be quite so stylish, nor quite so up in the world as you are, yet we have got money enough, money enough to give us everything that money can buy, and Westenra will have a right good time with my son Albert and me. Come, Albert."

Albert Fanning gave me a piteous glance, but I could not reply to it just then, and I let them both go away, and felt myself a wretch for being so cold to them, and for their society so thoroughly.

When they were gone, and the sound of wheels had died away in the street, Jasmine turned to me.

"What does it mean?" she cried. "It cannot be true—you, Westenra, engaged to that man! Jim Randolph wants you; he loves you with all his heart; he has been chivalrous about you; he is a splendid fellow, and he is rich and in your own set, and you choose that man!"

"Yes, I choose Albert Fanning," I said. "I can never marry James Randolph."

"But why, why, why?" asked Jasmine.

CHAPTER XXIX

HAVE I LOST YOU?

I told her everything, not then, but on the evening of the same day. She came into my room where I was lying on a sofa, for I was thoroughly prostrated with grief for my mother and—and other great troubles, and she held my hand and I told her. I described Jane's anxiety in the boarding-house, the debts creeping up and up, the aspect of affairs getting more and more serious; I told her about Mrs. Fanning and Albert, and the chocolate-coloured brougham, and the drive to Highgate, and the rooms all furnished according to Albert's taste, and the garden, and the proposal he made to me there, and my horror. And then I told her about mother's gradual fading and the certainty that she would not live long, and the doctor's verdict, and the one caution impressed and impressed upon me—that she was to have no shock of any sort, that everything was to be made smooth and right for her.

I described, further, Jane Mullins' agitation, her despair, her difficulty in going on at all, the dreadful news which had reached us with regard to Jim, the almost certainty that he was drowned.

Then I told her of the awful day when I went to try and borrow a thousand pounds from the Duchess, and how I could not see the Duchess, for she was too ill to see any one, all on account of Jim's supposed death; and then I told her what I found when I came back—the awful greasy little man in the dining-room—the man in possession. I described his attitude that day at dinner, and the surprise and astonishment of the boarders; and then I explained how he had gone and why he had gone, and I told her of my visit to Albert Fanning in Paternoster Row, and what Albert Fanning had said, and how kind he was to me; and, notwithstanding his want of polish, how really chivalrous he was in his own way, and how really he loved me and wanted to help me. I made the very best of him, and I went on still further, and told her of the man who had burst into mother's presence in the drawing-room, and rudely demanded payment for his debt, and then how I had yielded, and told Albert Fanning that I would marry him, and how, after that, everything was smooth, and all the worries about money had disappeared as if by magic.

"I gave him my bond," I said at the conclusion. "I said that I would marry him at the end of a year, and he was satisfied, quite satisfied, and he paid up everything, and mother went to her grave happy. She was sure that all was well with me, and indeed I gave her to understand that all was very well, and she died; and never guessed that 17 Graham Square was an absolute, absolute failure—a castle in the clouds, which was tumbling about our heads."

I paused at the end of my story. Jasmine had tears in her eyes; they were rolling down her cheeks.

"Why didn't you come to me, Westenra?" she said; "my husband is very rich, and we would have lent you the money. Oh! to think that a thousand pounds could have saved you!"

"I did not think of you," I replied. "You must acknowledge, Jasmine, that you were cold and indifferent, and did not help me with a cheery word, nor with much of your presence, during my time in the boarding-house; and when the Duchess failed me, troubles came on too thick and fast to wait for any chance help from outside. I just took the help that was near, and in my way was grateful."

"I see," said Jasmine; "it is a most piteous—most terrible story."

"Do not say that," I answered. "Help me to bear it; don't pity me too much. Help me to see the best, all the best in those two good people with whom I am in future to live. Albert Fanning is not polished, he is not a gentleman outwardly, but he has—O Jasmine! he has in his own way a gentleman's heart, and his mother is a dear old soul, and even for Jim I would not break my bond, no, not for fifty Jim Randolphs; but I love Jim—oh, I love him with all my heart and soul."

I did not cry as I said the words; I was quite past tears that evening, and Jasmine continued to sit near me and to talk in soft tones, and after a time she relapsed into silence, a sort of despairing silence, and I lay with my eyes closed, for I could not look at her, and presently I dropped asleep.

At an early hour the next day I wrote to the Fannings to tell them that I would go with them to Switzerland. I went and saw Jasmine after I had written the note.

"I am going with the Fannings to Switzerland on the 4th of August," I said; "will this interfere with your plans? I mean, may I stay on here until they start?"

"Oh yes, you can stay on here, Westenra," she replied. She looked at me fixedly. I thought she would say something to dissuade me, but she did not. She opened her lips once, but no words came. She simply said—

"Is that the letter?"

"Yes."

"I am going out," she said then; "I will post it for you."

"Thank you," I answered. I went back to the drawing-room. I heard Jasmine go downstairs and out, and then I sat quiet. Everything seemed to have come to a sort of end; I could not see my way any further. In a fortnight's time I should have truly stepped down out of sight of those who were my friends. I should have left them for ever and ever. It would be a final stepping down for me. Nevertheless, the faintest thought of being unfaithful to the promise I had made, I am glad to think now, never for a single moment occurred to me.

Jasmine returned to lunch, and after lunch we went to the drawing-room, and she asked me if I would like to drive with her. I said—

"Yes, but not in the Park." Perhaps she guessed what I meant.

"Jim has come back," she remarked; "I had a line from him, and he wants to see you this evening."

"Oh, I cannot see him," I answered.

"I think you must. You ought to tell him yourself; it is only fair to him. Tell him just what you told me; he ought to know, and it will pain him less to hear it from your lips."

I thought for a moment.

"What hour is he coming?" I asked then.

"He will look in after dinner about nine o'clock. I am going to a reception with Henry; you will have the drawing-room to yourselves."

I did not reply. She looked at me, then she said—

"I have written already to tell him that he can come. It is absolutely necessary, Westenra, that you should go through this; it will be, I know, most painful to you both, but it is only just to him."

Still I did not answer. After a time she said—

"I do not wish to dissuade you; indeed, I cannot myself see how you can get out of this most mistaken engagement, for the man has behaved well, and I am the first to acknowledge that; but has it ever occurred to you that you do a man an absolute and terrible injustice when you marry him, loving with all your heart and soul another man? Do you think it is fair to him? Don't you think he ought at least to know this?"

"I am sure Albert Fanning ought not to know it," I replied, "and I earnestly hope no one will ever tell him. By the time I marry him I shall have"—my lips trembled, I said the words with an effort—"I shall have got over this, at least to a great extent; and oh! he must not know. Yes, I will see Jim to-night, for I agree with you that it is necessary that I should tell him myself, but not

202

again," I continued; "you won't ask me to see him again after to-night?"

"You had much better not," she replied; she looked at me very gravely, and then she went away. Poor Jasmine, she was too restless to stay much with me. She was, I could see, terribly hurt, but she had not been gone an hour before the Duchess came bustling in. She was very motherly and very good, and she reminded me of my own dear mother. She sat near me, and began to talk. She had heard the whole story. She was terribly shocked, she could not make it out. She could not bring herself to realise that her god-daughter was going to marry a man like Albert Fanning.

"You ought never to have done it, West, never, never," she kept repeating.

At last I interrupted her.

"There is another side to this question," I said; "you think I did something mean and shabby when I promised to marry a man like Albert Fanning. You think I have done something unworthy of your god-daughter, but don't you really, really believe that you would have a much poorer, more contemptible, more worthless sort of god-daughter if she were now to break her bond to the man who saved her mother at considerable expense—the man who was so good, so kind, so faithful? Would you really counsel me to break my bond?"

"No, I would not," said the Duchess, "but I would do one thing, I would up and tell that man the truth. I would put the thing before him and let him decide. Upon my word, that's a very good idea. That's what I would do, Westenra."

"I will not tell him," I replied. "I have promised to marry him on the 1st of June next year. He knows well that I do not love him, but I will keep my bond."

"That is all very fine," said the Duchess. "You may have told him that you do not love him, but you have not told him that you love another man."

"I have certainly not told him that."

"Then you are unfair to him, and also unfair to James Randolph. You think nothing at all of breaking his heart."

"He was away when he might have helped me," I replied. "That was, I know, through no fault of his, but I cannot say any more except that I will not break my bond."

The Duchess went away, and in the evening Jim arrived. He came in with that very quiet manner which he always wore, that absolute self-possession which I do not think under any circumstances would desert him, but I read the anxiety in his grey eyes, the quizzical, half-laughing glance was gone altogether, the eyes were very grave and almost stern.

"Now," he said, "I have come to say very plain words. I want to know why you will not marry me."

"Have you not heard?" I asked.

"I have heard nothing," he answered. "I have been given no reason; you just told me you could not marry me the other night, and you were so upset and shaken that I did not press the matter any further. You know, of course, that I can give you everything now that the heart of girl could desire."

"Do not talk of those things," I said. "I would marry you if you had only a hundred a year; I would marry you if you had nothing a year, provided we could earn our living together. O Jim! I love you so much, I love you so much, so much."

I covered my face with my hands, a deep, dry sob came from my throat.

"Then if that is so," he answered, half bending towards me and yet restraining himself, "why will you not marry me?"

"I cannot, because—because——"

"Take your own time," he said then; "don't speak in a hurry. If you love me as you say you love me, and if you know that I love you, and if you know also, which I think you do, that your mother wished it, and all your friends wish it, why should not we two spend our lives together, shoulder to shoulder, dear, in the thick of the fight, all our lives close together until death does us part? And even death does not really part those who love, Westenra, so we shall in reality never be parted if we do so sincerely love. Why should not these things be?"

"Because I am bound to another man," I said then.

He started away, a stern look came into his face.

"Say that again," was his answer, after a full minute of dead silence.

"I am engaged to another," I said faintly.

"And yet you have dared to say that you love me?"

"It is true."

"In that case you do not love the man to whom you have given your promise?"

"I do not."

"But what does this mean? This puzzles me."

He put up his hand to his forehead as if to push away a weight. He was standing up, and the pallor of his face frightened me.

"I do not understand," he said. "I had put you on a pedestal—are you going to prove yourself common clay after all? but it is impossible. Who is the other man?"

Then I told him.

He uttered a sharp exclamation, then turned on his heel and walked away to the window. He stood there looking out, and I looked at him as his figure was silhouetted against the sky.

After a time he turned sharply round and came back to me and sat down. He did not sit close to me as he had done before, but he spoke quietly, as if he were trying to keep himself in control.

"This is very sudden and terrible," he said; "very inexplicable too. I suppose you will explain?"

"I will," I said. "I knew you were coming to-night; I was cowardly enough to wish that you would not come, but I will explain."

"You are engaged to the man I used to see you talking to at 17 Graham Square?"

"Yes," I said; "do not speak against him."

"I would not be so cruel," he answered. "If you have promised yourself to him, he must merit some respect; tell me the story."

So I told Jim just the same story I had told Jasmine that morning. I did not use quite the same words, for he did not take it so calmly. I had never seen his self-possession shaken before. As my story drew to an end he had quite a bowed look, almost like an old man; then he said slowly—

"It was my fault; I should not have gone away. To think that you were subjected to this, and that there was no escape."

"There was no escape," I said. "Could I have done otherwise?"

"God knows, child, I cannot say."

"I could not," I replied slowly. "If you had been me you would have acted as I have done; there are times when one must forget one's self."

"There are, truly," he said.

"Then you are not dreadfully angry with me, Jim?"

"Angry?" he said slowly; "angry? You have not given me the worst pain of all, you have not stepped down from your pedestal, you are still the one woman for me. But oh! Westenra, have I lost you? Have I lost you?"

He bowed his head in his hands.

CHAPTER XXX

THE DUCHESS HAS HER SAY

I shall never forget as long as I live that sultry 1st of August; there seemed to be scarcely a breath of air anywhere, all the air of London had that used-up feeling which those who live in it all the year round know so well. It was hot weather, hot in the house, hot in the outside streets, hot in the burnt-up parks, hot everywhere. The sky seemed to radiate heat, and the earth seemed to embrace it; and we poor human beings who were subjected to it scarcely knew what to do with ourselves.

Even in Jasmine's luxurious house, where all the appliances of comfort were abundantly in evidence, even there we gasped and thought of the country with a longing equal to that of thirsty people for water.

Jasmine and her husband were going away the next day, and the Duchess was going away too, and I was to join the Fannings on the 4th. I was to have three more days in Jasmine's house, and then I was to go, I knew well never to return. I had not seen Jim after that night, nearly a fortnight ago, when I had told him everything, and from that hour to now nothing at all had occurred to deliver me from my bondage and misery. Mrs. Fanning had come twice to see me; she was very bustling and self-important, and told me honestly that she had a downright hatred for that airified madam her ladyship. She said that we'd have an excellent time in Switzerland, going to the very best hotels, enjoying ourselves everywhere.

"And you two young engaged creatures will have no end of opportunities for flirtation," she said; "I won't be much in the way. You may be quite sure that the old mother will efface herself in order to give her son and her dear new daughter every possible opportunity for enjoying life. Ah! my dear, there is no time like the engaged period—the man makes such a fuss about you then. He don't afterwards, dear; I may as well be frank, but he don't—the best of 'em even take you as if you were common clay; but beforehand you're something of an angel, and they treat you according. It's the way of all men, dear, it is the way of every single one of 'em. Now Albert, for instance, I declare at times I scarcely know him. He used to be a matter-of-fact sort of body, but he is changed in all sorts of ways; and as to the way he speaks of you, you'd think you weren't common clay at all, that your feet had never yet touched the earth. He drives me past patience almost at times; but I say to myself, 'Thank goodness, it won't last.' That's my one consolation, for I cannot bear those high-falutin' ideas, although there's nothing Albert does that seems really wrong to me. He said to me only yesterday, 'Mother, I have a kind of awe over me when I am with her; she is not like any one else, she is so dainty, and so——' I declare I almost laughed in his face; but there, I didn't, and doubtless he has told you those sort of things himself. I don't want to see you blush. Not that you do blush, Westenra; I must say you take things pretty cool. I suppose it is breeding. They say it takes a power of good breeding to get that calm which it strikes me you have to perfection. I never saw any one else with it except that Mr. Randolph, who, I hear, wasn't drowned at all, but came back as safe as ever a few days ago. Well, well, I'm off now. You wouldn't like to come back to the Métropole to me and Albert the day her ladyship goes, would you, child? Say out frankly if you have a wish that way."

"No," I answered, "I have not a wish that way. I will meet you at Victoria Station. I would rather stay here until then."

"Well, well, good-bye, my dearie," said the stout old woman, and she embraced me with her voluminous arms, and patted me on my cheek.

But although she came, as I said, twice, Albert did not come at all, and I thought it extremely nice of him. New proofs of his kindness were meeting me at every turn. He wrote to me several times, and in each letter said that he knew perfectly well that I meant to be free until the year was up, and that he was not going to worry me with overmuch love-making, or any nonsense of that sort; but he thought I would like Switzerland, and the change would do me good, and although he would not say much, and would not even ask me to go out walking with him unless I wished it, yet I was to be certain of one thing, that he was ready to lay down his life for me, and that I was the one thought of his heart, the one treasure of his soul.

"Poor Albert!" I had almost said, "Poor dear Albert!" when I read that last letter. How much he had developed since the days when we first met. It is wonderful what a power love has, how it ennobles and purifies and sanctifies, and raises, and Albert's love was very unselfish—how utterly unselfish, I was to know before long.

But the days went on, and each day seemed a little harder than the last, until I became quite anxious for the complete break to take place when I should have parted with my old friends and my old life for ever. But I knew quite well that even if I did go away, the image of the man I really loved would remain in my heart. As this was likely to be a sin by-and-by—for surely I ought not to marry one man and love another—I must try to fight against all thoughts of Jim, and to banish the one who would not be banished from my thoughts.

I have said that the 1st of August came in with tremendous heat; every window in the house was open, the blinds were all down. Jasmine was quite fretful and irritable. She pined for Scotland; she said that she could scarcely contain herself until she got away.

She and her husband were to go early the next day to the North, and all arrangements were being made, and the final packing was being completed.

The Duchess also was kept in town owing to some special duties, but on the next day she was also to go.

She had asked me two or three times to visit her, but I had written to her begging of her not to press it.

"I must go through with what I have promised," I said, "and to see you only pains me. Do forgive me. Perhaps you will see me once when I return from Switzerland just to say good-bye."

The Duchess had taken no notice of this letter, and I concluded sadly that I was never to see her or hear of her again; but as I was sitting by myself in Jasmine's inner drawing-room on that same 1st of August, about twelve o'clock in the morning, I was startled when the door was thrown open, and the dear Duchess came in. She came up to me, put her arms round me, drew me to her breast, and kissed me several times. She had not, after all, more motherly arms than Mrs. Fanning, but she had a different way about her, and before I knew what I was doing, the feel of those arms, and the warm, consoling touch of her sympathy, caused me to burst out crying. Mrs. Fanning would not have thought much of the calm which in her opinion seems to accompany good breeding had she seen me at that moment. But the Duchess knew exactly what to do. She did not speak until I was quieter, and then she made me lie on the sofa, and took my hand and patted it.

"I am thinking of you, Westenra, almost all day long," she said solemnly. "I am terribly concerned about you. Have you got a photograph of that man anywhere near?"

"I have not got one," I replied.

"He never sent you his photograph? I thought they always did."

"He would have liked to. He is very patient, and he is very fond of me, you need not be anxious about me, it is just——"

"But it is the giving of you up, child, that is so painful, and the want of necessity of the whole thing. Sometimes I declare I am so impatient with ——"

But what the Duchess meant to say was never finished, for the drawing-room door was opened once more and the footman announced Mr. Fanning.

Albert Fanning entered in his usual, half assured, half nervous style. He had a way of walking on his toes, so that his tall figure seemed to undulate up and down as he approached you. He carried his hat in his hand, and his hair was as upright as usual, his face white, his blue eyes hungry. He was so anxious to see me, and this visit meant so much to him, that he did not even notice the Duchess. He came straight up to me, and when he saw that my cheeks were pale and my eyes red from recent crying, he was so concerned that he stooped, and before I could prevent him gave me the lightest and softest of kisses on my cheek.

"I could not keep away," he said, "and I—I have a message from the mater. Can you listen?"

I was sitting up, my face was crimson, with an involuntary movement I had tried to brush away that offending kiss. He saw me do it, and his face went whiter than ever.

"Introduce me, Westenra," said the voice of the Duchess.

In my emotion at seeing Albert Fanning, I had forgotten her, but now I stood up and made the necessary introduction. Her Grace of Wilmot gave a distant bow, which Mr. Fanning gravely and with no trace of awkwardness returned.

"Won't you sit down?" said the Duchess then; "do you know I have been most anxious to see you?"

"Indeed," he replied. He looked amazed and a little incredulous. He kept glancing from the Duchess to me. I do not know why, but I suddenly began to feel intensely nervous. There was a gleam in my old friend's soft brown eyes which I had only seen there at moments of intense emotion. She evidently was making up her mind to say something terrible. I exclaimed hastily—

"Albert, if you wish to speak to me, will you come into the next room. You will excuse us for a moment will you not, Duchess?"

"No, Westenra," she replied, and she rose now herself; "I will not excuse you. You must stay here, and so must Mr. Fanning, for I have got something I wish particularly to say to Mr. Fanning."

"Oh, what?" I cried. "Oh, you will not"—she held up her hand to stop my torrent of words.

"The opportunity has come which I have desired," she said, "and I am not going to neglect it. It need make no difference to either of you, but at least you, Mr. Fanning, will not marry my dear girl without knowing how things really are."

"Oh, please don't speak of it, I implore you, you don't know what terrible mischief you will do."

"Hold your tongue, Westenra. Mr. Fanning, this young girl is very dear to me, I have known her since her birth; I stood sponsor for her when she was a baby. I take shame to myself for having to a certain extent neglected her, and also her mother, my most dear friend, during the few months they lived in 17 Graham Square. I take shame to myself, for had I done all that I might have done for those whom I sincerely loved, the calamity which came about need never have occurred."

"As to that," said Albert Fanning, speaking for the first time, and in quite his usual assured voice, "it could not help occurring, your Grace, for the simple fact that the boarding-house never could have paid, the expenses were greater than the incomings. If you have ever studied political economy, your Grace will know for yourself that when you spend more than you receive it spells RUIN."

The Duchess stopped speaking when Albert Fanning began, and looked at him with considerable astonishment.

"Then you knew from the first that the extraordinary scheme of my young friend could not succeed."

"I did," he replied, "and I bided my time. I suppose you mean to say something disagreeable to me; you do not think I am in the running with her at all, but as far as that goes I have money, and she has not any, and I love her as I suppose woman never was loved before, and I will make her happy in my own fashion. And I'll never intrude on her grand friends, so that her grand friends can come to see her as often as they like; and as to my mother, she is a right-down good sort, though she wasn't born in the purple like yourself, your Grace; so, as far as I am concerned, I do not know what you have to say to me. I suppose you want to tell me that Westenra here, my pretty little girl, who is going to give herself to me on the 1st of June next year, does not care for me, but she will care for me by-and-by, for my feeling is that love like mine must be returned in the long run, and if after a year she don't tell your Grace that she is the happiest little wife in the length and breadth of England, I shall be greatly surprised."

Here Albert Fanning slapped his thigh in his excitement, and then stood bolt upright before the Duchess, who in absolute astonishment stared back at him.

"That is not the point," she said. "You do not want to marry a girl who not only does not love you, but who does, with all her heart and soul, love some one else?"

"Why, of course not," he replied, and a frightened look came for the first time into his blue eyes. He turned and faced me.

"Of course not," he repeated, his eyes still devouring mine; "but Westenra cares for nobody, I never saw a girl less of a flirt in the whole course of my life. It is not to be supposed that such a very pretty girl should not have men fall in love with her, but that is neither here nor there."

"You ask her yourself," said the Duchess; "I think from your face that you seem a very honest good sort of man; you are a publisher, are you not?"

"Yes, Madam, I publish books, bright, entertaining books too."

"I repeat that you seem a very honest upright sort of man, who sincerely loves my young friend, and honestly wishes to do his best for her, but I think you will find that there is more behind the scenes than you are aware of, and, in short, that Westenra ought to tell you the truth. Tell him the truth now, Westenra."

"Yes, tell me now, Westenra," he said; "tell me the truth;" and he faced me once more, and I forced myself to look into his eyes.

"I know you don't love me just yet," he continued, "but it will come some day."

"I will do my very best to love you," I answered; "I will try to be a good wife to you, Albert."

"Ay, ay—how sweetly you say those words. May I hold your hand?"

I gave him my hand—he held it as he always did hold it, as if it were something very precious and sacred, letting it lie in his palm, and looking down at it as if it were a sort of white wonder to him.

"But ask her the question," said her Grace, and then I glanced at the Duchess and saw that her cheeks were pink with excitement, and her eyes shining; "ask her that straight, straight question on which all your happiness depends, Mr. Fanning."

"I will, your Grace. You do not love me, Westenra, but you will try to be a good wife to me, and you will try to love me, that is, in the future. There is no one else whom you love now, is there? I know, of course, what your reply will be, darling, and it is a hard question to ask of you, as though I doubted you. There is no one, is there, Westenra? Speak, little girl, don't be afraid, there is no one?"

"But there is," I faltered. I covered my face for a moment, then I checked back my tears and looked at him as steadily as he had looked at me.

"There is another," he repeated, "and you—you love him? Who is he?"

"I won't tell you his name. I shall get over it. I could not help myself—I promised to marry you, but I never said that I could love you, for I don't—not now at least, and there is another, but I will never see him again. It won't make any difference to you, Albert."

"Yes, but it will," he said, "all the difference on earth." He dropped my hand as though it hurt him. He turned and faced the Duchess.

"I suppose you are talking of Mr. Randolph. I quite understand, he belongs to the set in which she was born, but he deserted her when she wanted him most. It can scarcely be that she cares for him. There, I don't want either of you to tell me his name just now. I have heard enough for the present."

He strode out of the room, slamming the door behind him.

CHAPTER XXXI

THE END CROWNS ALL

"I have done it now," said the Duchess, "God knows what will be the consequence, but I have at least delivered my soul."

She had scarcely uttered the words before Albert Fanning strode back into the room. He was not the least awkward now, he looked quite manly and dignified.

"Will you oblige me," he said, looking straight at the Duchess, "by giving me the address of Mr. James Randolph?"

"You are not going to do anything," I cried, springing up, "oh, you are not going to say anything? This has been forced out of me, and I have not mentioned any one's name."

"I will do nothing to hurt you, dear," he said very gently, and he looked at me again, and putting his hand on mine forced me quietly back into my seat. Then he turned to the Duchess, waiting for her to give him what he required.

Her face was very white, and her lips tremulous. She tore a sheet out of her little gold-mounted note-book, which always hung at her side, scribbled a few words on it, and handed it to him.

"I am dreadfully sorry to hurt you, you must believe that," she said.

He did not make any response. He bowed to her and then left the room.

"What does it mean? This is terrible," I cried.

The Duchess looked at me.

"Will you come home with me, Westenra? it is best for you," she said. "Come and spend the rest of the day with me."

"No, I cannot," I answered; "I must stay here. Albert may come back again. There is no saying what mischief you have done. I cannot think, I am too miserable, too anxious. Oh, suppose he goes to see Mr. Randolph, and suppose, suppose he tells him."

"I believe in his heart that man is a gentleman. Even if you marry him I shall not be quite so unhappy as I would have been," was the Duchess's next speech, and then seeing that I was not inclined to say anything more she left the room.

I do not know how the rest of the day passed. From the quiet of despair my mind was suddenly roused to a perfect whirl of anxiety, and I could not think consecutively. I could plan nothing, I could hope nothing, but it seemed to me that my journey to Switzerland was indefinitely postponed, and that my future from being settled in every detail, month, week, hour, and all, was as indefinite and vague and shadowy as though I were standing on the brink of the other world.

Jasmine entered the room at tea-time and asked me what was the matter. I replied that I had nothing at all fresh to tell her, for I felt that she must never know what the Duchess had told Albert Fanning. She gazed at me as I spoke as though I were a source of irritation to her, and then said that my stepping down had changed me so absolutely that she was not sure whether I was a nice girl any longer, and whether, after all, the fate of being Albert Fanning's wife was not the best fate for me. Then I said stoutly—

"Albert Fanning is one of the best men in the world, and I am fortunate to be left in such good care." Jasmine got really angry and offended then, and went out of the room. She presently came back to ask me, if I would mind dining alone, as she and Henry wished to spend their last evening with some friends. I said that, of course, I did not mind. In reality I was very glad.

Jasmine went out, and I was again alone. How I hated the house; how I hated the dreary, and yet beautifully-furnished drawing-room; how the heat oppressed me, and seemed to take away the remainder of my strength! I wondered if it were true, that I was only two-and-twenty, just on the verge of womanhood. I felt quite old, and I stretched out my arms, and gave a dreary sigh; and felt that the sadness of youth was just as *great* as the sadness of age; and that one of its most painful moments was the knowledge that, in the ordinary course of life, I was so far from the end. Yes, I was young, and I must bear my burden, and I was strong too; and there was no chance under any ordinary circumstances of my not living out the full measure of my years.

Just before dinner the drawing-room door was again opened, and Albert Fanning for the third time that day made his appearance. He looked quite brisk, and bright, and like his usual self, except that in some extraordinary way his awkwardness and self-consciousness had completely left him; he was evidently absorbed with some business on hand, which made him a new man for the time.

"Will you come for a walk with me, Westenra?" he asked gravely.

"What, now?" I inquired in some surprise and trepidation.

"Yes," he answered, "or, at least, I want you to drive with me now, and to walk with me afterwards. I have a great desire that we should spend this evening together; and I fancy, somehow, that you won't deny me. I have a carriage outside; I bought it for you, yesterday, a smart little victoria. I will drive you to Richmond, and we can dine there. You will come, won't you, dear?"

I paused to think, then I said, just as gravely as he had addressed me—

"Yes, I'll come."

"That is nice," he remarked, rubbing his hands, "we'll have a good time, little girl. We won't mind what the Duchess said; we'll have a right, good, jolly time, you and I."

"Of course," I answered. I went up to my room, dressed, and came down again.

"I am ready now," I said.

He took my hand.

"It is very good of you, Westenra; we shall have a delightful evening; all that thundery feeling has gone out of the air, everything is crisp and fresh, and you'll enjoy your drive."

None of the servants saw us go out, and it was Albert himself who put me into the victoria. He sat beside me, took the reins, and we were off.

"Don't you think this is a neat little turn-out?" he said, as we drove down in the soft summer air to Richmond.

I praised the victoria to his heart's content, and then I told him that I thought his taste was much improved.

"It is all owing to you, dear," he replied. "You like things to look *gentle* somehow. I could not see myself looking at you in a place with *loud* things. It was only this morning I was saying to myself, early this morning, I mean"— he gave a quick sigh as he uttered these last words—"I was saying to myself, that we would furnish the house at Highgate over again according to your ideas. We would just leave a couple of rooms for mother, according to her tastes, and you and I should have the rest of the house furnished as you like. Liberty, Morris, all the rest, everything soft, and cloudy, and dim, and you walking about in the midst of the pretty things, and I coming home, and—but, never mind, dear, only I would like you always to feel, that there is nothing under the sun I would not do for you, nothing."

"You are very, very kind," I murmured.

"Oh, it is not real kindness," he replied with great earnestness. "You must not speak of it as kindness; you cannot call it that, when you love, and I love you so much, little girl, that when I do things for you, I do things for myself; you can never call it just *kindness* when you please yourself. That is how I feel about the matter. You understand, don't you?"

I nodded. I understood very well. Albert thought me kind when I said gentle and affectionate words to him, but he thought himself rather selfish than otherwise, when he poured out his whole heart at my feet.

As we were driving quickly in the direction of Richmond, he told me many of his plans. I had never heard him speak more freely nor unrestrainedly. Amongst other things he mentioned Jane Mullins.

"She is a capital woman," he said, "and she and I have gone carefully into the matter of the house in Graham Square. Jane wants to give it up, and it is quite too big for her to manage alone. I am starting her in a little boarding-house in Pimlico, and with her business-like instincts she will do uncommonly well there. She spoke of you when I saw her yesterday, there were tears in her eyes."

"She must come and see us when we are settled at Highgate," I replied, but to this remark of mine he made no answer.

We got to Richmond, and had some dinner, and then we went out, and walked up and down on the terrace outside the hotel. There was a lovely view, and the stars were coming out. Albert said—

"Let us turn down this walk. It is quite sheltered and rather lonely, and at the farther end there is an arbour, they call it the 'Lover's Arbour.' Beyond doubt many lovers have sat there; you and I, Westenra, will sit there to-night."

I had been feeling almost happy in his society—I had almost forgotten the Duchess, and even Jim Randolph had been put into the background of my thoughts; but when Albert proposed that he and I should sit in the "Lover's Arbour" as lovers, I felt a shiver run through me. I said not a word, however, and I do not think he noticed the momentary unwillingness which made me pause and hesitate. We walked between the beautiful flowering shrubs, and under the leafy trees to the little arbour, and we entered. I seated myself; he stood in the doorway.

"Won't you come and sit down, too?" I said.

"Do you ask me?" he answered, a light leaping into his eyes.

"Yes, I do ask you," I replied after a moment.

He sat down—then suddenly without the slightest warning, his arms were round me; he had strained me to his heart; he had kissed me several times on my lips.

"Oh, you ought not," I could not help exclaiming.

"But why not?" he cried, and he did not let me go, but looked into my eyes, almost fiercely it seemed to me. "You are my promised wife, may I not kiss you just once?"

"Oh, I know, you have the right to kiss me, but you have always been——" I could not finish the words. He suddenly dropped his arms, moved away from me, and stood up. His face was gloomy, then the gloom seemed to clear as by a great effort.

"I have kissed you," he said; "I vowed I would, and I have done it. I shall remember that kiss, and the feel of you in my arms, all my life long; but I am not going to think of my own feelings, I have something far more important to say. Do you know, little girl, that I received an awful shock to-day? Now, listen. You gave me your bond, did you not?"

"I did, Albert, I did."

"Just come out here, dear, I want to see your face. Ah! the moon shines on it and lights it up; there never was a face in all the world like yours, never to me; and I vowed, that because of it, and because of you, I would lead a good life, a beautiful life. A great deal, that I did not think was in me, has been awakened since you were good to me, Westenra."

"You have been very kind to me, Albert," I said, "and I will marry you. I will marry you when a year is up."

"You are a good girl," he said, patting my hand; but he did not squeeze it, nor even take it in his. "You are a very good girl, and you remember your bond. It was faithfully given, was it not?"

"Very faithfully, Albert."

"And you always, always meant to keep it?"

"I always did. I will keep it. Albert, why do you question me? Why do you doubt me?"

"I will tell you in a minute, darling. Now I want to ask you a question. Do you love me the least little scrap? Look well, well into your heart before you answer. I know that when you said you would marry me, you did not love me. You were willing to be bone of my bone, and flesh of my flesh; my dear, dear wife, till death us did part; you were willing to be all that?"

"I was," I said.

"And yet had you *never* a kindly feeling towards me?"

"A very kindly feeling," I answered, "very kindly, but I——"

218

"I know," he said, "you are a good girl. I won't press you too hard. Still my questions are not quite over. Had you, Westenra, at the time you promised yourself to me, any sort of idea that you cared for another?"

"He was dead, or at least, I thought he was dead," I said, trembling, and turning away. "Had I thought him alive, even for mother's sake, I could not have done it, but I thought him dead."

"And now that he has come back, you are sorry you gave me that bond?"

"Do not question me," I replied; "I will do my best for you; you will never regret that you have taken me to be your wife, but you must not question me."

"Because of your sore, sore heart," he said, looking very kindly at me; and now I looked back at him, and saw that in some wonderful way the expression on his face had changed; the look of passion had left it—it was quite quiet, a very kindly face, a very good face; never were there more honest blue eyes.

"I pressed you hard," he said, "I should not have done it, I see it all now, and you were so good and so unselfish. You gave me that bond for your mother's sake. I meant to put you into a corner; I meant to force your hand. It was unfair, miserably unfair. I did not think so at the time, but now I see it. Well, my dear, you are so gentle, and so different from other girls, that you have opened my eyes. There is a good bit of pain in having one's eyes opened sometimes, but there is also great joy in giving perfect joy to one whom you love, as I love you. So, if you will promise, little girl, faithfully, that never, never shall those debts which I paid for you, be paid back again to me; if you will allow me, for the whole of my life, to feel that I was the one who saved Westenra in her hour of bitter need; I was the one who helped her mother in her last moments to go down to the grave in peace, if you will promise all that, Westenra, there is an end of everything else. You have your bond back again. I don't want it, child, it is yours to do what you will with. You are free, Westenra. If it is hard on me, I am not going to talk of myself; but, I hope, I am manly enough to bear a bit of pain, and not cause the girl I love best on earth to suffer pain to her dying day. You are free, Westenra, that is all."

"But I won't be free," I answered passionately, for at that moment all the heroism in me, all that my dead father had given me before I was born, all that I owed to him, sprang to life in my veins, and I saw Albert Fanning as a hero, and faintly, very faintly, I began to love him in return. Not for a moment with the love I had for Jim, but still with a love which might have made me a blessed if not a happy wife.

"I won't be free, Albert," I cried, "I gave you my bond, and I will keep it; I will marry you."

"Never mind about that just now," he said; "but do you think—" he sat down near me as he spoke, and looked me in the face. "Do you think you could bring yourself to do one last thing for me?"

"It won't be a last thing," I answered, "it will be the first of many; I will do everything for you; I will marry you."

"It is not such a big thing as that," he replied; "but it is a big thing, at least a very big thing to me. It is something that I shall prize all my life. I took you in my arms just now and kissed you—will you kiss me just once of your own accord?"

I did not hesitate; I raised my lips and pressed a kiss on his cheek. He looked at me very mournfully and quietly.

"Thank you," he said, "I shall always have this to make a better man of me."

"But I am going to be yours; you won't cast me off," I pleaded; "I said I would marry you on the 1st of June next year, and I will."

"But I would rather not, my little girl. The fact is this, Westenra, I would not marry you now at any price. I would have married you had I thought I could have won you in the end, but I won't have a wife who loves another. I could not do it on any terms, Westenra. I am low down enough, but I am not as low as that. So I refuse you, dear; I give you up—you understand, don't you?"

I did understand. A wild wave of joy, almost intolerable, surged round my heart, and the next moment Mr. Fanning took my hand and led me out of the arbour just where the moon was shining.

"I asked Mr. Randolph to come down," he said quietly, "I guessed that perhaps he would be wanted. I think this is he."

Footsteps were heard approaching, and Jim Randolph stood in the moonlit path.

"How do you do, Mr. Randolph?" said Albert Fanning, with that new dignity which self-denial gave him. He looked almost grand at the moment.

"I have just been telling this young girl, Mr. Randolph, that I have heard a certain secret about her which she was bravely trying to keep to herself, and in consequence of that secret I can have nothing more to do with her. She wanted to marry me, sir, but I have refused her; she is quite free, free for any one else to woo and win. She is a very good girl, sir, and—but that is all, I have nothing more to say. I have given her back her bond." And then without a word, Albert Fanning walked quickly away through the gloom of the shrubbery, and Jim and I found ourselves alone face to face with the moonlight shining on us both.